I0582259

Demonic Depression

Ross Pollitt

Ross Pollitt Publishing

Book Cover by Alejandro Colucci

Illustrations (Photography) by Ross Pollitt

1st edition 2023

Contents

Acknowledgements

Without the help of two people, this debut novel would not be possible.

A huge thank you to Elizabeth for the edit and Kate for the proofreading.

There is a place I have found that is 'safe space and no blame culture' as she would say.

she would say.

A belief held for me that no other could ever achieve.

This is for Rosa.

About the Author

Ross is a writer of necessity. Chronic fatigue syndrome, depression and anxiety ruled his life before he found something he could complete. Having nearly finished a degree in Chemistry he found he could not go on, many nights were spent thinking about his life. A natural writer from a young age, he wrote little stories inspired by small events. Then through therapy, he was forced to begin a story of himself that turned into a novel. It felt cathartic so he wrote this one. Still crippled by fatigue and mental health issues he had to storm on and continue to plug away day after day, word by word to the finished product. Ross is lucky, the nights and days spent thinking about stories while stuck in bed have proven so valuable. Now he has found what he loves and turned a hobby into the physical novel you see now. Perfection is a way off, but undeterred, the words will flow.

Poetry never really flowed the same for Ross. A group changed that. He now writes nonets daily for his Facebook and Instagram pages, thank you to the people who read them. In time Ross hopes to help others through the writing and telling of bed imaginations.

Chapter One

I have nothing now,

Left to gift to this world of,

Death and dark despair.

There is a cloud covering my mind's eye, but from where it came, I do not know. The cloud is not light, white and fluffy; rather it's dark and full of rain and storms to come. It blankets me now, putting a fear in me that I have not experienced previously. It is not painful but prevents me from achieving anything during its spell. I tried to use magic, but the power needed to alleviate my symptoms is entirely beyond me now. I feel weak and near vanquished; raising a hand seems too much to bear. I have no hope left that the end will reach me on its own. I cannot even will the gods to take me far from this mind that has become rotten with the filth of its thinking. Death and despair are all I ponder these days; they grow in size and repel all the other thoughts I am sure I once had. I cry for a reprieve, howl for an amnesty, but neither is forthcoming, so I lie back down under the covers of this bed-come-tomb, and wait for a reckoning to find me and finish this. Invariably nothing comes of this pleading, and I groan under the weight of these thoughts. I must escape this sinking feeling, I say to myself, before falling into a restless dazing daydream. I shudder to imagine what the rest of them think of me now, so broken, so lost. I am terrified of this place, and will myself to make a movement that snatches me from the depths of dreams.

My eyes open to a sight I have grown accustomed to; walls. They tower over me as the claustrophobia sets in, and they feel as though they come closer every time I blink. I roll over and wonder what is happening beyond this room. The people, my people, wait for me somewhere out there. I could reach out and touch them once upon a time, I sigh, but no more. I know this land very well; I could step upon the dirt and stone once and stride out, powerful and strong.

In the early days, when I was young, I tried to fit in with my kin. I was hardworking but with a little feral streak. They sent me on pointless 'missions', I suspect to rid them of my presence. I helped build the towns in which they slept, however, after I finished completing the houses, there was not one for me. They would laugh and say, 'Go to the next town, I am sure they will have space for one such as you.' I pondered for a moment. Wasn't I one of them? 'Such as me', eh? What could that mean? It soon became apparent that I was not welcome in any of the towns, and I think this was when a spark was created where before there was nothing. With my jobs at an end, and being laughed at every time I passed, it was time to leave. I decided to roam the land in the hope there were others who would be more accommodating. I wandered far, and finding a still pool one day I peered in to see my face. I looked down into the water but it didn't look like me . . . did it? A face, an appalling reflection appeared in front of me. It was a grotesque mess of skin and bone. I had been born into this world by the gods – why would they give me such an unsightly appearance? I panicked, and, terrorised, I ran. I had never felt the need to touch my face before but I did then, discovering lumps and bumps that grew from all sorts of unnatural places. I cried as I ran. What had happened to me? This is why my kin denies me. I am not perfect like them. Yes, I am tall and muscled, but deformed. I wept some more, and then found myself in the middle of a great, old forest. The beauty was discovered not in where I had come from but from the place in which I was now.

There was an opening in the trees, and I walked forward into the light. Suddenly there was a large rustle in the bushes, a ruckus, and then the screams started. A deer leapt out of the bush, bleeding and limp, followed by a large wolf. It snarled at the sight of me, but I was not afraid. I charged at the wolf and promptly threw my fist at its face. Shocked into collapsing, the wolf then rose from the carpet of grass and staggered away from us. I knelt next to the screeching deer, possibly believing it was in its last moments. I bandaged the cuts as best I could and decided to try something new. We are magical beings, so why couldn't I try to use magic on this poor creature? I laid my hands on its leg and began to feel a warmth spreading through me and I hope the deer felt the same. It bleated out horribly as I heard the bone crack and come back to its rightful place. Immediately the deer rose, turned to look at me, and licked my face. Then it scampered off to the dense forest in search of shelter. I had never experienced such power and I felt a great wave of emotion flowing through me, jubilation. What I had done far exceeded our witch's powers, I knew. I had seen them try and fail on demon kin. But I succeeded! Joy spread from my hand and I jumped up and down with tears in my eyes.

The animal's paths led me far, to a hidden refuge, and I decided this was my safe place and began the toil to create a home of my own at last. I ate only from what I could grow in the earth. It was hard labour, but I took to the task with ease, and the wholesome crop of vegetables and fruit I could collect pleased me greatly. I could cook soups, bake bread on the fire and keep myself feeling strong. I made friends with the animals, copying them, and found that the plentiful amount of berries were also delicious to eat. I had found my real kin, and I would protect them for all time, I decided. I did not see any other demon for a long time, as none were explorers or adventurers like me. I felt immensely proud in those days and ready to open my eyes to the world of nature.

You see, this land, this seemingly endless land, is an island. Once flourishing, with forests for miles and vast wild meadows that seemed to have no end, to their size and their beauty. I have stretched to the far reaches and seen all the nooks and crannies, treasures and troves hidden in the land's vaults and caves. The island stretches a hundred miles in all directions, not far when you have the time. I never grew tired of exploring, I remember that. The animals roamed free, and I sat many an hour watching the eagles soaring the cliffs or the butterflies making their way to some unknown destination. I crossed paths with the deer and owl the most, never ceasing to be amazed to feel so close to nature and its perfection. I found peace there, watching an otter fishing in my waters or peregrine diving down a cliffside. I fell in love with the island and her delights, which never came close to easing. It was a perfect, enclosed land where I could press my face to a tree for long spells of time, and feel nature's beating heart. This is how I spent many years, just being in the world, present and a part of the land. Eventually, the animals grew accustomed to my presence and let me closer than any demon had ever been to them. I looked after them if they were sick and leapt with them when filled with joy, something rarely experienced by any other being. I remember the feeling vividly. The land had taken me in as its child, she pleased me, and I hope in return I pleased her; caring for the land was of utmost importance to me. I used what I had to, no more, and planted again where I had received her gifts of wood or wheat. I was sure never to take more than she could replace – the world was in balance, and we kept it that way for many years.

I can recall that era because I am an immortal being. Time was all I had in abundance, and I felt like being in nature was a way of living that suited me greatly. I always was a bit of a loner, and I preferred my animal company to those of my kin. We demons, or whatever is preferred, are not unkillable, but we don't degrade in time as the other animals around me seemed to do. The deer, for example, would come from fawn to adult and then perish within an age, but this was nothing but a blink in my eye. I cried each time it happened to them, but I could do nothing to stop this march towards the grave. I tried my magic and more physical means, but to no avail. I was very attuned to the land, and even the great trees that I had watched spring up from seed withered in time and became hollow. Maybe that is what is happening to me. I wonder if I am just a cavity in myself now. My body stays strong and never falters. You see, compared with the human's lifespan, I am incredibly old indeed. Their time on this land is truly short, so I drift along and watch them grey and grow into frailty. I am now very jealous of this journey. I lack the ability to die with such ease; my time never comes. I used to enjoy this fact, and for many a year, I watched the kings and queens fall into shadow and die. Their time is minuscule compared with my longevity. They eat, sleep and take their last breath in the same time I could be pressed, hugging a tree, communing with nature. How jealous they grow, unknowing of the burden that comes with my age. Unknowing of the terrible malaise I find myself in. The harsh reality has set in – I will never breathe my last, unless someone, I pray, comes to end my suffering.

I was the first to find the human explorers on their sailboats. A ramshackle bunch, but I was pleased, in the beginning, to have more company. So I was overly welcoming when the first boat landed on shore. I believed they were animals, like my deer friends, to be kept safe when sick and guided them through the land as such. I taught the first travellers which berries would be tasty and which would be poison to their veins. Initially, they were grateful, and starving. I brought them to water but the first red flag came when they tried to kill my friend the deer. I should have known then that this island was not for them. But I am caring and nurturing, and regret now that I let them loose on her, my home. They asked many questions and I was pleased to answer them, teaching all I knew. In return, they thought they could teach me things. Foolish traps were first, but it was here I learned about the sword and bow. The sword immediately took my attention. So shiny and sharp, and the feel of swinging it made me experience something I hadn't felt much of before – anger. I was enraged with my kin for shunning me and leaving me out in the cold. So, I learned swordplay and archery. Finding a natural talent, I worked on a new craft called 'war'. I liked it immensely and listened round the fire to their tales of battle. I was taught to kill, not to be afraid of forcing my victims to journey on to the next world. I took a sword as a gift, a mighty falchion I named Brandfire and felt a deviousness growing inside me. I liked it, the act of harm. I found myself enchanting Brandfire with the souls of those that lost their lives to her. In return, she would turn to flame with the essence of the dead screeching and whining, but a whisper to her and they would follow my lead. First was a bear, then the wolf who had preyed on my friends in times gone by. Their souls were strong and made the gifts I had potent. Each soul taken breathed fresh life into me and allowed me to become faster and tougher to harm, with lightning reflexes part of the reward. I could feel nature turning from me, but I cared not – I had found my true passion now. The humans did not shy me away from this path but encouraged me to follow it. I felt amazing when a boar let out a high-pitched squeal and attacked. I drew my blade and cut it in half. We fed from the remains and felt powerful.

I showed them the way to our towns on maps I had drawn in previous years; the whole island, I gave to them freely, sharing all the delights we demon immortals possess. Food, warmth and a little magic were given at will and they took in all they could. More and more travellers arrived until the towns groaned and bellowed under the weight and noise. My kin grew rude, there were just too many humans to care for properly. The demons didn't mean to upset them. But it was time for the guests to take their leave, the council decided, and head back on the boats that brought them here from a harsh land where no seed would grow. For them, utopia had finally been found, and they weren't to go without a challenge. In retaliation for the insults, they started to kill, taking down the system of government in just a few days. My kin were unused to war, having never seen it, and none but me had taken up a blade in anger or violence. It was strange in those first days; I was busy in the woods, perfecting my new craft. Meanwhile, our people were being slaughtered. I pondered on helping the humans; taking the souls of my kin would make me stronger. I had reached a point where I did not care for life anymore. I joined the humans. Nearby the little western fiefdom I had carved out, I found a modest township of my kin fighting humans, hands against swords. I joined in, with fire and steel; thousands of humans had descended, and the sheer numbers were overwhelming. They slashed through the bodies of the demons and I stood triumphant with them, bathed in blood. Then something strange happened: a handful noticed me and charged screaming 'demon!' into the night. I was taken aback, wide-eyed I parried the first blow before anger took over; it was my turn to cleave bodies. I did not stop with those few, the cheering army turned to blood and flesh that day, and I found power.

As only a handful of my kin were warriors of sorts, witches and wizards, they stayed to protect the escape of our people. I had heard they were leaving and was happy for them to. I was not ready to quit my land; my thirst for strength expanding. There were many human souls on the island to add to Brandfire; besides this was my fiefdom. I was prepared to keep it firmly in my grasp.

There was a march west to the coast by my kin, I knew that much, and I did not say goodbye or wave them off. They fled in fishing boats, and to this day I know not what happened to them. My hope is that there was a prevailing wind and calm waters. The sheer amount of humans suggests there are other islands, so I live in hope that in the future we will meet again and I may beg for their forgiveness. I further hope that they made it to a distant shore and started again; they were a resourceful bunch I believe, maybe they are happy in their new lands. Not sinking into a feeling that binds us down and breaks our spirit. It seems likely they are like me, and it is my greatest fear, carved out and dead inside. Falling into darkness and the depths of this void of life. It is what has happened, I am sure now – they fled and have just come to find death's open arms. I imagine them calling out for relief, drowning in spite of the power we possess. Yes, I feel them here now, and if I could I would reach out a hand this time and beg for mercy. So frightened, so broken, I don't know what help I would be, but we could do it together if only they were still here, standing by my side. Yet, the humans seem immune to this malaise; they trot around my bed and give me food and water when I need it, then disappear into oblivion through the door when I am finished. They have a strength I have not, a power beyond my own. I broke, but they believe that I must still have power within me, or they would slit me up and be finished serving a master who cannot control them anymore.

Chapter Two

I betray all those,

Who called me friend and ally,

Kill me for my deeds.

I will say, these humans have spirit, and controlling them was not easy. The Thrallium surrounding my keep still works, enslaving them to my will. It is a powerful spell, after all, one that remains even though I am incapable of lifting the sheets from my bed. They continue about their tasks thinking that they are free, thinking that they control their destiny. The first few who arrived at my keep did not know what was in store for them. I tried conventional ways to subdue them of course, but this wicked spell, after many failures, seems the best way for all. I used to muse with them about how they felt in their servitude – it gave me immense pleasure. But now I will only use them until the cloud lifts and I am the free one once more. Whether or not it ever lifts is a problem for me to deal with. They are dead-eyed beings to me now, props to hold me up while I cannot stand. Though it would be nice to have company, I fear I would have nothing to say, if I could talk at all. I have not spoken since becoming bedbound; words feel heavy on my tongue and I dare not try to use them. Sluggish and heavy are the only feelings I have; my head will not yield to the cloud, and will not break into sunshine as it once was able to.

I breathe a sigh, all I can muster, and stare at the wall once more. I was a being of great power, at least, I was before the cloud came. When my people began their voyage, I had given up killing humans or demons for the moment and instead wandered my forests. I caught the wolves, slitting their throats or eating the flesh of the deer that came my way. So hungry I was for death then, evil reigned in my eyes and I missed my chance for salvation, gorging on hollow feasts of flesh, while my people sailed into the night. I heard and felt their cries on their journey westwards, but it was of no use then. The sounds merely bounced off my mind's eye, so I shrugged them off and continued my campaign of hate. That night it left me empty, simply killing animals, and I knew what must be done, so I slinked down to the river and washed the blood off. The humans must have found the remains of the battle and would come for me now, I could hear distant horns sounding. There was no need to search out my prey. I enchanted the river water and sat on the only crossing, waiting for their march to my fiefdom.

I think of that day much of the time, how I waited in the rain, breathed silent breaths and became calm. In my mind, I have a vivid memory of smelling the sweet air that only comes before a battle. The birds stopped singing, almost as if they were in anticipation of my undoing, but I knew different. I had tasted human flesh and knew them to be thin-skinned and weak. Bones that break and skin that tears so easily. With Brandfire on my lap, I meditated on how I would fare; there were at least ten thousand on their way, I could feel it in the ground. I pondered my existence for a while, holding my hands and really feeling the beat in them. It relaxed me to know they were coming. The ground shook slightly, but I knew I was safe here. The waters would protect the flank and Brandfire would protect my front. Being a rather clever being, I had chosen my stronghold because of its excellent fishing grounds, fertile soil, the fact that no one else had found it yet helped immensely and also the colossal mountain range that swept down the valley between us and the sea. This meant there was no other choice but to face me at this place. It would be a tough call to break them all and hold them back, but I could do it in theory I knew. They weren't masters of tactics and would invariably just attack through the crossing, maybe not even trying the water. They were only animals, after all, I thought, and would add to mine and Brandfire's power soon.

I shake back into life and the world as it is now. I never leave this bed. It is my tomb, my penance for all the wrongs done in past anger and deviousness. I killed yes, but also enslaved and tortured beings for my own pleasure. A single tear falls from my eye. I never cry anymore; I don't see the point in trying to now. I really don't believe I could properly sob and hurt myself as I did at the beginning of the malaise; that pain is gone, and all that is left is a void of darkness. A deep, molasses-like black. It coats my being and lets no light in, nor anything shine out. I am in a catacomb of torture, far from the demon I once was. Far from strong, far from the light. I am sure if the king or queen knew of my crippled situation, they would send an army here to take me to the afterlife. I have no way of telling them that it is the case and they should send at least an assassin. For the sake of the gods, how could I get a message out of here? I can't bring myself to shout out, not that calling would help. I am trapped by my own hand. The town below my keep has humans not under my control, but they would never dare venture up here. More than likely they are busy whittling their lives to the bone. Farming or fishing, and always making those children who would do the same thing, and will die also in their own time. All for nothing, no point, yet I envy them deeply.

I will concede that this grave I wait in gives me plenty of time to think, but here, I cannot will myself to move. I cannot see the point anyway – my people are dead and I am the last of my kind, it would seem. They sank, drowned or wasted away on some foreign beachhead. How should the last of a species die? I am still alive enough to think and plan my death. I would like to bleed out of wounds, I believe. Seeing my precious blood weep down my arms and legs, becoming deep red and wet with it, before falling to my knees and letting the rest flow. Maybe I should use Brandfire – she is not as sharp as she once was but will still cleave a man in half if she was asked to. My soul would be within her then, along with the others, they would torture me with screams and give it the place it deserves. I still hear the howling from the sword even though she is in her scabbard attached to the wall. Just a slight noise nowadays, but I remember when it began to send shivers through me. I hadn't heard them before that time and I don't recall why I started to listen, but I did. At night they would make me cry, knowing the spell is irreversible, and the souls will still be with her when all has rusted to the hilt. I begged them to stop on quite a few occasions, removing the sword from her waiting place and crying as I saw them in the reflection on the metal. Waves of souls weeping and wailing to let them out and go to their place of peace. I whispered that I was sorry but couldn't undo the magic. This angered them and she burned me that day, my hands blistered and red, and it was the first time

I slept in bed and did not wake for a few days. Yes, maybe that is when it all began and this journey I am sailing through, started. She did this to me, so it is only apt that I end it with her cutting through bone and flesh alike.

The heavy golden curtain shivers in the wind, waking me from my dark thoughts. The curtain's movement periodically allows some sunlight to beam directly into my eyes. It burns; I have not seen full daylight in many a . . . well, for some time I imagine. The days are lost to me now, so I wave the sun away and beg internally for a cloud to cover its light and let me rest. I will it, yet nothing occurs; my strength wanes and I let the sun burn me over and over again.

My captives bring me water and soup, and for a while I am distracted from my thoughts and feelings. A reprieve is most welcome and I sigh and lie back once finished, as they clear up after me and take their leave without a word. The sun's light eventually dissipates, and in its place the moon rises, casting a different shine through my window. It is softer and more peaceful, and I find myself just watching the light beam down on me; I feel it may take my soul upwards with it, but no such luck. I am doomed to lie here and wait, it would seem. I flick my toes to make sure they actually work and they crack into life; my legs I am not sure work as legs should, or that they could carry my weight now. Not that I dare to touch the cold stone floor and test them out. There is no point. Nothing matters now, the only thing to manage is my dying light and how it is to be extinguished. A being such as myself deserves a big funeral march. I smile; there are none I know who would turn out for such an occasion, maybe a party to celebrate freedom at last, but no funeral, nobody to carry me to a grave and curl me up in a hole. Or burn the body so I may float to the gods and be finally free.

But in any case, it is morning again. I shake my head – it came too quickly, so I must have slept somewhere along the way. I roll over away from the window, pleased I managed such a manoeuvre. The pleasure is fleeting and hollow, like a tiny spark that extinguishes all too quickly, and again the malaise hits me hard, turning my face into a sorrowful image. If only I had kindling for that spark, an ember that would flourish and bring me back from the darkness. I stare at the wall once more, before taking my gaze to the portrait hanging to the left. It is grand – I had one of the local artists create it. Full of purples, blacks and reds. I look opulent, but the face remains. After much infuriating discussion, they painted me as I am. I wear my face with pride now; many who laughed at the beginning are now in possession of Brandfire. No one laughs now. Most bow their head in some human custom to their lord, but would never dare to look into these eyes. My slaves come in, no laughs from them either, not since the spell took their minds. I am fed again, as breaking fast early is a custom too. The food keeps coming so I am kept alive here. I have not walked to the town in a long time, and have no need to, as the beauty that once was my home has now diminished as the town grew larger. Forests were cut to make their homes and fires, and I was displeased at first but needs must. I allowed all to come into my realm eventually, the ones who are outcasts in their previous homes. I created a place for them to go, a place where they could be free to start again. I only took a few into servitude, the rest able to go about their little lives in peace.

I know it is winter since bed coals are brought every night out of some strange but not unpleasant human tradition, to keep their lords warm. The winters here are hard for the town, and without the forests the animals have moved on. Nothing grows, and the winds from the mountains bring much snow and gales of cold air. But hardy folk they are, and manage along in their new homes. Most were murderers and thieves I believe from what little I've heard about them. Given a second chance though, most keep to my rules, and I have only a few. The main one is to give all their fair second chance, a clean slate if you will. They can be whatever they wish to be, and a lot of artists have emerged from this rule. Also, to work as a community, for there would be nothing without them working together to build a better world. I set up the first guilds and a group to watch over whom I named the elders, not that they were old. The thieves and assassin guilds do very well but I taught them to use their skills against the rest of the island, not their own homes. They bring in gold for the coffers, which seems to please the people of the town, especially at this time of year, when we may have to trade with the towns further afield. Death – I taught them to bring death, didn't I? That is my main legacy. I embody death I suppose, not that the people of my town remember who I really am. Most who remember that time are long into the afterlife, and only watch down on us. I am also a killer, just like they are, a murderer, a thief of souls and I am so regretful of my choice to become what I was back then.

My mind twists and turns backwards in time to that night on the bridge. It wasn't a warm evening when the knights of the human realm came for me. They must have marched for the entire day, as when I finally caught sight of them fully armoured and shouting, waving their pitiful spears and swords, they looked tired. I smiled, this was perfect for me, being well rested and ready for battle. I would make them bleed heavily. Their cries of: 'Die demon!' was the main chant and when they caught sight of me, I stood and took Brandfire from her scabbard in preparation. The rain flowed from the heavens, and I still waited on the bridge to my home. I laughed at the chants, and bellowed back, screaming that they should turn around while they still could. I heard a cheer as they formed into ranks at the foot of the bridge. Thunder cracked and lightning lit up the humans for a split second. Ten thousand was quite right, but that would not be enough. I felt my anger grow, and rage spilled into my mind. The berserker in my head was ready. I knew well that they don't fight as such, they use weight of numbers to crush an enemy taking down what they can with them. But I was a master at fighting, my senses honed and my blade sharp, it was time to whisper my words to Brandfire. She burst into flame with the souls, and I heard a resounding gasp from across the bridge. I goaded them, hoping for a reckless charge of their bodies.

'Come to me, my children, and feel the steel I hold!' I roared in a voice so dark it shook the ground beneath them.

They fell for it, and charged without orders or discipline, some into the water, most to the bridge. The waters under my control did their job of drowning all who dared try to wade into it. They were swallowed up in heavy armour incredibly easily. The rest charged the bridge, which I cut swiftly and cleanly, taking bodies and heads all the same. They were bottlenecked. Numbers made no odds against me and I held the bridge, growing stronger and angrier with each human soul taken. Soon they were screeching and chanted no more, the disciplined drum beat of footsteps became a mash of noise as they ran from me. I did not give chase, knowing I had the ground and more may well swell across the bridge once more if their leaders could convince them. I sat cross-legged again and waited. Once most had run into the night, one of their leaders cautiously crossed over to me.

'What do you want? My men are beaten, give me your terms!' he shouted, still many metres away from my sword.

I looked up into his eyes and shouted back, 'Leave my land! Take your soldiers home and never return here! I hold it and there is no changing that.'

He nodded, bowed and left the bridge. No army ever did dare to come back. So I have not kept my own army, as the fear of that night still resonates to this day. The king of the humans sent me a messenger not long after, agreeing to leave my land to me as long as I did not encroach on theirs at any point in the future. I nodded to the messenger and told him I would abide by the agreement.

I still follow their rules – I haven't set foot on their soil since the agreement, and my adventuring days were at an end anyway. I had all the power of souls I needed, and I didn't believe I could get much stronger. It poured from me, and I built the keep by hand, mining the stone from the mountains and carrying it to this place I had chosen in a clearing on top of a small hillock. A bonus came when after mining for some time I discovered pure veins of Thrallium, from which I knew what could be made. The very mineral that gives the power over minds, with the right spellcasting of course. Useless to most, it has no value to anyone but myself so I collected as much as I needed and eventually when the first humans came, hungry and cast out, I brought them to the keep and used them to serve. More arrived, and I had no use for them but something in me resonated; I heard them tell of being hated and just needing a new place to start. Would I have them? The animals feared me now and I was longing for a little company. I agreed and sent several humans to message the island, town by town that there was a place for the beggars, thieves and murderers. They came in a trickle at first, then waves of the broken started to arrive. I was astonished there were so many like me, alone in the world, or so we all thought to ourselves. I could still talk to my servants in those days, but it wasn't until I had a full town's worth of humans that I truly felt like I had a family to look after. They did not show looks of disgust when they arrived, only a shared pity, or maybe just pure elation that they were actually being welcomed for the first time in their lives.

They lived in ramshackle huts to begin with, and from my keep, I watched them a while. It was spring and the air was fresh and clean. The snowdrops had begun to grow and birds started to sing, a noise I hadn't noticed in a long while. I thought it was an omen; these humans could live in harmony with nature, and my anger waned at last. So, instead of just being the overseer, I decided I would be the benevolent god. I walked among them and heard some of their stories.

'I stole a loaf of bread for my starving family,' said one and I looked at the children, so small and delicate. They deserved to eat, I thought. So I taught them to fish and bake their own bread from the wheat field not far down the valley.

'My parents died of illness when I was young. I have been begging since but no one took pity on me,' a youngling girl said. I nodded to her.

'And what would you like to be?' I asked, to which she replied, 'An artist, I can draw!' She beamed and took out of her satchel scraps filled with drawings of people who had not even noticed her.

'Amazing,' I said. 'Would you like to do this in a proper studio?' I asked and she nodded with glee. It was the first house to be built by me since my people left. I knew how to make the perfect studio for her. After I was finished, which took me a week or so, she hugged me at less than half my height, and I crouched down and reciprocated. It brought warmth to me.

'What shall I call you?' I asked, curious.

'Well, my name was Charlotte, but I prefer Fern as ferns are my favourite plant to draw,' she said in a noticeably quiet, ashamed voice.

'Why do you sound so embarrassed child?' I asked.

'All used to make fun of me for the name, sir.' She replied.

'Fern, you shall be the artist for the town. I name you, so all shall know where to come to find real art.' I spoke softly and stroked her hair.

She cried, and I took my hand away thinking it was because of me, but she pulled me in close and once again gave me a hug, deeper and more devoted now. I held her a while before slowly letting go and sending her to set up her studio. She did become the artist in residence, which pulled more artists into my realm, a safe place in which to practice their work.

The first murderer arrived, and he spoke to me of voices in his head, which I had never heard of before. How they belittled him, caused him rage, and there was only one way to appease them.

'I didn't mean to kill them,' he said sorrowfully.

'My child, you are safe here, but you must learn to listen to the birds and nature, which speak to me all the time, instead of these voices who harm you. Come to me anytime they bother you and I will help you through it,' I said with a massive hand on his shoulder. I wept with him, seeing the pain in his eyes.

Witches made up most of the population in no time at all, properly persecuted by male humans. I found this repugnant, as a lover of magic in all its forms, and took them in letting them know they could either continue to practice their skills, or if falsely accused, to do what pleased them the most. Unfortunately, it became apparent the men were for the most part liars and these women had no skill in the craft. So it became that I taught them some basic spells. Only enough to get them started, after that it was up to them if they wanted to explore more from real witches arriving of which there were only a handful, but I must admit I was disappointed in the level of skill of the humans. It was like they had no connection with their power inside, that it had been beaten out of them, literally, from a young age. Unlike myself, who was nurtured to explore magic and curiosity, before I was cast out and became the hate-filled predator I am today.

In any case, the witches that chose the right path were able to build the town without much help from myself. I gave orders, of course, just aesthetical deviations, and would make right any changes I saw fit. Soon, we had a small hamlet to be proud of. A fountain sat in the central cobbled marketplace and homes stretched out in a star formation, which pleased me greatly. It is true that we cleared forest in order for this town to flourish and have the space it deserved but at the time, I believed it had to be done. I hate myself constantly for ruining the old trees and habitats that I had cherished in my youth. It was my fault after all, my doing, my hand that stretched out and gave way to all this chaos and misery. How the trees must have screamed as we ripped them from their homes and cut and cut until only timber remained. We never planted a new forest in compensation – it never occurred to me. Progress; we were progressing to a state of freedom and second starts.

Chapter Three

Is there a future?

The past is a dense forest,

I cannot escape.

I bring myself to my senses, feeling the sheets of the bed once more, no longer travelling in the past. I gather my strength for quite a while, waiting for the moment when I can lift myself up to sit against the headboard. I complete the task in stages, and it grieves me that this is what it has come to. I manage and eventually reach for my letter opener, barely grasping it in long, shaking fingers with nails like claws. I hold it carefully in my right hand and look at my reflection in the mirrored metal. *Can I bear to do this again?* I look round at my pristine shoulder; yes, I can. I bring the knife across slowly, steadily and with precision, and begin to cut. Little slices at first; the blood pops from my skin so I open the wound with my fingers and it starts to flow, black like my heart. I don't cry, there is no pain anymore. Just relief as I watch the trickle, then pain the small wounds heals quickly. I have hurt so many, it is definitely time I bled for my corruption. This time, for the cut, I go with the tip of the blade, dipping it deep into the muscle and starting to pull along the shoulder. This is pain, I think. 'You can feel something,' I repeat in my head. A little more and I stop and breathe out sharply. The blood is now a stream of colliding trickles forming a proper river by the time it reaches my hand. It is not the pain I crave, only the rush from seeing my bloodied arm. The first time I did this I was scared, but now it has become a ritual and it gives me power over my mind. The relief pours from me and I wipe the blood onto the sheets, settling back down to curl up, my mind spinning and swaying under this cloud.

My internal voice attacks me. 'Stupid demon, pretending to be a human, where are the forests now? What did you do, you evil, vindictive being? You are devoid of nature's connection and now alone in this bed forevermore. It is your penance for the blood you spilled all over the land. She knows, nature, she has seen what you did to her and she weeps. Are you proud as you once were? Hide in the covers, maybe you will die soon and even the gods will send you away, everyone does and you know that very well.'

I shake and bend further into myself, bringing my head right to my knees. I can't stop it – my mind assaults me constantly now. Obsessively and continuously, it screams at me to do the right thing, not just to bleed but to kill. I wish to be far from this place of worshipping death, but it is to no avail. Hideous in face and in nature, that is what I am, I know. A wretched soul, tortured and twisted into a grotesque, dark energy. That is all I have left to give to the world. I am a plague on this land, destroyer of the good and pure, everything I touch turns out like my face – torn and broken. None would dare look at it now. Even those who serve me are turning out like me, fallowed, with yellowed faces and nothing behind the eyes. As my strength wanes, so does theirs and there is no help for any of us. We are all prisoners of my doing. Why did I think it was right to subdue such poor souls? It was not my place to do so. I have changed now, the malaise has broken my anger and I feel it no more. No being would have to be scared of me now, whether it be a deer, human, fox or bear. Even my kin. I wonder if my pestilence has spread to the town. They may also be under the cloud that envelops me. It is getting darker every season, I see that now. It could spread out, powerful as it is, and capture their minds too. It would crush any not as strong-willed as I am. They will bleed out aswell, cutting and slashing at their bodies until there is not even a trickle flowing out, and finally, lose their souls to their gods. Once they were so happy here, fresh-faced again and unburdened by their past. Mine had caught me, but they were free and peaceful, grateful to me for the chance to be who they really are. I look to the ceiling, just for a moment, and pray. Pray that the cloud leaves them alone as it is all my fault, my doing – torture me! Oh, not them, please gods. Not my children.

However, I must accept that my human children, whom I took in and made whole, have been burned too. I cannot see from the window, but I know in my heart they will be troubled and tortured till madness takes over. Maybe they will storm the keep in anger, but that would be a terrible move on their part; the spell would simply take over. No, I need someone wise enough to break the circle of Thrallium underneath the ground. But who could be so clever? No-one. I alone hold that power, I believe. So I will just wait. At least my bleeding has ceased finally, and the sheets have soaked up what they could, becoming cold, wet and uncomfortable. No matter though, my servants will bring me a change without a word. If only they would ask what happened, but I know the spell – no questions will be forthcoming. They do their duties and care not for my actual well-being. The time has come to be fed and watered again, so I order the sheets removed and new ones to be brought. They simply nod and go about the task. I don't move, I can't, so it is an arduous task. I see my naked body; it has been a while and I look misshapen – bones can be seen, bulging out of the skin. I would say sorry to it and promise to do better, but I know the truth is that my body will have to stay this way. I am covered again eventually and breathe a sigh; I do not have to look at the unsightly mess of bones any longer. They leave in silence, as expected, as ordered long ago when the cloud first came and I did not realise that I needed any help.

I cannot pinpoint when the shadow of the cloud first came over, but I do know I had felt far from nature and the animals for some time before that first day. The sluggishness kept me in bed longer and longer, till it was all I was, a demon in a bed. On the days I could walk, I only made it to the town, no further. Exchanging talk with the market stall holders about where they had come from, was my respite from town life.

'My Lord! Try these oranges, they come from Cotres, best in the land you know!' one said, calling me over. I came and inspected the fruit. It was like nothing I had seen before and such a vibrant colour.

'Oranges, you say. Tell me of Cotres.' I speak in a slow and deep voice but with a hint of meekness.

'It is my home on the south of the island. Oh, you should see the orchards! Right by the sea, Lord, goes well with duck. Try one please,

I beg of you,' he said with pleading eyes, knowing I could buy his cart if I wanted and he could go home a happy man.

'You have forests?' I asked, tasting the sweet juicy fruit.

'Oh, Lord, if I may you don't eat the peel and pith, here see.' He peeled back the layer of pith for me to reveal the lushest part of the fruit.

'Tasty. Do you have forests?' I queried again, peering deep into his eyes with some hope.

'Of course, sire, the apples and oranges grow on trees in the orchards,' he replied, still clinging to the hope that maybe I would purchase his wares.

My mouth turned sour. 'Stupid man – forests! With animals and leaves and ferns and real trees!' I spat out the flesh of the fruit and moved on. His face dropped, and he looked quite scared at offending me.

I searched the market for anyone with stories of real forests, not farms, but none had a clue what I was talking about. I must have seemed crazy, and I returned to the keep defeated. I think that was the first time I cut myself. It hurt then, but I felt a compulsion because of my anger at myself – I had let this happen, brought this onto the island. Farming had taken over it would seem, no use for forests except for their timber which they must have cut and slashed for. So I cut and slashed in reciprocation, bleeding and crying for what I had done to her, my goddess of nature. Where would the birds and animals live now? Picking through pieces of whatever was left behind in the wake of human progress. I slept then, not a restful sleep but full of nightmares and tossing about the bed, sweating.

My goddess of nature seemed further and further away; none of my lands contained the old forests now. There were fields of course, but farmed animals used them and you could see them expand across to the horizon. Not a tree in sight – even the eagles and peregrines that used to hold court on the cliffs had moved on or died from hunger. It was this realisation that I think, perhaps, first brought on the malaise. Quite a thought, and maybe in some way it holds the key to my freedom. I cannot access it though, it seems so clear sometimes but quickly I lose grasp of it and give up.

I stopped walking out of the keep. I would stretch and walk around my bedroom, but that was as far as I went. The door handle to the outside got heavier, so I ordered my servants to bring everything to me.

'Keep me alive,' I told them, and in their way, they nodded and then I said, 'silence only when in my chambers.' I can remember thinking I could not bear to hear words from humans any longer.

Maybe I should have gone out in my fiefdom and planted trees, looked after the animals like I once had. It felt like too much to do though – the humans had progressed so far that I could not take their food, I had brought them into my land, after all. I was torn inside, ripped apart by guilt, and so never again wandered the halls or caught sunlight in any great measure. I had the power to do it then, and should have been braver, but I can no longer look in the mirror at what I have become. In any case, the trees that were chopped down for building supplies were ages old, would I really expect a change by planting saplings? Even if the animals had shelter again it wouldn't bring them back, not with so many hungry humans in this world now. They have an insatiable hunger for war and killing. I found myself the same, greedy for destruction but it was not always this way was it? The seed was planted in my mind from an early age, I suppose, and has turned me into a hate-filled, angry but woeful adult. I embraced it with all my might and it has left me hollow and falling deep into the ground beneath. If only I could be swallowed up by my goddess and a tree come from my body. I imagine the roots sprouting from my arms and legs, slowly sapping my energies, then from my chest a seedling would shoot upwards towards the sky. It would be painful to grow the sapling, but I would bear it and thrust my chest out to help it reach its goal. Then a beautiful and grand tree would emerge and take my place on this island. Nature may forgive my sins then, for a tree that could not be cut and would give shelter to all animals, seeding more trees around it until a forest would grow once again. It is a great dream, though misguided and false. She will never take me into her ground and nothing can grow from me but darkness.

My mind is drawn deeper into shadow once more; the cloud wraps round my thoughts. My heart was once pumped full of love, and I almost remember the feeling. It was definitely there, it must have been – I cared, I looked after the humans and loved them for all their faults and the failure to comprehend my being. When love is not reciprocal though, it can turn dark and shrivel. That hurt my mind; I would have survived the disappointment though. Now my mind constantly berates me for a reason I cannot fathom. I hate myself now, not just a fleeting hate but a long, deep and spiteful hate, so angry at what I have done and become. I hit my legs in frustration till they bruise and pain begins to surface. I am a stupid being, worthless and useless. Good only for timber for the fire, incapable of love or doing anything useful – what have I done recently that was useful, even to myself? Nothing, is the answer I hear in my head. Cruelty is all I know so I will embrace that, pick apart this pathetic body till there are only the bones left to show that a demon died here. Love – what a ridiculous, fleeting feeling. I was silly to imagine it would continue to reside in me, a complete idiot to believe in anyone. I am alone. Mostly I have been alone all my poor life, but not lonely like I am now. Not craving attention like a beggar on the streets of the towns far from here. I sense them; we share a common feeling. I am so lonely, it splits my heart in two, that none come to my aid in these darkest of days. The servants come in for supper, 'what great timing,' I think.

'Please help me,' I meekly manage to voice in a hoarse, rasping tone. But they continue their jobs, dead-eyed and perfect in their duties. I reach out a hand to grab one but miss; I am too weak and slow nowadays and they seem so far away. Nothing from them, then I remember I have told them to be silent. Even if they had some kind words, they could not speak them. It is as if I have sewn their mouths shut. If only they were stronger, maybe they could break the spell themselves but no, I chose them because they were weak! Stupid thing, you didn't see a need for them to be company. When now all I long for is someone to breathe life into me and help me out of this malaise.

I think that is the only way now – I am obviously too broken and encapsulated in this cloud to manage on my own. Why did I not think of this before? I need help, that is the only way to salvage this. Or death. That is an option, I know. I could stop eating and that would do the job in a long, stretched-out time. I would find it hard to starve; our body goes into a state where it doesn't need much sustenance. I believe magic is at work here, but no matter. I wonder if the servants would force feed me though, after all, I did tell them to keep me alive . . . Brandfire is the only clean death but I fear for my soul, trapped like the others, and I change my mind. My soul doesn't deserve to be trapped. Let the gods decide the punishment. They will know what is to be done. Maybe I will come back as a tree, only to be repeatedly chopped down. I think that would be fair. The pain I put those trees through must have been excruciating, so I deserve the same. If the gods will oblige and are listening, those are my thoughts on the matter.

I need a plan, I need some way of contacting the outside township. Is there one with the power to withstand the spell by coming into the keep? Probably not. But they can destroy it completely. The Thrallium circle is a brittle mineral so I buried it deep, my stupid idea as well. How can I send a message to destroy what lies beneath? Slip a note out the window? No, no one would find it and my arms are too weak. If only the birds were my friends again, they could see my peril and send a message out to the world easily. But I hear no cheep or chirrup close by.

A spell, which could make its way to the town. It hits me all at once – a song! My song spells are strong enough to reach the ears and minds of the town's people. It can't be shaken out of your head until I break it. However, am I strong enough for the crafting? I need a tune, and I need lyrics. I will have to make it short and to the point, something that none can ignore and must investigate. I reach out a hand for my quill and paper and begin to write.

It is a frustrating task with many failures. It must be great; it must be a song for the witches. I give up for a few days, my energy sapped and no imagination left, and I believe it may be that I cannot do this. I bleed once more after a rest, and use the blood to write more and more till I have a song worthy of a spell.

The Lord awaits in his keep,
Until he is free you cannot sleep,
Break the spell around his home,
Dig till your fingers reach bone,
Destroy the crystal beneath the earth,
Kill or save the Lord in his berth.

I know it is a sin to stop them sleeping, but this is of the utmost urgency now. They will choose whether I should live or die here. I don't wish for either if I am honest – life is so difficult, and death, who knows what that will behold? Either torture or a blank nothingness, the latter could appeal to me most. A quietness, a stillness that expands forever, blackness like my soul with other souls there too, who have found themselves rid of the flesh and exist only to float in pure silence. But torture is a possibility, writhing in anger and a rage that my soul deserves, so I am afraid. Scared of death, and scared of life now, too. Caught in between worlds, neither holding any kind of satisfaction or love. So here I lie and will accept that it is not for me to choose one or the other. There are plenty who would enjoy my destruction so that they could take over my reign. Devious ones who wouldn't treat the population as well as I may have. But it is out of my hands. I will wait and see what the next chapter of my being holds. The elders will know what to do; they may be made up of ruffians but they are fair, for the most part. At least my dead-eyed slaves will be free, that I am glad of. Their time in servitude is ending, and they will be allowed back to the town to start anew, cursing my name all the way down the road. So they should, I think, I have kept them here while they grow old and frail. They will wake not in youth. I regret stealing their fleeting time from them, but they have kept me alive for a long time while I changed and repented my wrongdoings. Was it worth it? I wonder.

Chapter Four

In your memory,

There was time when you were well,

You will be again.

I scroll down the song. I just need a melody to go along with it. Something that sticks to them like oil and will never wash off until I command it. Reading the word kill, I shudder. It is the strongest possibility, I believe, and a tear creeps out of my eye and down my face. Yes, it may be that this will all be over soon. I will never see a tree again, never feel the firm but supple bark against my face. Never smell a wildflower, or leap with joy at the scent of the daffodil, or sight of the first bee of the season. It is hard to let these things go now. I grasp out towards them in my mind, and that will have to do. Memories of running through the forest with my deer kin, them leaping and bounding and me trying to do the same. I remember the first deer I saved, that lick on my distorted face, not caring for looks just grateful for the saving of its life. The tongue was rough but warm, tender and loving. To be back with that same deer, there in my decisive moment is all I hope for, I will replay the memory in my mind repeatedly until they come for me.

With the scroll written and ready, I hum to myself a tune that follows the words. It is challenging work and I lose my sense of it time and again. The trouble with writing songs as always. It is tiresome. Soon I lose my energy and lay back down on bloodied sheets to ponder a tune worthy of myself. I sleep and I dream of that deer licking my face and myself smiling, but then I look up and the clouds are coming down low, dark and bellowing thunder. I shout to the deer to run but it stands there, looking at me with a blank expression, then screams out as it melts to the ground into a pool of blood and guts. I awake sharply and hold my head. That is not what happened! I saved it! I cry properly for the first time in an age. I sniff, wipe my nose and tears with the bedsheets, then control myself. I must be disciplined now. I must finish the melody.

I continue to hum most of the day, and finally find a mingling of notes that rings true and is rhythmic. If it sticks in my mind, then surely it will stick in theirs. I take the scroll and it turns to blue fire – this saps my energy greatly, but I must hold firm. I sing the lyrics to the scroll and the words lift off the page, turning bright, burning red. I tell them to seek the villagers and with every ounce of my being I will it to go out the window. Slowly they drift, one line at a time and head towards the window; the wind catches them and for a moment I am afraid they will only imbue onto the curtains. Thankfully, they miss and slide out the open crack and swirl towards town.

I collapse backwards, exhausted with the effort. My last hope has started its journey and now I must wait. It may take a day to reach them, then a day for them to work it out, possibly a day to break the Thrallium and a night to kill me. So, I have three days to live. I can dream for three days till they come. I let out a short but sorrowful laugh, and weep again. Rolling over onto my side, I decide I will wait like this so they may make it quick should they choose. I hope I am not dragged through the streets like murderers are in human customs, bumped along cobbled roads and jeered at until I finally died. I would last an exceptionally long time that way, so I hope they think better of it. Better to just kill me quickly with a blade from the assassins guild. Maybe a thief will take what precious things I have collected over the years – not that I have any need of them now, anyway.

The best in my collection, which I hold most dear, is a locket I made from a fallen tree, not much use to a thief. Not even the Thrallium chandeliers are worth anything outside of their beauty. I do have a vast amount of gold, down in the vaults, that the people of the town gave me in thanks or in payment from the guilds. That will suffice for the thieves guild for sure, or the traders guild could do a lot for the town with that much gold. I hope they won't war over it, but humans are prone to such things. Maybe these will be my last words:

'Share the wealth, care for the people,' I will say.

A master assassin may heed the request but a thief would not. I hope for the former to arrive first; they are nimble and quick, so there is a good chance they will make it first. Assassins are used to creating a quick death, a quiet one so as not to arouse suspicion. If only the witches would come for me first – they know me and may actually help rather than create chaos. But stupid men always look for the glory and I am sure they have had their plans for my undoing tucked away somewhere.

The keep is not all as it seems, though. I built it for fun, but also for protection. The servants know the tricks because I taught them, but a newcomer could get lost in the labyrinth of tunnels and endless hallways with no doors. I giggle to myself, I cannot help but be amused that they may not find it so easy to kill a shadow. My room is not in the tower as you would expect, rather I chose a central room, not unlike the servants' quarters; it is not large, but unassuming and comfortable. I have a side table, a large bed, a few paintings and an easy way out of the keep, if one knows the route.

I created a trap door that leads to an underground tunnel and stretches all the way to the mountainside. It was just easier to get out before the malaise came, easier to avoid humans if I wanted to walk but not talk. There are a few trees there, pools and bogs that are unfarmable so I can be at peace, or, rather, I could go there when I used to be able to find peace. It holds nothing for me now – I don't believe in calm and harmony anymore. It was a falsehood that I fell for, head over heels in love with the natural world, but where is she now? I would watch in relish too, had the roles been reversed, I suppose. Now shunned by her I am lost, and my mind clouds over.

This first day has not yet found its end, and it is so frustrating that they haven't worked it out already. They aren't even trying to sleep yet, so therefore, must just have this weird melody and words in their heads. Infuriating. The song was not direct enough! I bash my legs and cut my arm in rage. This time I have gone too far though, and I feel a sigh of relief washing over me. The blood loss sends me into an almost unconscious state, not dreaming, just shaking in between worlds. I shift and toss about the bed, trying to find that relief again.

The night was full of dreams and sweating out the pain. It is the second day now. They have not slept a wink, so they must realise magic is at work, surely. I know humans aren't the brightest bunch, but no one sleeping points to a wizard or witch. I hope they don't blame the witches guild . . . That would be devastating, not just for my plan but for the world. Some of the most powerful witches reside here in peace, I hope the humans don't point a finger at them as they did in the other towns. But none of them are capable of such an act of magic yet – I know this as I would have felt their presence in the town. In any case, the elders will meet today to discuss the problem, and hopefully find a solution by actually listening to the lyrics. I hope the words are obvious. No one has knowledge of the keep's spell, they just know never to intrude or there will be deadly consequences. Some were brave enough in the early days, but they never returned of course, becoming servants in their own right. So the town's people got the message rather quickly, believing their brave, foolhardy men dead or in dungeons somewhere. I was pleaded with to return them, but refused. How I wish I had returned the young boy, though. I don't remember his name, and he is a man now, unrecognisable. He cleans out the horses every day and feeds them. I have heard some of his family call to him to return but to no avail, obviously. Must have been heart-breaking for them. Damn my bones, damn my head for its lack of compassion and empathy. But it is done now, and all I have left is remorse. His mother is probably dead by now, so he will see her again as a man, not the boy she loved. I have made a mess of things, taking children from their families and then their adult life away.

Chapter Five

Kings and queens perish,

I live in 'glorious' life,

What a waste I am.

It is the third day already, and they should have worked out what is to be done by now. Their tired bodies are digging in the dirt for my Thrallium circle. I hope they dig fast for I am impatient to see results of my work. I am desperate for this to be over and for the end to begin, but fearful of just what that end will be. I hear shouting from the town.

'My Lord! What have you done to us? Stop this incessant noise! We bleed and do not sleep!' I make it out as my hearing is honed but cannot shout back any words of wisdom. They have not worked it out yet.

Perhaps the melody was too strong, but I am too weak to try again. For our god's sake, dig! I scream in my mind. Bleeding was not part of the plan. I can go without sleep for weeks, but I know the humans tire every night and lay down to rest. They lead busy lives I suppose, and it fatigues them. Maybe that is why they die so quickly. If only they would slow down and take their time. If they bleed from their ears, how will they hear my song? Maybe it is not so, and the song will continue until I am brought to salvation. Noise, they called it. I audibly sigh. It is not a noise, you idiot, it is a song! Be mindful for once, and you will see the meaning!

What have I done for them? I gave them a new life, a clean start, it is not much to ask to help or destroy, after all I have accomplished for them. A great town, possibly the best in the land, is what I have done for you, fool. I feel a wave of anger rising in my chest but beat it down and back into me – it is my fault. I am hurting my children, but for good reason, albeit a selfish ploy. I am putting my own self above their wellbeing, but surely I will be forgiven given the state I am in. At death's door, the path travelled by all I suppose at some point. Ready to open that door and walk or crawl through, whichever I can manage, roll me if you must! Just let me go! I begin to cry, but not tears of sorrow – they are happy ones, because I will finally be free, as soon as those blasted humans follow my plan.

After weeping for some time I realise I can hear the sound of the pickaxe. Oh, joy of joys! Then more noises; they dig! At last the elders or someone has gathered the town to work on finding the circle. It won't be long now, I think with glee. I will be dead and they will have revenge on their master. The digging continues through the night. As I hear the clink of metal on stone, it brings a feeling of peace to me I thought I had lost. The relief is great to know – *hello, my old friend*. I sigh, and rest some more, as it will be morning before they dig deep enough to find the mineral circle.

It is the fourth day, and the sun rises on my last day of suffering. Light peeps through the window at me, almost teasing and playful in its nature. I dance my hands through the beams, feeling a sense of wonder again now that I know it is nearly over. I will miss sunlight on a dew-dropped tree. The digging sounds continue, much to my frustration. I did not tell them where the circle was – I should have described its location beneath the ground as well.

Maybe they dig too far away, scared to go so near. My voice is too weak and hoarse from lack of use to give this vital piece of information to them. But yes! I have it. The idea sparks like a flame in my mind. I will use the last of my magic and make the ground glow above the Thrallium. I think it is possible, after all, the spell covering the ring is still connected to me and I can use that connection.

It will definitely work. A bright light to guide the way to where the ring lies. There is no way I can fail now – they will be here tomorrow. I don't worry for the servants, for once the spell is broken they will stop serving and go about trying to live again. I wonder what they will be, who they were. Will they even remember? Poor villagers, but they are strong I am sure, and will fit in with the town's folk who will look after them when I am gone. They will have to go and find their purpose, whether it be art or fishing or farming. All are excellent choices as they serve the community well.

The noise of digging is halted, the town's people shout almost as one. After a short time I hear the ping of axe on stone once more. It really did work! I smile. So it will be tomorrow, I think with sadness. Tonight must be my last night in this hell, for better or worse. I will not sleep but muse on my life, and what it all meant. It is all I can do, believe that my life had meaning, that I gave something to the world that will last forever. My trouble is, I am death incarnate. I am no talented artist or hero to the people. No statue will be erected or building created for my legacy, nothing people can touch or look at in wonder and amazement that this person lived and changed their world. I will only be the tyrant who took children and cast a heavy shadow on the land, no better than a wolf or bear, hungry for prey.

The digging is incessant now, surely they are getting close. They are working fast to get rid of me, to free themselves of their plight. My servant comes in to put the coal basket under my bed, so clearly they are not quite there yet. She will scream at her old, shaky, warped hands and beg them to destroy me, I know this. They will remember all I have done to them, sucking the life force from their lives, making them prepare food and bathe me in earlier days. My slaves, they know the way to my bed chamber, so will it be one of them who gets to me first in rage, or will they be too overcome with grief? They will not make it quick, I fear that greatly now – the pain, the torture before the release. I have heard stories of something called crucifixion, where I would be tied to a post and left in the sun to die. Humans die in days. Me? I would die in many seasons. I used to love the sun, so maybe it would make me remember how to love again. There is always fire of course, burning alive from the feet upwards, choking on fumes as the flames lick you before consuming your body. I wouldn't mind that actually, it would be a final end, fitting for a lord they hate, and no blood would have to be spilled again. I would hate to choke on my own blood; I hope there are none who find me and beat me to my release. That would be an unfortunate option, as it would take a long time and lots of hands and boots to send me off. I hope the witches have brewed something special, something like 'forever sleep' – it is hard to make, but a single sip puts you into an eternal sleep. They could kill me quietly without screams from my lungs, just a slow slipping into the afterlife.

Enough of that, I think to myself. What did you do with life while you grasped it? You gave people a place to live, helped them out of their situations, whatever they were, and allowed them to change and grow into humans that they could be proud of. I made them rich enough, in their currency, to live comfortably. I shared wisdom – I think that will be my greatest achievement. Sharing my knowledge of magic with the witches so that they could instruct their children and so on, until there is a sort of everlasting effect. Yes, I am proud of that. I smile to myself, reflecting that they became quite powerful in their own right, at least by human standards. They can transmute, use telepathy on humans, change the weather for short periods of time, and the herbal remedies are excellent. They never did quite grasp how powerful nature is – it is where the magic comes from, and without her power they will eventually lose theirs. I wonder if they will figure that one out for themselves, and find a place to live inside a natural setting so that they can keep the magic alive within themselves. I chuckle; no, they probably won't. Probably shouldn't either – if I am gone, who will protect the land from the king's men? We are outcast people, strong, but without me, not strong enough to hold the land we have lived on for so many generations. The witches will burn and the men will kneel, and a new lord will come to replace me,

I assume. Horrible for all, but if they do kill me, it won't be my problem, I suppose. I will be busy figuring out the afterlife.

So, my life is one of two halves, really. In the beginning, when I was with nature, I was good and brave for her. Now I am weak and scared for myself. In the end, aren't all lives the same? Should I really hate myself so much for what I have become when in past times, I have done good work? Most lives are the same I would guess, the town's people could relate to that. Like a murderer who turns fisherman, or my little Fern, who painted me so elegantly, am I any different? I miss Fern, I miss seeing her natural works and how they made me feel at home. The corridors of the keep are strewn with her early pictures of trees and animals. They used to remind me of better times, and with enough paintings you could almost feel like you were there. She will be grown by now, a woman in her own right. How will she feel about me when she learns the truth of what I have done? Enslaving her human folk, to the point of death. Maybe she will paint my body after I am gone and they will hang it as a reminder of what happens to those who do the townsfolk wrong. I would like her to paint me one last time, I believe. I won't get to see her shining face though, before the end, nor her pretty curls, or those piercing eyes like a wolf's, always looking, always perceiving what others can't. I suppose that's what makes her a brilliant artist, the ability to see past what others would call plain and boring. She did ask to come to the keep once, to reside with me and paint, but I refused her, knowing the paintings would be controlled by myself. I can't see what she can, and I am afraid that the beauty she finds is far past my perception.

Not that I don't find the beauty, eventually. I have seen this island and found the tiniest flowers that only bloom at special times of the year. I never touched them, only marvelled at their brilliance. How I wish to go back and see them again. They were nearly pink with yellow at the centre – most would have trodden over them and not noticed, but I saw what nature had provided for the insects and bees. These bugs in turn fed the birds which fed the animals, making a lifecycle for nature. But where did I fit in? I should neither have been eaten nor eaten any animal. Maybe now, when I am gone, I will feed the insects? That could be my real purpose, to be brought into the circle at last, part of it and happy to give over my nutrients to the soil. I know we rot to nothing but bone, I have seen human remains. After my battle with them I laid them to rest on the fields to see what happened. I was very curious as to what the body did once it had no soul to keep it moving and alive. The birds, especially crows, fed, and after animals like the jackal ate the remains, the insects like the fly took the rest. By the time I had watched for a few days there was nothing left but the bones. They were hard to the touch and bright white in colour. I took one, and left the rest to fade. I still have it, but the shining white yellowed in time and became brittle, so I put it in a glass box to store and look at from time to time. I should tell them to lay me there where so many others were, so that I too can be picked apart. However, I am not sure I will have the energy or time.

The sun rises once more, and it is the fifth day. I hope I have not driven them into madness. Humans do not do well under these conditions. A noise shakes me from my thoughts, outside, comes a cheer – they have finally found the Thrallium! I hear the picking of the axe on the crystal, it is a sharp sound and I feel the strength of the spell waning with every blow. How marvellous it will be to be free soon.

The servants come to bring me food, they will soon be free and don't even know it. They file out of the room once my food is served. Now, I wait, my body stiffening as I continue to imagine what death will be like. I feel them now; they are close to breaking the spell. Well done, humans. The crack of crystal is audible as it finally gives and shatters. They will come for me now.

'Kill, kill!' I hear shouts from a mob of humans outside the keep.

Yes, indeed, I think to myself, kill away. But try to find me first – the maze will be interesting for tired bodies and minds. I hear the main door opening, and footfall on the stone of my keep; never have so many been inside. I wonder how long it will take now, and I grow irritated as I hear them going this way and that.

'Find him, he must break the spell!' one shouts from nearby, but not in my corridor.

I should really have signposted the place, too late now I suppose. By the time they reach me a rage should have built up and they will finish me as quickly as possible. Who will find me first? None are really clever enough to work out how the keep was planned. They will wander aimlessly till the lucky one finds a door that is slightly grander than the rest and open it to find me here, smiling at them broadly.

Smile I shall, and they will call their friends and break the spell one way or another. I hear a creak in my hallway – someone is carefully making their way to me. Too slowly; they must be tiptoeing, so it is the assassins who are the cleverest, however, maybe not the bravest. Do they believe I will put up a fight or not notice that someone is in my room? The footfall continues till they reach my door. It opens with a bang and an assassin jumps in the room and throws a knife towards me which misses my face by an inch. A fool has found me – why couldn't it be a competent assassin? Then I realise he was no fool, only distracted by his job. He never checked behind him, and he falls to the floor, choking, till no breath is left. Behind him stands an old woman in a bright red dress, hair mussed and messy, but I know her. I smile at her and lift my hands one last time to clap once.

'So, you found me. Now what will you do with me?' I ask quietly, but I know my voice is perceptible to her.

'I'm here to save you, you old fool.' She smiles and sighs. 'I am very tired, will you break the spell now?'

'So be it,' I say and gather the last energy I have to lift the spell that has kept them awake for so long.

Agatha, the head of the witches, walks to my chair and promptly passes out. I think it fair she rests now, and I hear the same happening all over the keep. Bodies crashing to the ground for rest. It is quite funny to listen to. They may sleep a while, I think to myself. Shame, really. I want to know what 'saving' means and why she does not kill me. Agatha is powerful in her own right. I believe she could rule if she wanted to.

So, it seems I am back to waiting. I will be patient now though, after all she did kill the man from the assassins guild, so there must be more to this and I feel a sense of curiosity building within me. Surely I am past saving, and a tyrant that needs to be removed from power after what I have done. A murderer, a killer of nature's way, lost on a path that may lead to the destruction of all. If I am left to live, I fear what I will do when I am able to walk again.

Chapter Six

Hope is the power,
You control whether you glow,
Blow on the ember.

They have slept for around half the day and still do not stir. I am lost as to what is going to happen and the trepidation puts a fear deep inside me. I curl up in bed and await my fate. When night is nearing, Agatha wakes with a start. Sleepy eyes open wide and stare at me in my stricken state. She yawns, rubs her hands together and stands on shaky legs. A step towards me – maybe she does have a poison after all, maybe she just wanted to be the one to do it? No, she opens her arms and as I turn to her, she hugs me deeply. Something I have not felt in a long time, the touch of another, and I begin to sob. It all comes at once, gushing out all the pain onto her shoulder. She strokes my hair and whispers in my ear.

'It's alright now, take your time, it has been a while since you spoke to anyone real, isn't it?' she asks, and as I pull back from her, I nod.

'Please kill me, it is what I deserve,' I say through the tears.

'My lord, my troubled one, you need my help as much as I need yours,' she says with shining eyes looking deep into me, 'you protect us, I am well aware, but you can't do it like this. At some point, the king will hear of your predicament and come for us all.'

So, that was the reason. I am their protector, the guard against the witch trials and murder's retribution. It is true there are about four thousand people in the town now, all of whom might have a reason to be against killing me, apart from the assassin's guild, apparently, who think they can do this alone.

'How can I be saved? How can I make up for all my failures?' I say to her with hope.

'We will talk, and I also have some medicine. I'm not sure it will work on you but there is no harm in trying. It works on humans so I am hopeful – it is called Saint John's Wort,' Agatha says.

'I know this plant. I had no idea it could ease pain,' I reply, curious to know that there is something that can bring me back from the brink of death and this despair.

'My dear, you don't understand yet, but you will. The poultice I have brought may ease a mental pain, but it won't fix you. All we can do is talk and see where this pain you speak of is and try to fix it together,' she says, stroking my hair once again. A tear comes from her eye. 'I have lost one close to me through this same sickness of the mind. I am glad I have found you before anything happened to you as well.'

She is right, I don't understand. I feel like a youngling again, so helpless and fragile. I don't know if I am ready to talk, it seems pointless to try, nothing matters anymore and I don't want to live like this any longer than I have to. I am a failure, a protector of no one, I can't even get out of this bed! How am I supposed to fight an army once more? Oh, it is too much, and I curl up again, holding my stomach tight.

'I can't, I just can't,' I moan, rocking back and forth.

'You are strong, you can do it, if you really want to be the man you once were,' she says.

'I am a failure and a tyrant! There is no saving, there is only pain where I walk.' I try to scream but fail, my voice too hoarse from lack of use.

'Yes, you have made mistakes, but that is why we are all here in this town, don't you see? You represent us.' Agatha sits back in the chair and awaits my reply.

I think about this, why we are here, how we are all lost children hoping for a second chance. Could this be mine? I don't deserve it, but who does? Who decides but the gods? I am lucky that Agatha found me; she seems genuine in her engagement with me. But will the town agree? Will they let me survive on another chance? I will put it to a vote I decide – any who wish me dead can have their desire if they win, the ones who wish for my protection, well they can have it freely once I am strong if they have enough votes. I no longer wish to be a lord, though, I know that now. I wish to be free of this prison which has corrupted me, allowed to wander the land without dealing with the day-to-day running of the town. The elders have been doing that all the time that I have been in bed anyway, I am sure. So what need of me do they have but as a fighter? I start to cry again, can I bear to become a killer again? A death dealer? Maybe so. These people don't deserve to die – maybe there will be no fight if I am at full capacity. The agreement still stands after all, no army can step foot here as long as I do not trespass on their land. Then I will be able to walk to the trees again and feel that bark on my face and the sun beaming on me.

'I suppose I am one of you. Do you believe the king will come? I have no fight left in me. I am so sorry, Agatha.' My tears shed as I tell her what I am thinking. 'I am broken, I have little to give at this time. How can I get strong? I just don't know.'

Agatha shakes her head and stays silent for what, to me, seems an eternity. I cannot shake the feeling that she is losing her faith in me, if she had any at all, now she has seen the state that I am in.

She speaks carefully and slowly. 'Yes, I do believe the king will come.' She pauses. 'So, it is up to me, not you, to get you back to health. But you have to want it, you have to feel it again, that need to live and be free from those who would grip on your throat and squeeze till you are dead.'

I nod in reply, mostly to myself, thinking about what I actually want. I have been heading to death's door, and building the courage to knock. However, every single time I almost do, something pulls me back. Something strong-willed resides in me, I suggest to my mind. But the want to live? That is another question altogether.

'Bring me Fern, I could live to save her,' I suggest to Agatha, who nods and rises from the chair.

'I will be back shortly. You must rise to protect yourself if there is trouble, there are still some who would do you harm and we are not finished yet. Can you do that?' I nod in agreement, 'I will bring the poultice as well, it may come in handy,' she says as she closes the door.

So, I am left only with my thoughts once more. But this really is the last time. This is the last I will think by myself, and I ponder. I can't believe some still care for me – it is strange to know that there are a few who would actually help me. It warms me; I feel a rush of blood to my unsaturated heart once more, and I glow. I smile to myself and hold my arms around my chest. I felt Agatha's warmth, I can still feel it, and it eases the mental pain for the first time in what feels like an age. I could be even loved. I don't know about this but it is possible the town's people could come to really love their protector. Not a lord in a cage but a just and right being that guards, like a sentinel, the fiefdom we have created. It was not only me who created this place. I see the beginning as an accomplishment, but the rest was them! They are strong and do deserve to live in peace, and my mind keeps coming back to this point. They have earned their peace given all that they have been through. Weathered the storms of normal human life and come out fighting. Should I also come out fighting? It seems appropriate and mirrors them in a way. That is why I asked for Fern – she embodies all I know about humans and their struggles. From the streets to being a free artist with a warm home and plentiful food, she is surely thankful for what I did in the beginning. Maybe she will hug me? I can hope for that, to feel warmth repeatedly and settle myself in for a fight with my own mind. That will be my course then, it is decided. We will be strong and a collective that no army can stand against. No king to rule us, tell us what is right and wrong. Only we decide that. I will give the keep over to the elders and build my own home, a real home, not cold stone but warm wood.

While thinking, I seem to have neglected my senses. I have been staring at the window for some time and it is only now I notice that I am not alone in this room. I turn my head in shock, eyes open wide at the appearance of a man standing at the foot of my bed, crossbow in hand.

'You may not live any longer. You savage, corrupt demon!' His voice becomes louder with each syllable.

'Why not? I made this place, you are safe here,' I reply, eyeing the fingers held on the trigger.

'Safe? You stole my son and made him work the stables until I can't recognise him anymore. He is broken, barely speaking and lost to the darkness that you created.' His fingers tremble as he speaks. He has never killed before, I realise, so maybe he can be reasoned with.

'I am deeply sorry for your loss. You are correct, I was corrupted and darkness reigned over this keep. But no more, no more.' I repeat these words to him, over and over.

He begins to cry and lowers his bow.

'I will heal the wounds I have created. I can help your son if you just let me live and change what I was and have done,' I continue as he drops to his knees.

It is the first time I have moved from the bed. I am crying too as I shuffle my body to the edge to hold his head.

'I am sorry, but I will help your son, I promise. Just help me. I need all the help I can get.'

I feel his head nodding, then he looks up at me.

'How? You can't turn back time. I lost my boy, don't you see?' he says, face streaming with tears for time lost that I did not truly understand until now. I have all the time, and his son has less and less, the longer I keep him as my slave.

I am right over him now. I can barely hold myself but reach out to hug the man and also in my mind, the boy whom I stole time from. My tears drip over the bow. He raises it and before I can move, fires a bolt into my abdomen. He runs from the room and I collapse onto the floor with a grunt. At least I am out of bed, I think, smiling. I deserved that, even if it is not a killing blow. I pull on the bolt with what little strength I have, and free it from my body after much twisting and yanking. Blood now pours out of the wound and I grab onto the bedsheets and tug them down to my level, putting pressure on the hole in me. I have little magic left, I used it all on the spell to free his son. Agatha has the power to heal me, and I know I must hang on until she arrives. Back to waiting, I think with a smirk. The sheets are now a deep red and I worry this is possibly fatal in my weakened state. I put my hand over the wound under the sheet and try to use my magic. I feel the warmth of the blood and concentrate on it, slowing the flow, so that I may survive many hours albeit in physical pain. I put more pressure back on my belly, and it hurts less than before so I am hopeful. Agatha must really hurry up, though.

By the gods, it has been a while. I cough, but no blood comes up so I am sure the bolt did not hit anything vital to my survival. I am on the edge of passing out when the door creaks open.

'You are too late if you are an assassin,' I whisper.

'Gods, what happened? I told you to stay safe while I was gone!' Agatha curses and then comes to my side. She lays her hands over my stomach and whispers words. I feel the warmth again, this time much stronger and I can feel a lot more pain but the blood slows to a trickle. I look down at her handiwork. She has managed to stop the bleeding from inside but a hole still remains. She goes to the bed, ripping the rest of the sheets off and tearing strips to wrap around me.

I look backwards towards the door. A shaky Fern stands staring at me, and I wave her over.

'Come in, it is okay. I will survive.' I smile warmly and she takes a few steps towards me before running to hold my head in her arms. She is a grown woman now, no longer the child I built a home for. With braided hair she looks so different, so beautiful, and I could have her hold me all the time. It feels so good and I am reassured that I will survive with her by my side.

'Who did this to you?' Fern says, looking deep into my eyes.

'Just a devoted father,' I reply, smiling. I shake off the pain and nuzzle further into her hands. 'Thank you for coming.'

'Of course I came, you silly thing. I would have come sooner but I could not find your room. Then I had to return home to sleep as someone put a spell on me!' she says with the hint of a smile and shakes her head at me. 'It was a good tune, although "kill or save?"' She raises an eyebrow. 'You should have sung "help me, please", it might have gone a bit better. You really angered the townsfolk, you know.' She strokes my hair.

'Enough of that, it doesn't matter now. You will live, you are quite correct, but the wound will take a bit of time to heal up. I am afraid my magic only sealed the insides,' Agatha says, patting the bandage. 'Here, take this now, it will help your mind with a bit of luck. You must be thirsty, too. We brought water and some food, that is why we took so long.' I drink the poultice and some water after, as it tasted disgusting. 'Now, let us get you back in bed.'

I shake my head. 'I am out now, I won't be going back there. Can you two drag me to the chair?'

They nod in agreement and pull me, much to my discomfort, and help me to my knees so that I can clamber into the chair with a lot of effort and groaning. Now sitting, I hold the wound and look at both of them panting. I grin at them and laugh a little before coughing in pain.

'What is so funny?' Fern asks between breaths.

'Thank you for coming,' I reply, and she comes to hold my hand. I look up at my portrait. 'That was the old me. I have decided to live for you and your people,' I say, gruffly.

'Good. A little progress, but we have much to do. Eat now while I rest.' Agatha takes to the bed.

I look to Fern now, and say, 'Have you noticed the corridor?'

She nods and looks enormously proud. 'You kept them all, all these years. Thank you.'

'They remind me of better times. You are such a talent, and now a grown woman! You will need to paint some more for me,' I say with a strong nod.

She nods back and musses my hair.

'I like your hair, you should keep it long,' she says with a laugh.

'Not as nice as yours, my dear.' I reach up to feel the braid. 'You know, you are like my daughter. I am so glad you came and are well.'

'Oh, you old fool, you gave me this new start away from those rotten streets. I will always be here for you, my lord,' she says, and cheekily slaps me lightly on the face.

'I am no longer your lord, call me by my name. Ariel. I would much prefer it. It suits me much better,' I say with a grimace, knowing I shouldn't be higher than anyone now. A lowly servant of the people.

'Ok then, Ariel. It is a nice name for you. I never knew! You should have told everyone a long time ago. You don't need to be a lord to have respect for yourself and others,' she says, turning my face back to a smile.

She is correct, of course, I need not be much except myself to have their respect. I don't want their fear any longer. It doesn't serve me now. Respect for myself will be a much harder task though. I definitely lost that feeling a long time ago, I think as soon as I killed my first animal. I do not believe I am good at heart – only darkness resides there. I must contain it and be brave for them. When I have their respect, however I manage to get it, I will work on myself and find that belief again. That steadfast knowledge that I can live and be truly at peace. I long for that now, but at the moment any feeling will do. Just the touch of a caring hand has done wonders for me already.

We wait for Agatha to wake, as she will know what to do next. I hope we don't have to leave the keep yet; that seems scary and painful to face, as of this moment. Out in the world, there are those who would harm me, but now we three are here to care for my body and mind and that has a certainty to it that settles my head. The world seems too big to take on, the sky goes up and up, and a never-ending wind could whisk my soul upwards forever and I would be lost. The land stretches for miles and I don't think I can take the sight of all those fields, where there used to be forests and flowers. Nature has been corrupted all over the island, so where can I go from here? There is nowhere to hide but in this room, where I am safe and insulated from the knowledge that it is all gone and that, in the name of progress, we have lost so much. Even my would-be assassin has progressed – crossbows. I never thought the humans would be able to manufacture them but they obviously have. Further weapons are coming for me, I know this, and I will have to build up my body to withstand the onslaught.

'May I eat, Fern? Pass me something from the basket. I fear I will have to grow strong quickly if we are to stop the king's men from taking all we have made here.' I sigh as I speak. It is a large task that starts with one small step – eating.

'Of course, what would you like? Maybe some cheese or ham? They seem good choices if you want to get your strength back fast.' Fern passes me the food, and I sit and look at it. These were animals, the ham, a pig or boar. And the cheese, how cruel to steal the milk from the cow to feed ourselves. But of course, she is right. The food is delicious and I feel stronger after a few bites.

Once my strength returns I will no longer hunger for animal flesh, but live off fruit and vegetables like I once managed. Once, I would never have thought that there is power in meat, nor would I have wanted it. But now, knowing what I have to do, I will sacrifice this poor slaughtered pig and later honour it by creating a place for them to be free. Yes, that will be a fair bargain, don't you think, nature? No more pens and livestock bred for the butcher, but living alongside each other. If I garner enough respect maybe some of the people shall indeed see the error of their ways and follow me in eating what we should have been all along. That is a far-off dream, it feels. I weep as I eat more and more, Fern handing me plentiful amounts of food for my fragile figure to build up again. I am a lot less bulky and muscled than I was. It won't take too long for the body to return. I have starved before when I did not know what to eat. Once I found the fruit on the trees, I laughed and tasted my first bite of something pure. The energy was not great, but I could survive quite nicely on what nature provided. It is my mind, cracked and brittle, that I worry for. It will not be repaired by the apple or pear or cherry but through some kind of means that only Agatha seems to know. If she has indeed seen this malaise in humans, she has greater knowledge than myself, and I must bow to her.

Agatha does not stir until the next morning, when I have had my fill of food and Fern has crashed out onto the same bed as Agatha. I wait and watch the sunrise so that I can feel its brightness once more.

Agatha yawns, looks over at Fern, and then turns her attention towards me with glowing eyes, like she has a plan. I really am hopeful that she does or we will all perish by the king's fist. Before speaking a word, Agatha gets up and eats some leftover cheese and bread, and drinks water in complete silence. I watch her with curiosity. What is it she thinks will help?

'Agatha, how will we get out of this predicament? My mind feels so lost and darkness prevails,' I say, carefully.

Agatha looks me up and down and slowly begins to speak at last. 'Well, I think the best plan is for you and me to talk a while. We have many days, so take your time and we will find what is troubling you. I can see you are in a tricky situation regarding your mind. So, tell me about it.'

We begin at my first breath, up to my people neglecting and being repelled by me. 'That is when I first knew I was different. I saw my face and understood why they didn't want me around,' I say in a quiet, sombre tone.

'I see, so you never experienced love in your early days. In fact, it was the opposite, and they are the ones at fault, not you. You must ingrain it into your mind that you were only a child and deserved to be loved no matter what you look like.' She speaks with a certainty that begins to resonate within me.

So it was them, not I, that was at fault. I grow quiet and become deep in thought. Agatha only eyes me carefully, not pushing too hard but letting it all sink in slowly. They punished me and sent me away repeatedly after all the hard work I had done to please them. They think of themselves as God's children, powerful and strong. But I was less than them in their eyes, just a child with a broken face that disgusted them to the point where they thought they were better off without me around.

'I was not loved you are correct. The animals became my friends, my confidants and I betrayed them for power,' I say with a whimper, 'even now, I betray them every second with my eating and being, what I have made. This town lies on the grounds of a forest, which I spent many a year in. I loved it and it loved me. What have I done?'

'Yes, I see. You have made mistakes but they do not define you. You are not your mistakes no more than you are your thoughts. You are separate from them, you can observe them. I want you to close your eyes now, if you will,' Agatha says and I proceed to shut my eyes tight. 'I want to look at your thoughts, without judgement, and see that they are a part of you but they are not you.'

I try to imagine this, a place where thought is only that. It is not me, I repeat to myself, with eyes still closed. I look at my thoughts and feelings, especially the ones of dread and see them for the first time with curiosity and wonder. The darkness is only one part of my mind, I start to learn. There are other thoughts here, too. Some come and go quickly, but others come back again, the trees, the animals, the birds and the insects, all living with me in harmony. The place I feel safe and well. The darkness comes in waves over me, thoughts of death and why I am here when I was never wanted in the first instance. I shake them off to return back to the forests – my home, the real home.

'I want to return to the forests, but they are gone now. We planted crops and reared livestock, built homes of wood and cut and cut till there are few spots where I could breathe in that air. You see, Agatha, it is a wondrous place, full of life and warmth.' I spread my arms out to the side and look at her with pleading eyes. 'Can you bring them back? Can I? I don't believe it is possible now.' I sit back in the chair again, feeling the pain, not just from my wound but inside my mind and I cradle my head in my hands. Holding it here, it feels safe away from eyes who now know what I have really destroyed.

'I know my dear, it is a sad fact, but there is still forest to the north of the town. Build a home there when you are well. We will be fine, you don't have to protect us constantly. We can call on you if needed and leave you in your peace.' Agatha looks hopeful, as if she had found the key to my well-being.

'I could build a home there, but it won't change what I have done. Will nature forgive me?' I ask the floor.

'You will find Mother Nature cares only for what you do now. She does not live in the past as you have been, but in the present where you could also be.'

To live only for now . . . well, that was a thought. Could I forgive myself? Could it be that all this time I have been living in a dream world, where the past only haunts me but is not real, is not me? In this present state, I open my tearing eyes and look straight at Agatha. It is true that I have fallen into a chasm of my historical failures, but they do not define me? I am different having gone through this process; living through the malaise has been enlightening. I do not know what I must do, but I know there is much to be done. Nature goes on regardless of what has happened to her, so could I do the same? Living with her once more would be an honour and privilege I did not believe I had earned but maybe I don't need to.

'What are you thinking?' Agatha asks, softly.

'That the past is exactly that,' I answer. I feel stronger in myself, thinking with an unfamiliar perspective.

Nightfall is coming so both Agatha and a very sleepy Fern return to the town.

'I will be back in the morning,' Agatha says with a warm smile.

I nod and hug Fern goodbye as best I can.

'Look after yourself and come and see me soon,' she says, tugging on my hair.

'I will once Agatha lets me out of the keep,' I joke.

I am left alone with my thoughts, but I do not fear them this time. I drink more of the poultice and shake my head as it goes down my throat. Terrible stuff, but if it works, maybe it's worth it. I eat more and actually stand on my legs for a short time. They feel wobbly and weak, and I have to sit again after a few seconds but it is an improvement from lying in bed. So I stretch them in the chair. I stretch my arms out too, feeling a bit of strength returning. I think in a few days I will leave this room, which has kept me safe for so long. It pains me that I will have to come face to face with the sons, wives and daughters I stole to keep me alive. Yes, I did that, it was very evil of me but necessary. If I had not, I would have died and the king would have come and they would all be dead. It is not an excuse, I think to myself, because some servants may have come to help willingly and for pay. From what I have seen from Agatha and Fern, there must be more who would have helped. Fool, I say to myself. Subduing them in the beginning. I really did not care, but I do now. I feel for all the lives lost under my spell. I will make my amends and live in the present, no longer a shade hiding in the past. I can sort the boy out, I know that – he sounds like his mind is still trapped and I have a few spells that can bring it back from the brink. As for the rest, they must be in need of something, and perhaps I can help them back to living.

Chapter Seven

Remember I am,

Strong-willed, capable, but kind,

I will not judge you.

Agatha has not yet returned when the sun begins to rise, I drink my poultice again. She comes in the late afternoon, sighing and looking worn out.

'What happened to you?' I ask.

'The elders, they will vote on your future soon. I have been arguing your case. It was very tiresome. They are old men now, all men I might add, and believe you are still a threat to them. We must leave the keep sooner than I would like and have you on the stand to talk. Will you be ready? You are the only one who can save us from the king, after all.' She does not seem as bright or hopeful as yesterday.

'It's okay, Agatha, I will be strong enough to talk to them soon. I must show them I am willing to make up for the mistakes of the past,' I say, solemnly.

'Yes, there is a lot to do. But we must get your mind well too. I wish we had much more time to talk and figure this out as I fear, if we do not, that it will only resurface in the future, you see?' She really does care for me.

I propose to myself that she does see the same mind markers as her friend who died of malaise.

'Tell me about your friend who died, Agatha,' I say, hoping it will shed some light on my situation, as well as let her talk about her problems.

'Well, she was called Revel, a beautiful woman, strong and silent for the most part. How she must have suffered under her stoic demeanour. I found her in bed, like you, in a terrible malaise. A horrible state, much worse than I had ever experienced before. The darkness had a tight hold of her, so we spoke for many weeks about what troubled her. I gave her the poultice and hoped for the best. Unfortunately, she killed herself not long after . . . it was just too much for her to bear, I suppose. I wish I had done more, saved her soul, but that is in the past and remember we live in the present.' As she finishes, I understand why she is helping me.

'I am sorry about Revel, it must be painful for you. But I am not her, I have decided to live and stand by it,' I say confidently.

'She said similar words to me the night before she died. I shouldn't have trusted her, but I do trust you. I have faith that there are ways to find you your peace.' She's nearly whispering, her voice croaking and cracking.

I rise, holding my wound with one hand and reaching out the other. Agatha comes towards me, sobbing as she dives into my chest.

'It will be okay, I will protect you all. Even if the elders do not wish it, I will do my duty. But I believe they will see me as a weapon, to be used when needed and that works for me at the moment. We will go and see the sun again, Agatha, in all its beauty.' I hold her close as I speak.

No longer afraid of consequences, I am allowed to think of a future. I will stop the king's men and then be free to rebuild my life. It is nearly time to leave the room but I am not quite steady yet, only standing as Agatha is basically holding me up. I can do this, or I think I can. I can be a great figure to these people and steadfast. If only they could be reasoned with, and talk to me like a man, not a demon or lord, but one of them.

We hold each other silently for a while before I have to sit down again. It is much more than I thought I could manage and I am pleased with myself. I hold my legs, the semi-functioning tools that I need to walk out of this room. They will come back to me, I will remember how to use them. They will carry me off to better places, and I will find my peace out there somewhere. I am no longer afraid of the outside world; I can't be now, there is much to do and little time to prove my life is worth saving.

'I am almost ready, Agatha, but these legs won't work properly. I will need help to face the elders,' I say with a strength I did not know I still had. I will go to the elders and speak – it is a daunting thought.

'I will fetch you something – it works for the old and frail, so it should work for you for the time being. I am so sorry we don't have the time to talk anymore. I hope we will in the future.' She says this with a lot of care but full of sorrow. I now know she needs me as much as I need her, and together we might just make it out of this.

As night draws in close, Agatha leaves me once more. In silence this time, and I know she has much on her mind. What will I say in my defence? What will I tell the elders that will make them see that I must live? I will stand by a vote of the people, to exile me or not. Death is slipping further from my mind so I doubt I will let them burn me now. It no longer has the same grasp on me as it did, and I look to my blood-covered sheets and the place where I lay for so long. That will not be me, I am not Revel. She had much more pain than I and maybe less to live for. Don't be stupid, I think. She was strong and this malaise can take any of us at any time. It matters not who you are, what power you hold, or who is there to help, you can be taken and that is the point of it. I may well have used Brandfire given the strength of will. But I was weak and could not reach for her. Oh Brandfire, how evil I made you. I will need a new sword, it won't do to take souls any longer, the ones left trapped are bad enough. What can I do for them? I must make my amends but the power to break them free is beyond me. I don't know of any magic that could set them free. Maybe I should bury the sword in a grave of sorts and hope nature finds a way. But a new sword, how should I enchant it? It needs to be sharp and piercing, a sword to keep the people safe, a sword *of* the people. There will be a blacksmith in town still, I am sure of it. He or she will make me a grand weapon. It will be a weapon of nature too, and I must ask her for this favour, but I am afraid she remembers me. Agatha is sure she will not, but I have not seen the forest for myself yet so cannot be so definite in my thinking. What power my new weapon will have I do not know, that is an exciting prospect, new spells to keep the people safe. Hopefully enough to stop an invasion. My magic alone is great, but not enough. Last time I needed Brandfire, and they will definitely have progressed by now from the savage barbarians I met on that bridge.

Agatha finally returns deep into the night, with wooden poles of sorts that I will use under my arms, I suppose. She comes to me and helps me stand then puts one each under my armpits. She shows me how to walk with them. On my first try, balancing nicely, I push forward and fall, clattering to the ground in a mess.

'Be patient and practice. Tomorrow we will go out and see the elders so tonight we must prepare,' she says, helping me up once more.

'So, what do they think of me?' I ask once back in the chair.

'How are you feeling now you can walk?' Agatha asks avoiding my question.

'Ok, Agatha, but what is going to happen tomorrow?' I repeat.

She turns and looks me in the eye. It is a look of shame and grief. 'There will be no vote, the elders alone will decide your fate. As a protector, or death by hanging.' She lowers her head.

'They can't possibly think I will stand by this, the people should decide as one' I reply, shaking my head. 'I have come too far to give in now. You have shown me love, I will not let it go.'

'I am afraid you may have no choice. Quite a few misguided witches are controlled by the elders, they may be strong enough to take you down in your weakened state.' She looks to her feet and shakes her own head. 'I am sorry there is nothing I can do for you now, it will be up to you to convince them.'

I think about this. Is it possible magic could contain me? Bind my form? I know of the spells to paralyse, but did not know the humans had worked them out on their own. Clever beasts.

'You must, I repeat must, prove your power beyond all expectation. They believe you can't stop them now, but I know you are strong still, it is within you to talk, don't run away from this.' Agatha pleads with me.

'Quite right,' I say, resting my chin on the crutch.

There is nothing else for it. When the sun rises I will take myself to them and see if I can have a vote allowed. I have charisma but I am afraid I will need much more to persuade the men. I don't want them to fear me, but it is a tool at my command. They have to really know I have changed, become a better being, a pure being.

'Call for Fern. I should gather the people on my side and say goodbye to her if I must,' I say with a sigh, still holding the crutches. Agatha nods and leaves the room.

I practice walking again. This time slowly, carefully, making sure I am supported. It does not look good for me, coming in like this, but I have no choice – emaciated legs will take much more time to build.

Fern arrives quickly, out of breath and sweating quite a bit. I laugh at her appearance and she scowls at me in jest.

'I may have to say goodbye,' I say quietly, head hung downwards.

'They've set up a gallows for you! I can't believe this is happening – you must convince them to let you live. I testified for you this morning but they would not listen to me. I'm sorry, Ariel, what can we do to help?' She falls down to her knees, despondent and in failure.

I do a balanced walk over to her and hold her head. 'It is okay, Fern, do not worry about me. I am sure I can talk them through this. But if I can't I wanted to say thank you for being my friend and becoming what you are. You are a woman now, and still see the beauty in the world. I must admit, I am rather jealous.' I stroke her hair and she gets up and looks at my face.

'You will see beauty again, just stay alive, okay?' she says.

'It will be fine. In this life or the next, I will find beauty and peace, I promise you,' I say through the pain of the wound as I stretch to walk properly with these sticks, 'Sleep now, and in the morning we will go.'

We wait till dawn. Few words are passed between us. I sit in the chair as Fern sleeps on the bed, occasionally waking to check I am still there. I hear the birdsong before the sunrise, I have nearly made it through the waiting. Fern wakes with a start and comes to stand beside me.

'Beautiful sounds aren't they?' I say rhetorically, 'The afterlife awaits Fern.'

'No, don't go! With you in the afterlife, what would I have? I would miss you and probably be killed as a witch of painting when the king's men arrive.' She laughs a little and I chuckle, knowing both our fates are now in the hands of old men. I feel for her, it is something women have to escape from their whole lives it would seem, old men carrying out their whims.

I cling to her as we walk down the corridor. I admire each painting and feel a sense of hope that maybe I could find that spark once more. That fire in my belly, for being alive and living. I guide her to the quickest exit, and move towards the outside world. I hesitate at the gates – it seems so unreal. I peek out at the sky, still its same deep blue like an ocean. I wonder at it, it is such a special world – I can't lose it now. Not like this, anyway. I am not ready to die and pass on, the army would come and send the witches to the slow death, hanging or burning, which all fear. It is not the actual death I find that humans fear, but the way in which they will die. Old and in their sleep is preferable, compared with the tortured confession and burning of the witches that I have heard so much about, mainly from the town's people in earlier days when I could walk amongst them freely. I have no idea what I am stumbling into now.

The town's people will not gather for me, I see as we walk down the hill towards a great gallows pole. It is massive and wooden, a curse upon nature that I find repulsive. They have chopped trees in preparation for killing me, slowly. I feel I am walking towards a slow death. There is no way they would have built this if they hadn't already made up their minds about what to do with me. How can I make them see I have changed? What proof is there other than my word? I have not had the time to be with my humans and help them instead of enslaving them.

Chapter Eight

Send out your love to,

People in the world even,

Those who anger you.

As we pass the gallows, a crowd has gathered around it. So, they have

come for a spectacle, one which I am sure now that the elders will give to

them. I am to die, something I wished for, something I told them to do,

I suppose. Damn myself for being so slow, damn the malaise and damn

all those who now jeer and throw fruit and vegetables at me. Of course,

they cause no damage and they have a right to be angry but I am not that

demon anymore.

Fern shields me as best she can as we stride towards the great hall and my doom. I see at least ten witches lined up, geared for action. They scowl at me, this time not in jest, but in hatred. I have never seen this before from humans in my town. Not that it is my town anymore, I think. I would have left it to them freely – this death is not necessary, not justice for the folk who will die at the hands of the king, why do they not see this? The doors are opened for us and we come into the trial. Much like a witch's, I think, sneaking a look behind at the women at the ready. We pass by the seated humans who want to listen and see what will happen, practically slobbering over the idea of killing one so powerful. They sit in pews apparently taken from the church. This was a banquet hall once, where parties were held and joy was felt. The tone is quite different now, no ale will be drunk till all the breath has left my body. How will they do it, though? I am still strong, I feel the magic in me growing even now. Several of those witches might be able to stop me, I suppose.

The head elder, a grey and incredibly angry-looking man waves us to be seated on the right of the hall behind a large wooden dock. Hastily built, it wobbles as I finally get to sit after my travels. I let out a long sigh and groan at my wounded self, and I hear chatter, grumbles and laughter from the back. The five elders all sit in various opulent robes of silk, faces greying and frail. Soon they too will be in the ground, hopefully a slow death like mine, and just out of spite I wish I could see it.

'All stand for the vote and verdict,' says a man from the side of the now courtroom.

'Wait a minute! You haven't even heard my argument!' I shout, coming shakily to a standing position.

'You have no power here, my lord,' says the middle elder, and he lets out a laugh before waving his hand.

Suddenly, I find my legs tightening, my hands pinned to my sides and myself unable to speak. If I could look behind me, I am sure I would see the witches binding me. I can no longer move or speak, tied in this position. I know it is over. The decision will come out in a moment and it will be a guilty one. There is nothing to do now but hear my crimes read out. Although to be fair I probably am guilty for much of it in the past, I no longer live there. I have transcended my past behaviour and come to the present only to find it horrifying. I probably shouldn't have come down the hill from the keep, but I believed I would have a chance to explain, to make them see how I could be so useful to them. However, it seems it is not to be and all will burn with my death. The king will definitely come after hearing of this from the traders. He will kill them and all that will be left is a ghostly town, a reminder to the populace of the island of what they do to thieves, murderers and witches. But that is not my problem anymore. I must concentrate on the next life now, and whatever that entails. Will the gods look kindly on their child? Or punish me for my previous missteps? I have done my best to change, and that is what I hold onto. The idea that they can see into my mind and the transformation that has occurred over the last while. I do not wish for this death; it is a slow death, a craven death, one that should never be allowed to happen. I try some magic and there are a few sparks but nothing to worry the witches. It seems they have learned to bind that too, very much the clever beings I had realised they have become. I don't think anyone even notices I am trying to free myself.

The elders all rise to cast their votes. All raise their hand and say 'Aye.' I guess that this is the time to pray that I will die and be freed from this body, that my soul will indeed go towards the sky, and find the gods in good humour.

'The vote is cast, he is guilty. You, sir, will hang until no breath remains and you are dead. Who will carry this demon away?' The middle elder spoke again and there was a rush of people grappling at me, tugging me towards my doom.

'No! Let him go! You must listen to him or we will all die!' Fern has sprung into life and is fighting the people as they drag me further out of the hall.

I shake my head slightly at her, being all I can manage but she persists until three men grab her and pull her out of my sight. I hope she will be okay, and know that this is the time to leave the town before it is desolated. There are shouts and screams of death, from what I can make out, but it is very loud out here. I now care not for the body, it is withered and useless, my soul is what I think over. You must reach the sky, I tell it, go to the gods and tell them of the malaise and how it changed you, made you a better being. My hands continued to spark as the gallows come close.

'Hold him!' I hear a shout from the hall.

The bind becomes ever tighter, they may as well kill me this way. I laugh inside my head; there is no need for the rope. But the humans do like a show, I believe. I wish I could gift them one. I will all be still, I hope they realise that there will be no noise or movement, as I assume they won't let the bind go until they are sure I am gone. So, it is nearly here, my time to let my soul rise skywards. I wonder if my kin, who were so repelled by me, will feel it. Will they notice the world has changed? Has it changed? Or is my ego obscuring my vision? Am I really this easy to kill? All the questions come at once, fast, and are gone in a second as they drag me up the staircase to the wooden platform. I forgive them of course, they deserve my forgiveness. After all, is that not what the town is built on? I smile as the noose is forced around my neck and the pulling begins.

It takes ten men at least to hoist me up to a standing position. The shouting continues but my smile remains. I forgive you, I think forcefully, knowing at least some of the witches can indeed hear my thoughts. I spread the thought loudly in waves across the crowd. The noose tightens as my feet begin to leave the ground, and I feel it start to choke the life force from me. Hoisted up, it is only less distance for my soul to travel. I continue to smile as I reach the full height of the gallows – there is no struggle, no movement, simply a smile that broadens with every inch I am raised.

'Why does he smile so?' someone shouts from the crowd.

'He forgives us!' I hear Agatha's voice. Thank you, I think to her – she must be listening.

A hush follows, the mob quietens down and the shouts are no more. I am thankful for the peace while I die. It will take many hours, so they will have to wait with me. My feet start to tingle from the lack of oxygen, I assume. Not that it matters now, only my clean soul must rise and be with the gods. I am so sorry for the hurt I have caused, is my next thought. Agatha starts to relay my message.

'He apologises for the hurt he caused and wishes he could make it right. He is happy his soul will be with the gods within the day.' Her voice is clear and crisp on this fine morning.

'Let him go!' the crowd begins to slowly chant, feet stamping on the ground, and even I feel the vibration. However, the noose remains tight.

'We have voted and this is the penalty! No more will this thing rule our lives!' Presumably an elder shouts this, but his call is quickly lost to the crowd's voice.

This is no longer my story. I hope there is another that can take on the role of protagonist and help these people. My great fear is there is no witch, no assassin, no thief who is even close to being as strong as me, and as kind now. But I will have to leave them to help themselves, if they can. The king will be here soon and wash away all that stands in front of him. This will become a ghost town once the fire's rage has quietened. All these humans wasted. I cannot believe it is going to happen, but all will fall under the sword or the trials of the witches. This town will become a symbol to the populace of the island of what occurs when you cross the king's laws.

My feet are becoming unbearably tingly, and I wish I could fidget and let it wash over my whole body. Then maybe this would be done with quicker. I am not angry, only annoyed that this sensation will not abate. The crowd begin to mourn my passing, I can hear the crying. This is good. However, they will not realise the full weight of my death until the men at arms come for them. But it is nice to know they do actually have a heart and care for me. They shouldn't be upset though, I am travelling far upwards and am happy now, as I have longed for this deep in the back of my mind. It was on the surface not too long ago, but I buried the feeling and a single tear rolls down my cheek.

This is not a quick death, and some of the crowd even begin to leave. The sensation in my feet finally starts to spread up my legs, and to my hands. I am not close to death, I know, however, this is an important sign that is not all right with my body. My feet start to feel like they are on fire. I can almost feel it beating through the skin. Then it bursts. The crowd gasp, and I can smell the heat and smoke from down below. Surely hanging is enough; a fire really is not necessary. I am still bound so cannot express the pain I am in. The fire spreads upwards and I can feel my skin bubbling and bursting. Much to my surprise, the binding on my legs breaks and allows me to move my legs, kicking them outwards, and I burst into full flame. I am not dying, I am self-immolating! The fire releases the binds on my arms and finally, the noose burns too and breaks. I fall. Crumpled on the ground, barely able to breathe, I rise. The gallows are on fire around me so I move quickly towards the closest elder.

'I will save you, even if you don't want me to.' The voice does not sound like my own but a mix of screeching and booming that shakes the ground.

I turn away as the crowd disperses in fear. I plant one foot in front of the other but soon am forced to run like an animal on all fours. I head north, and bound forward screaming and coughing from the flames, but still alive and blistering. I leave a trail of fire behind me, darkening the ground once it has died down. I stop, look back and then charge on towards my goal. I must make it to the forest – it is far and I fear for my muscles. They burn too, but I cannot feel the pain anymore; there is too much of it and my senses are overloaded. I burn through the land, and whole fields start to turn to flame in my wake. I can see, through lidless eyes, a forest near the great mountains. I must continue on my journey and make it to nature; she will know what to do. I cannot stop this fire alone.

All the time I run, feeling like a blazing wolf moving at full speed. When I start to reach trees, I am smouldering still, and a raindrop hits my forehead, cool and cleansing. This is an old forest and the trees are wide and unbreakable, but still when I lay a hand on them, they become blackened and glow with embers I've created. I reach moss and dive into it; it is very moist and as I roll on the ground, the fire begins, finally, to dissipate. My skin is blackened and bursting with blisters. I will heal, but need time to rest. None will chase me here – I am finally safe. The rain starts and I look upward at it, feeling its cold, wet texture on my burns. It hurts, but I know I must endure this pain. Shortly the agony will dispel, and my skin will return to nearly its natural state.

'Self-immolation,' I say to myself, and chuckle.

I never thought I had it in me; realistically, I should be dead. However, here I stand, figuratively, as I lie deep in the mosses' embrace. I laugh. It is a bellowing and deep laugh, full of the joy and realisation that I do not want to die, that I am not ready yet. How I managed to pull this from my bag of tricks I do not know. It must have been a bodily response to being attacked like that. Luckily, I don't think anyone was hurt. Only scattered on the wind, back to their houses where they too are now safe. I will prepare for war and they can live their little lives, full of the happiness that life brings. Oh! It fills me with glee. I have it now, within my grasp and grab it with both hands, holding it tightly and I won't let go. Most would have accepted their fate, but not my body – it feels stronger, even now the muscles seem to bulge again, and beat with my heart, naked and bare to the outside world.

The rain soon passes, and I am cooled and refreshed from it. I start to hear birdsong now that they are free to roam after the downpour. It is a magical sound, one I have missed greatly. I listen with my head to every sound I can find; the rustle of leaves on the wind, the crack of a branch that an animal snaps by accident. I look round to see who my fellow is, and of course, it is the deer. My friend from the beginning. I wave and the deer runs, not knowing I am her best friend, and will never again taste venison.

Saying that, a hunger grows in me like nothing I have encountered before. I must find food, and I know where to look, I did it for so long before my fall from grace and nature's way.

Chapter Nine

Hard lesson to learn,

Even clouded minds need help,

Do not fear asking.

I stumble around the forest, picking up some berries, mushrooms and nuts. I gather till I think I have enough, then sit down with my food pile. The fresh feast is nourishing, and I munch happily, feeling better with every bite. I see a squirrel watching me, looking hungry too. I throw him some nuts, his favourite. He runs but quickly realises the nut is what he wants and returns to eat within sight of me. It brings me a lot of happiness to watch him; the both of us are a pair. After eating, the squirrel returns to its tree and me to my feet. I am shaky but can finally walk again without support. The run to the forest served me well, it strengthened me even though I still look like death. I wander the glorious forests for the day. Feeling the mosses between my toes; the leaves stroking my head as I go deeper in, is marvellous. When the day of beauty comes to a close, I rest. It is a peaceful sleep, hearing the sounds around me, I find it easy to drift off.

The morning comes and I sit up and yawn. I stare at my hands – the skin has already started to grow back in patches. I will wait until fully healed to go back to town and the humans; right now, I fear I would scare them too much. But I must convince them there is no retribution coming, only help and my loyal serving of the people. There are many dead already, and I wonder how I can serve them? Having technically killed them by stealing time, I must mend the wounds caused by my actions. I regret it and shake my head slowly. The dead will have to wait – the ones alive need me now more than ever. The king will come soon, I feel it deep within me; there are those that think I am gone and word will spread like wildfire. He will have to call the army of course, so that will take time, and make his way to my fiefdom. There he will find me, still alive and still as powerful as ever, maybe more now I have learned that my body has more to give than I thought.

During the day I find a place to hole up in to recover my skin. Shaded and cosy I find it easy to sleep. When night comes, I move to a clearing and lie awake through the night, the moss as my bed and watch the stars.

How beautiful, little lights brightening my night's relaxing time. So, the real question is, has she forgiven me? Does nature live in the present and help me? So far, it would seem so, but it still disturbs me that the deer ran. She should have come to my embrace like in the old times we had together. I understand though, that the world is a different place now. Full of danger from bands of hunting humans. Plus, the angry, constant fear of wolves with sharp teeth always ready to rip you apart. I am not surprised – I would run, too. Perhaps with time, they will recognise me as a friend and fellow, but for now, there are more important animals that need my attention. They are lost without me, and I must make my way back to the town soon. I dread it, but it must be done. Hopefully, they won't shoot at me with crossbows out of fear, but one never knows.

I move deeper into the forest the next day and find what I am searching for, an old tree, fallen from age, giving shelter to all manner of beasts. It is a recent fall which suits me better and I get to work. I rip a large slab of bark from the old tree, a shield, just in case they are very afraid and do something we will both regret. My magic is back and stronger than it has been in a long time. The forest seems to give me this power to wield. I am nearly ready. I only need clothes, and fashion myself with leaves.

I follow my black trail back towards town. I am especially anxious and shake a little as it comes into sight. I have walked all day, and I stop for a rest for the night, to sleep and regain my strength. The crusted, charred skin has all sloughed off, leaving me with new, bright skin. I shine in the light as the sun fades and settle beside a large oak tree, surviving on its own. I appreciate the shelter and thank it. I touch the bark and feel safe with it. It is hard to the touch and I knock on it; very strong. Soon, sleep takes me and I am unconscious for most of the night, only waking occasionally to look around to see if there are humans nearby.

The next morning, the sunrise hits my face and I wake smiling. Today, I will meet the people of the town. I hope it is with some welcome, but fear it will not be, especially if the elders have poisoned ears that listen. I walk casually now, down the hard, stony path that leads to the market square. I hear gasps and see the humans scurry from sight on the outskirts of town. But I plunge forward into the main square. The stallholders stare at me in fear but some of the people here smile to see my return. I must find either Agatha or Fern, they will know what to do, so I walk with a gathering of astonished stares to the building which spelled what was supposed to be my doom. But death is no threat to me at the moment and I open the large wooden doors wide. The courtroom has disappeared and instead, long tables have been set up, in preparation for another feast for the elders. The servants turn and look horrified at the sight of me standing in the doorway.

'We must speak!' I bellow.

An elder at the top table looks round; it is the middle elder from my trial. He does not look pleased to see me, but heaves himself up from the table and walks like a crippled old man towards me, as if holding up the world on his shoulders. His grey hair is tied at the back but it is his face I now look at; it is wrinkled and falling from the bone, and it will not be long before death takes him.

'What do you want?' he asks with a growl, nearing my frame.

'I only wish to talk and decide the future of this place,' I reply, no longer shaky but feeling strong against this figure who has lost his power.

'Fine, come,' he says sharply and turns, waving me into the hall.

We walk to the end of the long table, the elder lets out a long sigh and manages to sit in his chair. The other old men have gathered here, and none of them will look me in the eye as I take a chair beside the head elder.

'So, what would you have us do? We can't kill you, obviously, so what exactly do you want?' he repeats with a grimace, reaching for his wine. He sips it then bangs it back on the table.

'I would have you see that I am just like all of you, here, in this town. I wish no harm and I must make up for my mistakes,' I say carefully, and the head elder finally looks me in the eye.

'How?' he asks, peering at me.

'Allow me freedom of the town and I will protect it with my dying breath. You know full well the king will come – the traders saw what you did, and most think me dead or away from the town. Why would I protect you, who tried to kill me? But, I will. I will do all I can because we are one and the same. I gave you all a second chance, don't I deserve one too?' I take a long breath and hold it for his answer.

He takes another sip, lowers his glass down and rubs his withered face. 'I believe you. You did indeed give us all a second chance, but after what you have done, do you deserve it? I don't know anymore, the people will decide. It is out of our hands, obviously,' he says with palpable anger and some wine spills from his mouth. I find the ancient man laughable now, why was I afraid? He wipes his mouth with a napkin and looks away from me. 'Go help your people, sir. Good luck changing their minds.' He motions for me to leave.

The rest looked shocked at his answer but I will not take it lightly. I must prove to the people that I have changed and make sure they know I am no longer their lord, only a helper and protector.

I walk out into the sun once more. What should I do first? I must find Fern. She will help me gather the people and work out what I can do to help make things better. I stride out confidently. The elders don't care for me, nor do they believe I can help them, but that is okay, I am not here for old men. I see many people but one catches my eye – it is the man who shot me with the crossbow, and he is running away from me. I give chase and find his speed is no match for mine of course. My legs have nearly fully healed, it would seem. I grab his neck and haul him up, and legs still running I turn him to face me. He is terrified, I knew he would be. Watching me survive a hanging must have put even more fear in him that I would come back for revenge.

'It is okay. Do not fear, I have come to help your son,' I say as I place him back on solid ground.

'Please don't hurt me, Lord! It was a horrible accident!' he screams and falls to his knees, much like he did before he shot me.

I smile and help him up; no weapon is apparent this time, just a sobbing man afraid of his death.

'I told you I could help your son. Wouldn't you like him to talk again? Don't call me lord, as I am one no longer. Come, bring me to him and we will see what we can do,' I say softly, bending down close to his face.

He nods and leads me to a house, and a fine one it is. Sturdy and high, at least two floors, with a thatch roof that will keep out any weather nature has to throw at it.

'What do you do for a living?' I ask quietly so as not to frighten him.

'Carpenter, my lord,' he sheepishly replies as we walked towards the heavy wooden door.

'Ah, makes sense, a fine house you have built. Remember I am no longer a lord, only Ariel,' I say, reminding him my title has gone with the seasons.

'Yes, yes I am sorry, Ariel.' he coughs out.

We enter the abode and he takes me up the stairs to a room with a large bed, and in the covers, we find his son.

'What is his name?' I ask.

'George, my . . . I mean, Ariel.' He bows and I lift his head up quickly.

'May I have some food? I only eat from the land, so no meat or cheese if you please.' I ask this of him to remove him from the room for a while so that I can prepare.

'Of course, I will find what I can,' he replies and walks towards the door. 'Look after my son.' He begins to shed tears again and I nod my head towards him, bowing slightly.

When he has left I take to meditating, gathering my power on the rug beneath me. It is nice to feel sheepskin, so soft and warm but then remember unnervingly that a sheep died for this floor decoration. . . But still, I clear my mind of these matters and travel to a place of freedom and harmony. I ask my body and the powers within it to grow and help the boy, well, a boy no more, but the man in the bed. I vaguely remember the boy as he was before I took him as servant to the horses. He was happy and carefree, strong-willed and hard to conquer if I envisage him correctly. Yes, I do recall it, the moment I turned his mind to merely a tool. Zombified, he had no choice but to follow my orders and the horses needed looking after – I had no time for the labour. I really should have, they were my horses after all, but I was callous and arrogant then. I concentrate on the boy he was and how I might explore his mind as it is now. I rise from the floor and move to the bed. His eyes are wide open and I try to see the damage first.

'George, look to me,' I say, waiting for a response but my power over him has truly left his mind. He merely stares at the ceiling.

I put a hand on his head and start my mission. I delve deep into his mind where we may be able to talk once more. Travelling this way is demanding work, and thought transference by touch is the closest we may be allowed to come together. I imagine us on a plane of white clouds, soft and fluffy, a comfortable and safe place for him. It is here I wait. I sit and cross my legs, showing I am no danger.

'What are you doing to him?' shouts a voice from the outside. George's body is shaking as it tries to free itself from the mind.

I shush the extra noise and put out my other hand to stop the advance of the other party. This is between us, another entering or being trapped in the same way is not my intention. The extra noise cannot be allowed to touch the body or it may be dragged in by accident and lost.

'George,' I whisper in both worlds.

I feel another body squirming in my spare hand but I must hold it away and concentrate at the same moment. The body stops its spasming and from the cloud world, a man appears. He is large and muscled, fine blonde hair and clean shaven, with bright blue eyes that pull you in. It is how he sees himself now, not the emaciated body in the real world. I look up to him, and he stands towering over my cross-legged figure.

'George?' I ask.

'You, you did this.' He stares at his hands and looks to me again.

'Yes, I did. That is in the past, and I have come to bring you to the present,' I say with a little more force in my voice.

'To be your slave once more? Never!' he shouts down at me and moves to throw his fist. I hold the hand with a finger, moments before it strikes me.

'No, your father is here for you. You must remember your father, the carpenter?' I ask, still holding the hand. A lot of force is racing through both our bodies but I can still hold him.

He lifts his hand. 'Daddy? He is here too? Oh no!' He begins to cry.

I shake my head and put my hand back in the clouds.

'No, you are home and free now. I am sorry I took you, George. It was not fair or decent of me,' I say lightly with no malice in my voice.

'I am home, then?' George asks and falls to his knees.

'Come with me, back home,' I say and put a hand on his shoulder.

'Ok,' are the last words we say here and I draw him back out to the real world.

George bolts up in bed and turns to me. His eyes are wide and full of fear. I nod at him and look round at my spare hand. I have lifted the father off the ground and am nearly choking him.

'Get off my dad!' George leaps and I let go of the man.

The leap turns into a hug and the men hold each other. They both cry over the shoulder of the other. I see fruit dropped, spilled over the floor, and grab an apple to eat as my energies are drained.

'Thank you,' the father whispers to me and I bow low, and get up to leave the men to rekindle their relationship. As I exit I hear the boy, George, talking once again and I smile to myself.

'Daddy, I had the worst nightmare,' George says, and his father shushes him.

'You are safe, my sweet boy,' the father replies, simply happy to have his son returned after all the time lost.

Chapter Ten

Hold your own in life,
Break the spell that binds you down,
Through care and kindness.

I return to sunlight and wipe my brow, finish the apple, then continue on my journey to find Fern. I remember she had a house by a stream, that is all I have to work with. I wander the streets weakened and hungry. But with no currency, I cannot buy from the traders or simply take as I used to do, unfairly. I stumble further into the town, and the cobbled streets are difficult to walk on. I fall, and am helped up by two men.

'My lord, are you okay?' one asks politely, even though I must look a wreck.

'My name is Ariel, I am no longer a lord,' I breathe out to whoever is listening.

They bring me inside a house, and sit me down on a chair. It is uncomfortable but I have no idea how I could stand at the moment. The spell on the boy was an energy sapping one; it would seem I am still not up to full strength, and away from the forest I am much weaker.

'Here, take these,' says a voice and I am handed plain, homemade garments.

I struggle to put them on, but hands help me. The leaves fall from me and I am dressed, in a fashion, a little more comfortable. I feel the cotton against my skin, it is warm and soothing and I fall dazed into a sleep to recuperate.

I awake with a start. They moved me to a bed, how I don't know as I have only grown heavier with the time I spent in the forest. I look around, eyes finally able to fully open. The room is barren, nothing hangs on the walls. The door is thin and wobbly and as the soft breeze shakes it, it lets out a squeak. I continue to pull my head round and a woman appears, sitting beside me. She is red-headed and fair to look at, an angelic saviour I think to myself and cannot help but smile.

'Drink,' she says with a voice so soft it could soothe the greatest wounds.

I take a cup from her hands, slightly touching her which makes my heart pound faster than before. I notice this and raise my eyebrows; that has never happened before, and I hope there is nothing wrong with me. I drink anyway and my heart slows as I gulp down the freshest and most pure water I have ever tasted. I am weak, I think, I need nourishment.

'I need food,' I say in a hoarse voice but better for the water.

The woman turns and picks up a basket.

'I am afraid this is all we have, my lord. But it is yours,' she says and shows me the basket's contents. Some old fruit and vegetables. I smile.

'Exactly what I need, thank you,' I say and pick up the first piece my hands find. I eat the potatoes raw and the fruit I feast upon till the basket is empty.

The woman smiles hopefully.

'Could my lord help us in return? We are very poor and owe a lot of money to the traders. I fear they will come for us soon.' She lets out a solitary tear from her eye and sniffs.

'You will be rewarded, my dear, after the kindness your family have shown me. No one is coming to hurt you. Send the men to the keep, there they will find all they need, just take whatever you want. I have no use for it now. You must call me Ariel. I am no longer a lord you see.' I wink at her and get a smile in return which makes my mind soar and I feel much happier than I have in a long time. Her lips are red and a little raw from malnutrition, but her beauty still shines through for me. Her long hair, porcelain skin, and high cheekbones are too much for me to bear, and I reach out a hand and shakily stroke the kind face. She lets me do this for a while before taking my hand and putting it back on the covers. She raises up and floats over to the door. I hear voices; the men are excited and a door slams shut.

She returns to my side. 'Thank you, we will be okay now, I think. First, we will pay the traders, then rebuild this house,' she whispers and smiles again which makes me feel something I had not known was a feeling. It is like elation but something more. I cannot describe it, nor grasp its meaning.

'You are very welcome. I am glad you will be okay,' I say with a stupid grin on my face. I realise I am doing this and stop. She looks at me with curiosity and raises one eyebrow, before laughing out loud which sends me the same way.

For quite a moment we eye each other up, before I am the first to look away. There is one picture on the wall I have missed, a painting, one of a great old tree that draws me in and makes me flicker inside as I yearn to be with the forest again.

'Who painted this?' I ask, already knowing the answer, hopeful I am right.

'My friend, Fern, she is an excellent painter and made this for me as a present.'

'Excellent, I know her too. Tell me about you. I am sorry I have not even asked your name after you saved me, quite rude.' I sigh at myself and my discourtesy.

'My name is Di, short for Diana. I am just a maid in one of the houses further up the street, for an elder. I clean and wash their clothes. It was Fred, my brother, who found you first and my father helped bring you in. My mother died in childbirth, so it is just the three of us.'

'A perfect name for a woman such as yourself. I am sorry about your mother.' I bow my head. 'How on this island did they lift me?' I ask with an impressed tone.

'Thank you, you are exceedingly kind. Fern told me you were. They half-lifted you, I mean, you still walked a little . . . Ariel?' she asks back.

'Yes, Ariel, a demon of nature at my heart.' I bow my head once more. 'I must find our mutual friend, Fern, she will know what to do next.' I start to lift the sheets and rise.

'Ariel, you must rest, you were very weak and I am frightened for you. The elders are still plotting you know – I heard a couple talking. They will wait for you to show weakness, so please stay here at least until tomorrow. Then I will take you to Fern, I know the way well.' She puts the cover back over my massive frame, as best she can anyway. I am a bit large for the bed and I notice my feet hit the floor, but it is comforting to stay here a while.

'Okay, I will stay until the sun rises tomorrow and then we will go to Fern,' I say, and fall into a good sleep.

I am awoken by a pounding noise. 'Di!' I call out and open my eyes, to see her sitting by me.

'It is the traders, Ariel, I am sorry. Please help us once more. My father has not returned yet.'

I rise from the bed with sleepy eyes and bump my head on the ceiling. I stretch a little where I can and rip the trousers which have become shorts. I yawn and make my way to the front door. It flings open before I can reach the handle and three fat men burst through. They see me, and I see them, all of us a bit shocked. They go to turn and flee but I grab the middle one's clothes and drag him into the house, plonking him down on a chair which creaks under his mass. He heaves and puffs, holding his arms over his face.

'We must have the wrong house, my lord, we apologise!' he squeaks out and makes for the door once more, but a swift foot puts him back into place.

'I believe you are in just the place you desire. You come to rough up Diana and her family, do you not?' I ask, towering down on him.

'Yes, but, no, I mean, we came only to collect what is ours. Please don't hurt me, my lord.' He squirms more than a mouse would when a cat has caught it.

'You know, it is illegal for you to loan to the people. That was a rule when you first arrived to trade with us, remember?' I ask him, quite enjoying his fear. But I shake my head and let him go from my grip. I must be diplomatic, it is not right to use my title and power to put fear in humans any longer.

'Yes, my lord, quite illegal, thank you. It was only a misunderstanding I am sure.' He wipes his silk tunic down and coughs, staring up at me.

'The men will return from the keep with your gold. Do not be afraid. You will have your currency and we will be left alone,' I say and turn as a kerfuffle has broken out on the street. I step out into the light, and see the father and brother are fighting with the traders.

'Halt!' I bellow with a deep cry, and the fighting ceases. 'Pay the men and they will be on their way, correct?' I look round at my new friend and he nods repeatedly.

The men hand the traders one of my golden candlesticks, and I feel a pang of sorrow, but I need it not now. The traders run up the street and out of sight, and I motion for the men to return to their home. They go in and are immediately hugged by Di, who then slaps them both over the back of the head.

'Foolish father and foolish brother! Don't go around fighting them, it will only make things worse for us!' she shouts at them. The feeling comes back to me and I smile at her rage. She is indeed a strong woman, I think to myself.

She turns to me out on the street. 'You, in now. Get some rest.' She huffs and storms out of the room.

I do as I am told, after all, she knows where Fern is and I want to enjoy more of her company. I stretch out on the small bed and sleep once more. Full of dreams this time, and I find myself on a battlefield with fire all around me, men screaming in notes of agony. I am holding a sword but it is not my own. Did I make the fire? I don't remember creating it and putting my hand out to it, it doesn't burn me. I turn to see it is the town that burns, too. I shout for Fern but no sound comes from my mouth. I hear a clinking of armour and bring up my sword just in time to catch another's with the blade. Staring into my eyes, so close I can feel breath on my cheek, another demon concentrates and huffs at me, breathing heavily and pushing down on me so hard I fall. It is the king I realise – he has come for me. I lift an arm up as he crashes a blade down upon me. I wake with a gasp and sit up to look around.

Di shushes me and moves to hold my hand. 'Bad dreams? I have them sometimes too.'

'Yes, I think so. The king came for me and the town burned,' I say and flop back onto the bed. I rub my head and shake off the feeling of dread and fear.

'You're safe now, you slept the whole day. Tomorrow we will go and see Fern, I promise. You don't look so pale anymore, thankfully,' she says and leaves the room, returning with bread and water.

'Thank you, Di, it is much appreciated,' I say with a sheepish smile, not knowing what she really thinks of me. Does she actually like me? Or is she just using me to get out of trouble with the traders?

I can't tell which is the truth. Care for my wellbeing is rare, so rare that I can't believe she likes me or wants the best for me. I should be wary, but her eyes keep pulling me in and my heart feels like it is melting. Maybe I will see what happens, if Di does take me to Fern, then I can ask what she is really like.

I can hear shouting in the street and the movement of people, like a march.

'Has the king come already?' I ask, wide-eyed and in a panic state.

'No, the people here in town have seen my brother and family take from your keep. Now they all want something for themselves. They are maybe a touch greedy, but good people I promise you,' she says, bowing her head.

'Ah, they may have it,' I say, waving my hands, 'I will not be returning there, where I was stuck for so long. It is a hell I am glad to be away from.'

'Poor you, well thank you for sharing what you have. Why were you stuck there?' she asks with a voice that I am surprised by; it sounds like she is actually curious.

'A malaise nearly killed me. A cloud covered my mind and I nearly died, Di,' I reply.

She stays quiet, not saying a word, only taking my hand and kissing it. She looks up at me and I feel the warmth spreading through my body.

'May we go and see Fern now? I feel much stronger thanks to you,' I say, nearly crying.

'Yes, maybe it would be best to go now, here have some more bread and water first. It is not far but we don't want you collapsing again, do we?' Di says with care in her voice.

I drink my fill and eat the loaf, and it goes down so easily that I realise I must be starving. But I feel much stronger for eating so I raise myself from the bed and put my feet firmly down on the floor with a thump. I smile at Di and stand, well, crouch, and make my way out of the house. Di follows and then leads me, down the street then off the main road to tight, narrow spaces we squeeze in and out of until she stops and points.

'That is Fern's house. I will leave you to it, I must check on Father, he's always getting in trouble. I hope I see you again though, Ariel,' she says. Can I hear a slight bashfulness to her words? I hope so.

'Thank you for your hospitality, Di. I hope we do meet again, I would like that.' I bow to her and she waves then turns back the way we came.

I straighten myself to my full height and approach the door Di pointed at. I remember this place now and hear the rush of water from the stream as I knock politely. I stand back a little and wait in anticipation. The door does not open, instead a voice can be heard inside.

'Who is there? I don't have anything for you, please leave.' Fern's dulcet tones.

I cough and step forward. 'Fern? Could I come in please? I have nowhere else to go,' I say softly.

I hear the movement of furniture, and wood dragging on floors. Then the door slowly opens and I see a face that holds an amount of joy, but also trepidation. She waves me in with a flustered hand, and I follow quickly. I crouch to avoid banging my head on the frame. Fern then shuffles the wooden bench, a chest of drawers and a table back in front of the door.

'It's not safe out there at the moment and I'm afraid.' Fern's expression turns to panic and she checks the door for its sturdiness.

The room I am in is quaint, small but far from barren, and beautiful. I remember building this place, but it has changed a lot. There is a menagerie of paintings, most half-finished but all perfect or coming along well. Most are of nature but quite a few are portraits of people I recognise from the town plus some I do not know. The roof is higher here and I can lift myself to full height. There is a closed window at the back of the house; it has been boarded up but I can see by the stool and easel that it is where she paints, looking out over the stream. I imagine it is quite relaxing and wish I could see her in her element instead of what is in front of me now. She is shaking and I race to her and hug her deeply. It is my turn to stroke her hair. I hold her so gently and with care. The shaking stops for a moment and I take my chance, pulling away to look at her tear-ridden face.

'What is going on?' I ask, knowing full well the probable answer.

'Looting.' She sniffs.

'Because of the keep?' I enquire of her.

'Yes. Ariel, everyone has gone completely crazy. There is looting, but also fighting and houses being burgled I was told. I can't lose everything now, so I've barricaded the place as best I can. But now you're here! You will protect me? Please stay a while at least, I'm panicking.' I can hear the fear in her voice, so I nod and hold her again, my closest thing to a daughter. I caused this. Pain and fear once more.

'It will be okay. I am sorry, I think I did this. I let Di's family take from the keep and now everyone must want something.'

'I heard shouting about the keep. I was scared for you, but we will be okay together. I am glad you are here,' she says even though it's muffled in my chest.

'Show me your work, if you will.' I smile and take her by the hand into the middle of the room.

She smiles back at me and says with brighter eyes, 'I have all my work in here. Some are good, some are bad, but all mine.'

'And the portraits?' I ask.

'Yes, well I have to make extra money somehow. Allows me to live comfortably I suppose, but I long to paint the wilds again,' she says sadly.

'Good work, they are all beautiful, Fern. I am very jealous of your talent,' I say before turning to a banging on the door.

'Let us in, woman! We won't hurt you, I promise! Come on, you know you want to!' a voice from the outside shouts in jest, and I hear laughter following. I can hear that they do mean her harm and an anger grows in me. Wanting to protect my daughter, I rip the furniture from the doorway.

'No! Don't do that, we are safe in here,' Fern gasps as I open the door to reveal six burly men.

I stoop to come face to face with the leader. He backs off but I follow, my eyes on fire with rage and I grab him by the arms as I come out of the house.

'What do you want?' I snort into his face.

'I am sorry, I didn't know!' he screams and wriggles in my grasp.

I throw the man at his friends and they scatter, disappearing into the dark night.

'No one comes near Fern!' I shout into nothingness but I think the whole town will have heard the bellowing.

I return to her house and she smiles at me as I come in.

'You shouldn't have done that. They will just be back when you disappear.' She sighs before sitting down on her stool, looking very much defeated.

'I will stay as long as I have to,' I say confidently. I won't leave her until she is safe.

Fern nods slowly and rises to close the door, moving the furniture back into place. She turns to me, still shaken and tired looking.

'Have you slept yet?' I ask.

'No, how would anyone sleep through this?' she replies.

I nod and crouch by her side. She knows I am sorry, and there is nothing else to do now but hope no one is hurt. I pray Di and her family are okay, but I can't leave so I will imagine they are fine and in the same situation as Fern, blocking their doors till the storm of people dissipates. What a mess I have created. I mourn for all those normal people who are in harm's way because of my thoughtless act. I avoided violence and only generated more violence. But it is done, and we will have to wait till it's over. I wish I could change it all but even I can't seem to stop the human's proclivity for killing one another. I sigh and sit cross-legged on the floor. I hold my head in my hands and Fern comes over to reassure me, putting a hand on my bald head.

'I did this, I caused all of this,' I say in sorrow.

'It's okay, Ariel. You didn't cause everyone to go crazy. They should be able to control themselves, but this is just how people are.' She strokes my back.

I nod with grief and lean into her. I should stop them from their ways, but I am tired now. I can protect the humans from outside forces but, it seems, not from themselves. They will have to figure that one out on their own I suppose. They have their freedom and this is how they have chosen to use it. I can no more stop that than push back the tides.

Fern raises me up and silently leads me to the side room; she has a large bed and we settle down for the night. Hoping no one else comes to hurt her, I don't sleep well even though I am still weak from the spell. Fern cuddles into me, looking for comfort. I stroke her hair to encourage her to sleep, then lie awake with my mind for company. It spins and weaves, leaving me thinking dark thoughts. What if there is a fire that covers the town? I should stop it. I should have put an end to it already. I am a terrible being, I don't deserve to have a friend such as Fern. I can't protect her forever in this house. I hope the fighting dies down and the town becomes at peace once more. But I worry it won't, and all we built will come crashing down, never to be repaired. I started it all, thinking I could make things better for Di's family, for Di. Now the keep will be in ruins, and my precious artwork taken. I should burn it down tomorrow. That will stop them. They may pick through the rubble instead of destroying the town.

Chapter Eleven

I am not your friend,

I never helped you survive,

You did it alone.

The sun rises quickly to my knowledge – hopefully it will light the humans up and make them see that this is not the way. I roll out of bed and make my way back through to the studio room. The shouting has indeed died down so I move the furniture away from the door and step outside. The sun has only just risen, and is bright and cold. There is a redness to the sky that I pray has no meaning. I look around but my view is hampered by the small, close housing. Thatched roofs block what is happening on top of the hill. But I do see, I believe, some smoke coming from the general direction of the keep. Maybe they have done my job for me and burned the place to the ground already? It would be good if they have. Still, I can enjoy watching the sun, and let it shine on my face till it has broken free of the horizon and begins to warm the land properly. It shines through my body, giving me energy. I'm hoping that the worst is over and the humans have ceased their looting and vulgar ways.

I hear a noise from behind me. I have not noticed Fern has woken too and come through to the artist's room. I return inside, and stare at her; she is looking tired, but much better than last night. She yawns and waves at me as I come towards her.

'Would you like some food? It is very early, but I woke up when you left. Is it over?' she asks with a hope that is palpable.

I nod to both questions. 'I think it is done with. I see fire on the hill, and I am hopeful they have burned that damned keep to the ground and we may be left in peace.'

It is Fern's turn to nod. 'Good, then we can start the day. I have much to do and have commissions to finish.' She motions towards all the portraits stacked in the corner.

'That is fine, I will eat then scout the surrounding area to see if I can help at all,' I say with some trepidation about leaving her.

'Okay, but don't be too long. I think I can still help you. Would you like to learn to paint? I find it so relaxing and helpful for my mind in any case,' she says, biting her lip and peering at me with bright eyes.

'Of course, that sounds magical. We will paint together once you have finished the commission and I have helped anyone who needs it.'

Maybe there is hope if I can relax and help ease my mind. I eat some bread and drink some water. Fern also brings out some fruit for me.

'Not eating cheese or ham anymore?' she asks, looking at my half-full plate.

'No, I cannot stomach it now. I will return to only eating well from nature,' I say passionately.

'Okay, no need to sound so proud of yourself.' She giggles and sends me on my way with a full belly.

I leave the house and make my way towards the centre of the town, passing through tight spaces between homes. Some are damaged and I see a door that has been broken off its hinges, so make my way towards it. Stepping lightly, I knock on what is left of it.

'Hello? Anyone here?' I call into the darkness of the room.

'Be gone! There is nothing left here for you to steal!' A voice comes from the darkest corner.

'Be at peace, I think it is over. I am Ariel, your previous lord,' I say to the corner shadow.

A small woman comes out into the light of the doorway. She is old and greying, wrinkled and wearing a night dress of pink with white socks on her feet. Coming closer, I realise she has a black eye.

'What happened here? Can I help you at all?' I ask, knowing that the worst has already occurred.

'No, my dear. They stole all they could and left me with this.' She motions towards her eye.

'Who did this?' I ask of her.

'The traders came and damaged many houses. I don't know their names,' she replies and sits on the floor, weeping.

I walk into the room and hold her.

'It will be okay, all who have committed crimes will be held accountable. For now, shall I fix your door?' I ask and she nods, looking up at me.

I turn and lift the door back to where it should be. The hinges fit back onto their rightful place and I swing the door to check it still works. I nod to her. It is very little but the best I can do for now.

'I will see the traders, did you lose much of value?' I say, hoping nothing precious was taken.

'My necklace. My grandson, John made it, the blacksmith here. Can you return it to me?' she begs, and I can't resist nodding violently and bowing, then heading towards the door.

'Look after yourself, I will return,' I say as I walk from the house.

So, it is the traders. I knew the man looked foreign who tried to attack Fern. But I had not thought the traders capable of such violence. They must be punished but I will see the blacksmith, this John fellow first, and let him know what has occurred. He will be near the trader's square so I must be careful with my words. Blacksmiths are strong men, from beating steel and creating leather all day. He may well lose his temper as I did last night. I stopped myself, but maybe he won't, so I will tread lightly. I walk further into the town; many people are out on the main street shouting at one another and I can hear them clearly.

'They stole from us! We should hang them all!' says one.

'He started this! Opening his keep for a free for all, punish him I say!' one other replies.

The men shouting in the street are growing ever nearer and they turn open-mouthed to see me walking towards them. I notice now the second man is an elder, dressed as he is in silk and gold. Obviously, he was protected from the night's raid. I point a finger at them both and motion for them to approach my heavy frame. Standing towering over them, they appear so small and fragile that I feel a pang of guilt for bringing this on them. I want to embrace them and tell them they are safe now. But first I will show them I am not the enemy.

'I apologise for yesterday's events, I am truly sorry for the havoc I caused.' I bow to them both.

'Well, yes, well it is quite alright, my lord,' says the elder and the other man nods repeatedly.

'We have a problem, my lord. The traders attacked the town while, well, while the men were at your keep.' He glances sideways away from my gaze, obviously guilty that they left their people in order to prey on my wealth.

'I forgive you too, the keep is for the people now. I know the traders attacked and we will deal with them properly,' I say and march towards the main square.

As we arrive the traders are packing up in a hurrying fashion. Having taken their fill, I would guess they are ready to leave.

'Halt!' I shout and the traders leave their packs for running down the street towards the outskirts of town.

The people from the town launch themselves forward and give chase. I stand and shake my head; I am sure they will bring them back so I wait with the elder who has no chance of being able to run.

'You believe it is my fault and, to a certain degree, you are correct. I opened the doors to the keep and this mess would not have occurred had I not. How will you, the elders, deal with the traders?' I ask, not looking at him but at the crowd as they run down trader after trader, then carry them back towards us.

'They will have a trial, of course,' he replies.

'Like mine you mean?' I look down at him now, with a slight smirk on my face.

'Erm, no, a proper trial.' He coughs and looks meek.

'Good. Where is the blacksmith's home?' I ask and he points towards a large abode.

I turn and leave them to it. I have an important job to do. I knock on the door and hear again the sound of furniture being moved and lifted. The door peeks open and there is a man staring at me. He looks rough and like he has not slept. A large beard covers half his face and I see he stands taller than any human I have encountered before.

'Might you be the blacksmith? It is over, you are all safe now,' I say and the man further opens the door.

'Yes, I am the blacksmith. What do you require, my lord? I had to keep my family safe last night, I promise I was nowhere near your keep.' He says this without a smile.

I nod and press the door open further, half-whispering to him, 'It is about your grandmother, she was attacked last night.'

'No! Is, is she alright?' He begins to cry.

'Yes, but you may want to check up on her,' I say and the man looks round at his family. I see them now, hiding in a corner of the room.

'I will go, will you look after my family while I am gone?' he asks of me.

'Of course, go see her,' I say and he runs past me down the street.

I step further into the doorway and see a child, of around six or seven years, with dark hair and dark eyes. He looks puzzled at my appearance.

'What happened to your trousers?' he asks, as straight-faced as his father.

'Sash! Leave the man be, he is here to protect us, be respectful. I am sorry, my lord, would you like some tea?' the woman asks and I nod.

'It's alright. Sash, is it? I am afraid I am slightly larger than average humans and they ripped!' I bellow to him and he giggles.

The mother goes to a back room and the boy follows her, waving as he walks. I close the door and see all is dark inside. They must have been hiding in blackness all night. A window is opened in the back room and shines a bit of light on the situation. A chest of drawers hides the other window so I push it and reveal the wooden doors which I open and light pours over the room.

'Much better,' I say to myself and turn as the woman returns with a herbal tea that smells of pine.

'Good for your health, my lord,' the woman says, curtsying.

'No need for that, I am Ariel now only. What is your name?' I ask with curiosity and take a sip of the fresh tea.

'My name is Glen, Ariel, it is nice to meet your acquaintance,' she replies gracefully.

'A pleasure to meet you, too. I was wondering if your husband makes swords? I find myself in need of one.' I look at her; she has fine straight black hair and freckles on her face. A fine face it is, and as she looks up, I catch sight of sharp dark eyes, no fear in them. So, she is strong.

'Of course. He has not made one for a time, my lord. But I believe he would make one for you. Without needing payment of course,' she says with a smile, trying to be respectful.

'Hmm, I had not thought about payment. Perhaps there is an exchange to be had? What do you need?' I ask.

'Well, we need not for much, my lord Ariel. My husband keeps us in good stead. But Sash, the poor boy has been having terrible waking dreams every night. I know you use magic, do you think you could help him? We would be eternally grateful,' she says, hopefully.

'I can try. Let me place my hands on the boy's head and I will see what is going on,' I say and reach out a hand.

She turns to the boy. 'Now, Sash, the man is going to help you with nightmares. Come here, I will hold your hand.'

The boy shuffles forward and takes his mother's hand. I move towards him and he hides behind his mother's leg, peeking out at me.

'It is okay, I will make those pesky dreams go away,' I tell him, and he comes round the leg to stand in front of me.

'How?' he asks.

'Well, I use magic to find out what is going on up here.' I point to his head.

He nods vigorously, obviously impressed with magic and I smile, putting my hand on his forehead. I close my eyes with him doing the same and we delve deep into his mind. In the back of his mind, I find him. We are on a plain, the clouds are moving abnormally quickly and a storm breaks out. Thunder crashes and bangs, making the child jump. Lightning forks down in front of me, and the child screams out in a deafening, screeching tone. The rain starts, heavy and freezing cold. He is very troubled, I think to myself. The boy stands smaller than in real life, holding his hands around his body, dressed only in shorts and a shirt. He shakes uncontrollably in the pelting rain. I walk towards him and he screams again. I shush him and wrap myself around him. The rain no longer hitting his face, he speaks.

'Who are you?' He looks curious now, less afraid.

'I am here to help, my name is Ariel,' I say quietly, softly rocking him.

The boy nods in my arms. 'Can you make the rain go away? It is very scary here,' he says in a muffled voice which I can barely hear over the thunder.

'You can do it. Just imagine the sun shining and it will be so,' I say to him confidently, hoping it will give him strength.

He nods again, starts to make a high-pitched noise like he is concentrating with all his might, and then forces out a deep, vibrating tone. I can feel the rain weakening and the thunder bursts are quieter now. I look up and see some blue sky.

'That's it! Clever boy, Sash, there is no need to be afraid!' I shout as I look up further to see the cloud dispersing. I let the boy go and stand up to my full height.

Sash looks up for the first time to see the sun, and it beams down on him in a spotlight. He smiles and jumps for joy, reaching out a hand to feel the light. The clouds have gone now, giving way to blue skies. I feel myself retreating out of his world and waking into the real one with a start. Both me and Sash do a little jump as we disconnect.

'Is that it? Your eyes were only closed a second,' Glen says, looking at us wide-eyed.

'Yes, he is a bit troubled with fear. But together we worked through it,' I reply ruffling the boy's hair.

He laughs and skips up the stairs singing a tune.

'Well, he seems happier, thank you, Lord Ariel.' She sniffs, wiping her eyes.

'Not a problem, the nightmares are gone for now but you will have to build his confidence. He was very small in there,' I tell her.

Glen nods several times, and hugs me a thank you. I embrace her too, feeling strong after helping the boy. There is a bustling at the door and I walk to open it. I find the blacksmith with his grandmother on his back. They step in and he lets her down to the floor.

'Glen, Grandma will stay with us for a while. Can you make her a bed up, please?' the blacksmith says and turns to me.

'Thank you sir for staying with my family. What can I do to repay you?' he asks gruffly.

'He has already helped, John. He has broken Sash's nightmares!' Glen says with joy and walks up the stairs with a broad smile covering her face.

'Oh, well, thank you again. How did you manage that? He has been plagued for a long time. I thought it hopeless.' John looks at me with eyes of thanks and moves to shake my hand.

'I find myself in need of a sword, blacksmith,' I tell him, bowing down.

'Of course, I have not made a weapon for a while. What kind of sword do you need?' He nods his head to my bow.

'Long, longer than any you have made before. Straight and sharp is all I ask for.'

'Okay, I will get to work and let you know when it is finished. Where is your new abode?' John says hesitantly. He must know about the keep; I should go see the damage for myself.

'Do you know Fern? I stay with her now,' I tell him and rub my hands together, feeling a bit woozy and cold after helping Sash. The blacksmith nods, returning to his family.

Chapter Twelve

I sigh and I try,

To find the pure soul within,

It does not exist.

I let myself out into the outside world once more. I notice in the central square they have rounded up the traders so I walk over to see what is occurring. I shake off the feeling of weight that comes from using too much energy, and inspect the scene before I intervene. The situation has become dire – in so little time, a crowd has gathered and begun their chant for blood. It sickens me, as it reminds me of my own trial. I believe it will go the same way; I do not trust the elders to make a good and fair judgment on these men. Some will be traders who have done nothing wrong and I must protect them from my own people. I wade through the crowd, pushing past the masses to get into the square proper. Most of the traders have been stripped of their possessions, even their clothes, and are in the middle of being bound by the wrists.

'What are you doing?' I holler to the elders who have gathered.

'We are beginning to trial the men, of course.' The greyest elder speaks, the one in charge, I remember from my trial.

'And they are supposed to get justice this way? I think not. I will not allow this to happen again. Let me speak to the men, I will ascertain whether they are guilty by reaching their minds,' I say and begin to stride towards the men.

'Wait!' An elder shouts over the roar of the crowd. I disregard the call and continue my quest to find the truth and perhaps the blacksmith's grandmother's necklace.

Ignoring the mob, I begin my search, swatting the men away from the traders. I line them up and start. I put a hand on the first's head and delve into him, seeing his memories like they were my own. Tracking through to recent events, I can see he was a part of the group of men who attacked the homes. I see him standing back though, unsure about the situation and how to proceed. He is not a violent man, just an opportunist who thought he might benefit from this, but when the time came he was afraid and wished he had not come. I relay the message and the crowd goes quiet.

I turn to the elders. 'How would you deal with this man, knowing what he has done?' I ask of them.

'Hang!' is the shout from one in the crowd.

The head elder shushes them with a wave of his hand, and walks, almost rattles, to my side.

'You believe what you are seeing? Then the man is guilty and must hang,' he says to me in a stern voice.

He knows he has no power against my will and is trying to convince me to follow the crowd. But who am I to give orders now? Can I let this man die? A human who is kneeling, praying with tear-filled eyes. Completely disgusted with himself for bowing to peer pressure. If he could take it back he would, but that is past the point. He has committed a crime on our land, against our people. The people deserve justice.

'Banishment?' I query the elder.

The chant grows louder. 'Hang! Hang! Hang!'

The elder nods to himself for quite some time, weighing up the benefits of bowing to me or the crowd. He shakes his head in a 'no' fashion then looks up into my eyes.

'No, the crowd deserve their justice,' he says forcefully, and holds up a hand once more to create silence. 'Hang he will!' he cries out with all the frail energy he has.

I look down in sorrow, apologise to the man and move along the rank of traders.

'Who has attacked an old woman and has a golden necklace that was taken from her? This man will not be hanged but banished, so it would do you well to come forward now,' I shout to them and wait for an answer.

One trader looks round at the others and then nods at me vigorously. I stand over him and remove his binding, before guiding him to their loot.

'Give the necklace to me and you will not be harmed,' I say and watch as he rummages through the pile to find his bag. From it, he produces a necklace and slams it into my hand.

'Can I leave this cursed place now?' he asks and as soon as I nod, he runs.

The crowd sways in a wave towards the man.

'Hold yourselves! He is a free man, he will never return and justice has been served!' I continue to search minds, finding a mix of the guilty and innocent. The crowd will not be swayed by me though and I leave resigned and them to their fate. I stride to the blacksmith's house, leaving the rabble behind me, their thirst for blood making me hate them. I feel like I have made not a utopia, but the opposite.

I knock on the door and am answered by John himself.

'I am sorry, my lord, it is not started yet. I must tend to my family, you understand?' He looks sheepishly at the crowd. 'It is not safe to be in town, you should leave.' He begins to shut the door.

I hold the door and hand him the necklace. 'For your grandmother, I know it will take time for the sword,' I say and then let the door close on me.

I look round one more time at the crowd who are gathering wood for yet another gallows and pray for the souls of the traders who had no part in last night's debacle. I am sorry for all of them, but especially their wives and children who will never know exactly what happened to them, only that they never returned. It makes me incredibly heartbroken that the crowd does not understand; I saved them from such a fate, simply by creating this town. Based on the fact that everyone deserves a second chance, that was my rule, and yet they do not follow it for outsiders. Nor do they see that by sending these men to their deaths, they may start the process of losing their own lives should I decide not to protect them now. I am torn, between those who I know are good and the mob who seem to rule the town.

I am walking in the general direction of Fern's house when I stop. I look to my left and see a door I recognise, so I knock lightly on it. There is a lot of chatter inside but no words I can discern. I feel my heart start its heavy beat as the door opens, and the man standing in front of me is Di's brother.

'Is Di here?' I ask, feeling a strange shyness wash over me.

He nods and opens the door wider. 'Thank you for opening the keep, we are safe from hunger now,' he says.

'You are most welcome,' I reply as I step hunched through the doorway.

Inside is a delicious smell. It is the cooking of vegetables, and it warms my heart. My smile broadens as I see her; she walks with a grace I have not known before and I bow my head to her. She waves me in, and smiles back.

'Hello again,' she says, laying the table.

'Hello,' I say quietly, rubbing a foot on the floor, lifting my head slightly to look her in her beautiful, sparkling eyes.

'Come have some food with us, it is just vegetable soup. Not what you are used to I am sure, but it will fill you up, and there is plenty to go round, thanks to you.' Di looks incredibly pleased with herself and disappears back into another room.

'That is fine by me, I eat only vegetables now,' I say, and move forward towards the table. I take a seat after the brother motions for me to do so.

'I apologise, what is your name?' I ask the burly brother.

'Fred,' he replies and shouts through to the kitchen, 'your guest hungers! Come look after us, sister.'

I hear a laugh from somewhere inside the house; the notes are a song to me and I breathe them in happily.

'He will not starve! Do not fear for our guest, brother! I know it is only your own belly you worry for.' Di sweeps back in with a pot.

The father appears from nowhere, and sits. 'May you be well,' he says to the table and nods in my direction. He puts on a slight smile as Fred starts to dig in as soon as the pot reaches the table.

'Manners! Ariel is first, as our guest,' Di says, beaming at me.

I am incredibly grateful and use a large spoon to dish myself out some soup. I find it hearty and filling, so tasty I must ask for the recipe I think to myself. Fred gobbles a portion and starts his second endeavour.

'Is it to your liking, Ariel?' Di asks in a hopeful voice.

'Of course, it is delicious, thank you very much for your hospitality, Di,' I reply and take my own seconds to prove it.

'We will not go hungry again, thank you, sir,' the father says gruffly, but gratefully.

'There is no need for "sirs" father, this is Ariel, our friend,' Di says and wraps her hair behind an ear.

I smile and say, 'exactly,' before tucking into more of the vegetables.

Filled to the brim, I get ready to take my leave.

'Off so soon?' Di asks me.

'Yes, I must return to Fern. I have been away quite a while. However, I would like to see you again if that pleases you, of course?' I say to her bashfully, and the father grunts.

'I will come to Fern's when I have time, I promise. It has been too long since I saw her anyway,' Di replies giving her father a stern look.

I bow to them all, say my thanks and make for the door.

Chapter Thirteen

Show me a being,

Godly perfect specimen,

Who has not struggled.

The sun shines bright and I have to avert my eyes as I walk down the street. I am giddy with something. I cannot describe the feeling to myself, but something is different after seeing Diana. I feel complete, and I feel like I am blushing, a heat radiates from my cheeks. I stride quicker, my blood pumping, and begin to run for the first time since my escape to the forest. I arrive at Fern's door and knock quickly with a force that rattles the hinges.

'Hello? Who is that?' I hear from the otherside of the door.

'I have returned, Fern,' I say quickly, puffing from my run.

She opens the door. 'Took your time, everything is fine here though. Come in, you look pale. Is everything alright?' She looks concerned.

'Yes, something is happening to me and I am not sure why I ran all the way here from Diana's,' I reply.

'Di's? You know her? Beautiful, isn't she?' Fern gasps. 'You like her! Oh, I can see why! Come in and tell me everything now.'

I walk into the studio and sit on the stool.

'Like her? Yes, of course I do, she helped me when I was not well,' I say and I regain my breath.

'No, you *like* like her,' Fern says with a playful note.

'I have never felt these feelings before, Fern, it is very confusing,' I tell her.

'It's okay, Ariel. You can have feelings for people. And well-chosen, she is glorious, and my best friend here in town. Oh, I'll have to set you up! So exciting. This is great news!' She springs up and dances in front of me. 'You want to kiss her and make little Ariel and Diana babies!'

I am even more confused now; do I want to be with Di? I have never met anyone who could potentially be my mate. Is it possible I have found someone? Maybe. But I will have to get stronger first, and I have no idea how to woo a lady as fine as Di. Fern stretches out on the floor, tired from her movements. I hold my head in my hands, stuck in my own mind, spinning with the possibilities. All I know is that I feel different around her and after I have seen her. Is that love? I doubt love is so fleeting. I can only hope she does come to visit, and we will see where it goes from there. I smile and shake my head, looking up to see Fern has risen from the floor and is standing next to me, flushed from dancing. She puts a hand on my shoulder and giggles, still excited at the prospect.

'Come on, Ariel! Get excited! Don't hold your head down! Why don't we spend some time talking and relaxing whilst doing some painting?' she says and hands me a brush, then sets up the easel in front of me with a white canvas resting on it.

'I have no idea how, Fern,' I say, letting the brush go limp in my hand.

Fern turns and opens the window wide. Outside I can hear the birds chirping and the stream passing by. There is an old tree on its bank, and the grass surrounding it is a vivid green and rustles in the wind.

'Just paint what you see, silly.' She looks out onto the view 'It's not so difficult, just enjoy it and let it be whatever it wants to be.' Fern takes another stool and sets up beside me. She puts her hand to a brush and dips the tip into the water before choosing a colour.

'Okay, I think I see what you mean,' I say as I look directly at the tree, observing all its beauty and grizzly bark, worn from the decades of growth.

I diligently put my brush in the water and then in some green paint; it is as vibrant as the grass, so I'll begin there. I find it soothing to stroke the canvass with my brush. I smile, a long lingering smile that Fern notices as she continues to paint.

'Enjoying ourselves, finally?' Fern raises an eyebrow at me.

'I suppose, it is very relaxing. But I fear this time away will not solve my problems.' I let out a sigh.

'No, it won't, but you can remember this time together when you face hard times. What is it that concerns you?' she asks. I stop painting and turn towards her.

'How long before the king comes? My sword is not ready, and my powers are growing in different directions. Not for war but for healing, so how will I turn them against an army? The people are fickle and kill innocent traders in the square at this very minute!' I shout and point outside.

'Healing is a good thing, perhaps you will find it useful. People are bad, but you also see the good or you would not be here, right? And the king will come whenever it is time for you to fight. You are strong and capable, I believe you will be able to keep us safe, even if people are not perfect in nature and won't thank you for all you do.' She answers my questions and lays a hand on my knee, rubbing it slowly.

I look to her and try a little grin, but it's more of an anxious grimace still. What if I am still capable of past deeds? What if I fall into my previous behaviours? That cannot be allowed to happen. I try to clear my mind and paint, but it is darker now and the tree I am painting becomes ugly, like me.

'Am I ugly, Fern?' I ask with my head facing downwards and tears forming in my eyes.

'You are different, not ugly. But that is for you alone to judge, do not rely on others to give you confidence. Look to your mind's eye and see that you are special and beautiful in your own way,' she replies with a smile.

Fern pats my back gently as I regain control and sit up, wiping my tears with what is left of the shirt. I look at my clothes; not exactly a warrior's. I will have to ask more of the blacksmith, whenever he arrives with the sword, which I pray will be in a timely fashion.

I start painting again and see that the image is becoming better. Fern moves closer to me and holds my hand, helping me create each brushstroke to form a perfect tree. It doesn't matter what I look like, only what is in my heart. If people fear me, it is their problem, not mine. They probably don't, maybe it's just in my mind. It's a fear I have, and hold onto, that I will be banished again one day, as my people did to me so long ago. They had no remorse for what they did, no compassion for a young demon. Yet, I would still hug them and be cheerful if I found them again, they are my people, after all. It is a strange contradiction, and I can't bend my mind around it as I paint.

'What are you thinking?' Fern asks, looking concerned once more. 'You look so pained.'

'I am thinking about my people, the demons who roamed this land long before humans did. They taunted me, hated me for my appearance,' I say without looking her in the eye.

'Oh, I am sorry, Ariel, to go through that must have been hard. But you are with family now.' Fern again strokes my back and then grips me tightly.

A knock at the door brings us both out of our little world. A fair bit shocked, Fern rises and creeps to the door.

'Hello?' she asks when she reaches the wooden frame.

'Hello!' A soothing voice is returned; so she has come.

I am almost gleeful, the darkness in my mind retreating as the door is swung open.

'My girl! Oh! It has been too long! Come in, come in. I will make tea!' Fern hollers at her friend and lets her finally breach the door after a long embrace.

I cough, then stand and bow my head to Diana.

'So formal, mister! Say hello at least,' Fern says, sweeping past me.

'Apologies, Di.' I walk towards her and she to me, and we stand a few paces apart for a moment uncomfortably then back away. I am, again, bashful, and I smile at her through glassy, almost weeping, eyes.

'So nice to see you both doing so well, can I see your painting, Ariel?' Di steps forward and peers down at my work.

'It is not finished nor up to Fern's standard, I am afraid,' I say, rubbing my neck.

She laughs and says, 'Do not be afraid. It is coming along nicely.' She hums and turns towards me once more and claps her hands together.

She is definitely my favourite human in the town. I stare a bit too long and she looks at me quizzically.

'Everything alright? You look sad.' She pulls a face of dismay in jest.

It rattles me back into the real world and I say, 'Sorry, your beauty catches me off guard.'

'Well, thank you, I try,' she says, sweeping her hair off her shoulder.

I crack a smile, less shy and even more entranced. 'Please, take a seat, I am sure Fern will be back momentarily. Are you still okay?'

'You are very kind for asking, I am fine. My family are well but back to their old tricks though.' She clicks her tongue. 'They lost a lot of gold to gambling I am sorry to tell you.' She now looks withdrawn and stares at her perfect feet.

'That doesn't sound great . . .' I trail off as she looks back at me.

'I am thinking about leaving this place for a better one, but I don't know where.' She lifts her hands and shrugs, looking a bit forlorn.

'I have the same feeling Di, I wish I could leave for the forest, but I have things I must do first,' I say firmly.

'Oh, I didn't realise. I would love to live in the forest, so quiet and peaceful. What must you do?'

'I must defeat the king when he comes or else all will be put to the sword,' I grimly say.

'Well, not much then.' Di smiles brightly.

I laugh, a great and deep laugh that nearly shakes the house. 'Yes, not much at all.'

Fern returns with tea for us all. I sit down on the floor, as the women have taken the seats, which works as I am now the same height as them.

'You are getting on famously,' Fern says and points her tongue out towards me so that Di cannot see.

'I like Ariel a lot, you have a good friend there. We were just speaking about leaving this place, but it seems we both have responsibilities that come first.' Di slumps her shoulders and shakes off our conversation.

'Ah, yes, lots to do first. Then hopefully we can all escape! It would be so nice to keep us all together, don't you agree, Ariel?' A slight smile comes from Fern, and she tilts her head towards Diana and looks at me wide-eyed.

'I think it would be a good plan,' I say gruffly.

'Maybe, we will have to see what happens,' Di says shyly and looks to Fern. 'Tell me, what have you been up to? I have not seen you in so long.'

Fern looks to her friend and replies, 'Looking after this one.' She moves her head in my direction. 'He has not been well.'

I cringe and start to speak, but Di arrives first. 'Oh no, you have been through the wars, haven't you? What ails you most?' She has turned her attention towards me.

'A malaise caught me, but friends helped me get out of it for now.' I smile, but it is hollow, and the anxiety returns so I bend my head down.

'I am so sorry, that sounds awful. Plus, the elders make it worse! It wasn't right what they did. I stayed away, not wanting to be a part of such a farce.' Di looks stern and sorrowful at the same time.

'Thank you for saying that Di, it was indeed a farce. I believe the same is happening again. I am ashamed not to have the power to stop it,' I say and shake my head. Those poor traders must be hanging by the throat by now.

'It is not for you to stop the mob; you can only guide them.' Fern turns towards me and waves a hand.

'I agree, but what a show you put on I heard! Nearly dead, then breaking into flame, a bit overdramatic, wasn't it?' Di asks. Both the women laugh.

I look away and smile a little. It must have been quite frightening indeed; maybe I have something else up my sleeve for the king after all. My body will protect me, I must be confident in that fact. I am beginning to enjoy myself; these two women are strong and bright. I should really take a leaf out of their books and lose my sternness and anxiety.

'Perhaps!' I cry out and chuckle along with them.

Nightfall is coming, and I ask, 'Do you want to stay with us tonight? I am afraid the mob will still be roaming the streets.'

'I will be fine and back tomorrow for more of you two,' Di says, rising to leave. 'I will leave before it is too dark, enjoy the night and see you both soon.'

Diana leaves and Fern sighs deeply. 'You are rubbish at flirting, mister Ariel. You should be confident! I mean look at you, all muscled and fighting to protect us. That would get you a lot of points.'

I shake my head. 'I don't know what I am doing, Fern. I don't even know how I feel about her, all I know is she gives me this feeling in here.' I point to my stomach.

'It's called butterflies. She gives you butterflies. You definitely like her. Come on though, it's time for a rest. Tomorrow will be difficult for you again, I am sure.' Fern takes my hand and leads me to bed. 'You really must find better clothes by the way, and tomorrow morning go bathe in the stream.' She says.

I nod at her, and we climb into the bed. I will rest tonight and dream of Diana, I know this.

Before I have chance, light sprawls into the room, and I jut awake. I must have slept deeply, as I did not even notice that Fern must have risen already. I roll out of bed and make my way to the studio room. Fern has tea on and turns her head around to see me.

'At last! Now go bathe, you need to let me tell you,' she smiles, and continues, 'I am working on portraits today, but you can keep going on your tree. I will brew some more tea and have food ready when you are.'

'Okay, thank you, Fern,' I say and make my way out of the house and round to the stream. She is right, I am much in need of a bath. I find the stream; the water does not flow fast but it will do. I remove my clothes and dip into it; the water is cold but very soothing. It ripples round me, and I clean the past few days off. I look down to see my skin has fully healed, and I feel my head happily as the hair has started to grow back.

Once clean, I get up, dress and make my way back into the house still dripping wet.

'Oh, sorry, here,' Fern says and rushes off to the bedroom, returning with a towel.

I dry myself diligently and then take a seat beside Fern. I start to eat out of the basket provided, some bread and an apple. I will not gorge today, as my strength is feeling okay. I sip the tea and watch Fern concentrate on her work. She is painting a face I know, a face that disgusts me. The head elder.

'Why do you paint him? He is a coward,' I say and move away from the face.

'Gold, just gold, and he is ugly, so I am not enjoying it,' Fern says, not stopping her work.

'I suppose, he is my enemy though,' I say sternly.

'No, he isn't, he is just afraid is all. Your enemy is yourself and the king,' Fern replies, sounding happy with herself.

She is right, of course. The man on the canvass poses no threat to me. I must ready myself for the king.

I sit on the floor and begin to meditate. My mind clears and I think about what I must do. I must take my sword and thrust it down the throats of many men. I will fight with all my might and see if I can bury enough to break their advance. It will not be as easy as last time, and maybe I will need extra help. Nature has indeed forgiven me, so I must seek her, and ask for her favour. I know what I must do, and where I must go.

'The king is my only enemy, Fern. I must go back to the forest and find nature so that I may fight well,' I say and start to eat some food and finish a delightful tea.

Fern sticks her tongue out in my direction. 'Okay but look after yourself. Will I see you again?'

'Yes, of course, and can you invite Diana to stay as well? I would like to see her before I go to battle,' I say almost under my breath.

Fern makes a sound, cooing at me and says, 'Oh, of course you want to see Di! No problem, I will ask her to stay with me while you are gone.'

'Thank you, Fern, I know it will be tough. I need extra help.'

'On you go then, when you find nature, say hello from me.' Fern smiles and comes to hold me round the waist.

I settle a hand on her back, holding in my tears. I must prove myself worthy, or else she will be one of the witches burned. So, I take my leave, closing the door behind me. I know where to go now. I walk through the main square and see that the bodies still hang. It makes me extremely sorrowful; these men did not deserve this fate. I carry on regardless, and head for the fields. By the time I reach the forest, it is dark. So, I settle in for the night, finding a soft bed of grass and moss. It brings me a lot of comfort to be back here again. Tomorrow will be a difficult day, so I sleep while I can.

Chapter Fourteen

Always remember,
Nature breathes life into you,
Do not forget her.

I awake to the sunrise and stir my body into life. I start my travels deeper into the forest; the further I go the better, I hope. The birdsong is heart-warming, and I revel in the place I am in. I cross paths with no animals but a few squirrels, so I walk further in, sliding between trees as the forest becomes dense and smells old and musty. I do not know how much time has passed – the canopy covers the rays from the sun nearly completely. Spots of light come through but nothing to really mention.

I clamber about till I am sure I am right in the heart of the forest and sit to meditate. I put my back down on an old but straight tree, feeling the mossy bark touching me. Here I will find her, hidden somewhere in the depths; she still lives on.

I place my hands carefully down on the floor. I feel the life of the trees, roots deep in the earth come into being for me, and my magic beings to grow. I can feel it rising within me, ebbing one moment then flowing heavily into my skin and muscle. So, she has indeed forgiven me and will favour me over the king. I pray she hears my plea. I feel it now as a blue light inside me, a seedling that grows with every moment. I open my eyes to see many of the animals have gathered. I lift my hands out to them and they consider running, but then stop and approach me instead. The deer is, of course, first to reach me; being my friend from the beginning it is only right. She comes so close to my face, I feel her snorting and grunting at me, the breath on my cheek filling me with joy. She licks my cheek and I lay my hands round her neck.

'Thank you, I am so sorry I lost my way,' I say to all the animals.

Even the wolf is here I see, he is next and nuzzles into my shoulder for a good scratch. I laugh as he makes a low, growling playful snarl when I rub and stroke him. My people, I think to myself, my true home. I forget why I am here and enjoy the moment. A squirrel races down to be next, more come to me, the hare, the small birds, all eager for their turn to imbue me with their powers. Once the animals have cleared, I see light all around me, specks of dust catch the rays, making the place seem brighter and full of the life I thought it had lost. But it is still as strong as when I left it.

'Thank you, thank you all!' I cry out.

I place my hands back on the floor and close my eyes. I see images of tangling, creeping vines. The earth opening into a great maw, for swallowing men who attack me. I see visions of lightning and thunder that rumbles and breaks men down. I have the power to do all these spells now, I know it. A hundred other scenes flood into my mind. What a bounty she has provided for me. I am so thankful that I cry, tears rolling down my face to drop on the ground and be soaked up by the roots and mosses. I will stay here as long as I can, to be with her, alive and entwined together, the two of us.

When much time has passed, I rise and put a last hand on the bark and make my way to the edge of the trees. I am surprised to see it is light; I do not know how long I was in the forest. The king must have prepared by now, as I have, and be on his way here. The town needs me, I must protect those like Fern and Diana. They deserve to hold onto their second chances. I will do it for them and damn the rest.

I run through the fields and arrive at the town. There is a large kerfuffle, which I ignore and head straight for Fern's house. I knock, and the entry opens up to reveal the women whom I am to do this for.

'You've been gone a long time, Ariel. The king is definitely on his way, we had word from the hamlets.' Fern ushers me into the house.

'I thought he would be ready soon. Sorry, I was communing with the forest,' I say as I step over the threshold.

'This is not the time to speak to trees, Ariel. You must travel south, I know it is scary but please protect us,' Fern whimpers.

'My sword, I need a sword,' I say once I am safely in the room.

'Oh yes, the blacksmith dropped these off. He said he worked day and night.' Fern disappears into the bedroom and it is only then that I notice the other figure. She takes my breath from me and I splutter most inelegantly. She turns and waves at me to come to her, so I do.

'They are burning everything as they go, I have heard, from my brother,' Diana says, looking as radiant as ever. I barely hear the dark words, entranced by the movement of her lips.

'It will be okay, I will settle it,' I say and take her hand, 'I promise no harm will come to you or Fern.'

'I worry for you too though, you have shown yourself to be a kind soul. Don't throw your life away, alright?' she says with a bite to the lip that I stare at.

'I have been given great power by nature, and I am a match for any army now,' I say, proudly but softly.

Fern walks back into the room, dragging a sword and a large shield with her.

'Help me then!' she shouts as I run to her and grab the weaponry before she falls.

'Sorry. I must enchant these. Do you think I have time?' I ask and return to the bedroom.

'Oh, I would have just sent you to the bedroom if I knew. Yes, you probably have a little time. The king is not far though, we are all in grave danger,' Fern says as I take the weapons away.

I lay them on the bed and remove the sword from the scabbard. It is truly a work of art. Sharp and a long great blade, tall as any human. I take the hilt and run my fingers over the steel, then begin my work. I ask nature to favour the sword and name her Sophia, a kind name for a sword even though the work will be bloody. She feels strong in my hand and I concentrate on her, making her glow green and bright. Engraving starts to appear on the blade and reads, *Punish those who mean me harm.* The sword is now connected to nature, I see. Next, I turn my attention to the shield. I may not have much use for it, yet will use it with joy when I do. Plus, who knows what they have in store for me, maybe archers? Quite likely actually so I move to the shield and stroke its metal. It too begins to glow green and rings out a pleasant sound. I am pleased with the work and pick them up to see how they feel. Light but sturdy is the shield, and a much heavier sword sways at my side. I am ready now; I must leave and meet the army. I have no armour but it is of no use anyway – magic will keep me safe, I hope. I return to the studio room and show off my weapons with a warrior's stance. The women laugh but see I am serious and it dies away.

There is bashing on the door. 'Let me in! I must see the demon lord!' a voice yells harshly.

I go straight towards the noise and swing the door open to find the Elders awaiting me.

'Yes, is there a problem?' I ask sarcastically.

'You must go now! Please help us!' one shouts.

'I will protect as I have always done,' I say with a bow to them, then turn to the two women inside. 'Goodbye for now, ladies.' I tip my head even lower to them and they hold up a hand each.

'Safe travels, Ariel! Good luck, and thank you!' Fern yells.

Diana begins to speak but I am already thinking about battle and only catch the sweetness of her voice on the wind. I am sorry I did not catch the last words I may ever hear from her. I stride past the old men and brush them aside. I hear huffing and puffing as I charge through, but care not for them, they will be dealt with when I return. If I know anything, it is that we need new, strong, young elders who won't bow to the mob, but will serve real justice. That is my wish, and I will complete it as soon as I am back.

I break into a run, past the crowd that has gathered to see me off. I hear cheers and shouts of encouragement. I am deaf to them now. I must make the bridge if I am to hold them off easily. That old defensible place is far though, I feel a sense of foreboding; there are days between me and the place I could fight them. The road is long as I run, unstable beneath the pounding of my feet. In the distance I can see flags of red, telling me that I would never have made it to the bridge. I must find a better place to start the battle. I scout with keen eyes and pick a ridge not far away and move towards it. It will be part of my defence.

I am feeling strong, and sit on the ridge to watch the march through my lands. I can see a smoky haze which rises behind the army – they are burning as they go, then. Fire has some use though – they will not be able to retreat.

I can hear now the clanking of armoured humans and see a few wooden structures being hauled up the road. They are well-equipped this time, it would seem, and I wonder what tricks they have for me. There are at least four to five thousand humans in front of me. The clamouring comes to a halt, and the long line of humans begins to form into ranks. Disciplined, I think to myself, that will be a problem; less retreating and more fight in them. I can hear the cheers as a great man on a horse trots in front of the ranked men. I do not waver as the full cohort comes into sight. They are setting up crossbowmen and some kind of ballista; progress has definitely been made while I have been away. Lucky I have the shield and my magic to defend myself.

The man on the horse turns towards me, glinting in the sunlight, and lifts his sword high. The crowd of soldiers scream, in fits of elation, ready for battle. Little do they know, I have no intention of fighting myself; the sword is a conduit for nature's magic only. All their shouts mean nothing against such a foe, but I will let them have their moment thinking this will be easy. The horseman begins a gallop towards me, so I rise for him. He wears gold and a large plume of red erupts from his helm. This must be the king. I bow to him as he reaches the top of the ridge. He looks magnificent, and I am at pains to destroy him, but they have brought this on themselves. They could have stayed home with their families. I smile broadly at him and walk towards him. The horse rears up as I get close but the king holds the reigns, persuading the horse to settle.

'King, I suppose?' I say to him, reaching to the horse and laying a hand on it for comfort.

'I am the General Boeheim. King Roderick did not deem it worthy to come himself, as you are weak, and we will kill you on this day,' the man says smugly, and bows his helm to me.

'Bit rude,' I say, still stroking the now calm horse.

'Rude? How impudent of you, welp! You will face the full might of the army of the South today. We are few in number but fierce fighters.' He shouts this at me, spit flying from his mouth.

'Sounds like fun, but do not underestimate a demon who has survived for a long time under many kings' reigns,' I reply, and back away from the horse. 'The South, eh? Why not his whole army, he might need it.' I smile at the man, trying to figure out why he came all this way.

'The king asked his best fighters to come for you. Will you surrender or not? The people you protect are beggars, thieves and murderers who must face justice.'

'Indeed, what of the witches? They must surely be on your list. I will not be surrendering today, may I ask instead that you take your army back and off my land?' I bow deeply to him, but I know the answer.

'They will burn, it is true. So be it, we will battle here and once and for all destroy you and the people in that town.' He turns the horse, who looks at me in pain but follows his master's orders.

'It is okay, you follow your master. I will do my best to protect you too,' I say and the horse whinnies.

'Don't taunt my horse, demon. We will be ready in a moment to reign hell upon this ridge.' He rushes off and travels back to his army.

The men scream once more as he returns. So be it. I will fight them; they think me weak, as I have been away so long. But I am far from weak now, and death will be the deal of the day – no more human aggressors on my land.

I hear a hooting and hollering as the crossbowmen come to the fore. The wooden contraptions are pulled forward as well, and loading begins. I sigh and sit back down. I raise the shield in preparation and touch the ground, hoping nature can also help me. There are shouts to load and aim then the sky becomes black as I peek over the shield, then hide myself behind it. I hear the sounds of bolts thumping into the ground. They miss. The ballista also miss and I hear calls to move and aim once more. The arrows fly true this time and again beat down upon my shield. The bolts thud harmlessly into the ground or stick to the shield. The army groans as a whole. I have not succumbed, and they must charge.

I throw the shield away and stand, my sword removed from its sheath. I hold it up high so they may all see the bright green it glows. The colour flashes and shimmers in the light, and I hear another gasp and groan from the crowd.

The cavalry are next. I see them lining up with their polearms, shields raised against whatever I will throw at them but I have no intention of doing so. There is a hooting of a horn and they begin to trot, then gallop towards the ridge. Poor men, poor horses; it is hell in my mind to do this, but I cannot defeat such a force on my own. There are only spells left. I stab Sophia into the ground, deep and up to the hilt. Then I simply wait. It is a nerve-wracking moment as nothing happens but the charging of horses and the glint of metal coming at speed. Then, there is a great rumbling, and I breathe out in relief. The spell has started, and the ground I can see at the bottom of the ridge begins to shake. They have nearly reached it and are fully committed now. They must be sure they will complete their goal quickly – who could fight off such a force? The ground shakes harder and the men start to fall off their horses. The ones who manage to keep a balance are close to the bottom of the ridge.

'So near, yet so far,' I say to myself.

The ground begins to open underneath them so quickly that none are able to jump or escape the gaping maw. They fall into the deep. I hear their screams and those of the horses as well. I wince, knowing the next step. I remove the sword from the ground. The gap starts to close over them till there is only silence on the field. I see the rank of swordsmen back off as one but they are shouted at and they do not retreat. You would have thought, after such a showing they would realise how strong I am, but no. They are arrogant, presumably having never been defeated before.

The men begin their march to a horn again. I raise Sophia once more and ask for nature's favour, which she gives. A bright light shines from her and into the eyes of the men marching. I can see them wavering now but the horns give them some kind of confidence. I let them come closer then allow the magic to do the work. Tentacles of green spring from the ground around them – the vines have come. They wrap round the men as they try to cut them away and set themselves free. But the hold is strong and more come from the ground. Some men try to run, but are caught and dragged back into the mess. There is an audible choking noise from thousands of men at once, as the vines wrap around faces and chests, crushing armour into bodies as they go.

There will be no retreat today then, no one left to tell the story as I lift the sword and then aim it at the general's retinue. The clouds come in imperceptibly quickly, and the thunder rumbles as the men below scream. The horsemen with the general try to run but there is no gallop that is quick enough. Lightning strikes down upon them, and a black haze is what is left. When it clears, the horsemen are grounded, and a rain begins to fall. The swordsmen at the bottom have given up, limbs ripped out – they are living no longer. There is a stillness to the field now, a silence that fills my body. I begin to cry into my hands. What have I accomplished? Killed, nae, murdered thousands of men to protect the town's folk and myself. Was it worth it? Should I have been allowed to do this?

No; it was no fault of mine that they came to this field of death. I gave them the chance to leave the meadow. The king should have known better and kept to the agreement – the fault lies with them, I am sure.

Chapter Fifteen

Heal my broken mind,
Bring my body back to life,
I will protect you.

I turn and drag myself back towards the town, sheathing my sword and leaving the shield to rust as I cannot carry the weight. The magic has seeped out all my energies. I am in a daze, and look skyward for some assistance. My legs are as heavy as bags of rock, and my arms hang down and sway in the wind. My eyes no longer focus and I feel like death is upon me. However, there is a place in my mind that struggles on, forcing my legs to move in the right direction, carrying them from the dead men, closer to hope. I can vaguely see a town shape, smoke billowing from chimneys and shouts from humans there. They must have spotted me. I stand in a field of some sort, and fall to my knees. Hands grapple me with shouts but I can't pinpoint the words. My mind is too full of death and the despair I feel creeping in. Hands again pull me up to standing and I lean on bodies to get to the market square. If they are to kill me, now would be the perfect time, a voice from inside calls. I may have said it out loud, I am not sure. More hands drag me forward and my senses begin to come back.

'Are you wounded? Are you wounded, man?' A hollering in my ear rouses me.

'No, it is done,' I say, weakly. 'Take me to Fern's house.' I am promptly towed down the street, eyes still blurry. I can make out the sun and nothing else.

I am dropped by accident, but picked up again and the march continues. The houses are becoming clearer, and I can hear the sound of the stream burbling. We must be close. I also hear a banging noise that hurts my brain.

'Oh my god!' a shout cries out, 'get him in, now!'

I am dumped into a bed and I sleep almost immediately.

I awake to darkness.

How many days have I slept now? I wonder. I feel a coolness on my head and reach to find a cold-water compress on it. I fling it away and roll over, falling from my comfort. I land with a thud, and hear the shuffling of footsteps.

'What are you doing? Stay in bed, you old fool. You need rest after saving us. We heard what happened from the people to the south. Quite a mess you made, it would seem.' It was Fern's soothing tones, and she helped me back into the bed.

'Oh, Fern. What have I done? Killed so many. I feel as only a death dealer, no more,' I say to her, quietly.

'Don't be silly, you have much more to give.' She covers me up to my neck.

'I don't know anymore. Why am here? What did I do to deserve such a fate as this?' I have tears in my eyes as I speak.

Fern has no words, instead she hums a song to me and strokes my newly grown hair. I find it relaxing, but something disturbs my rest, a niggle in my mind. I can actually feel the darkness creeping in, so lay my head back on the bed and wait for it to take me. There is no escaping this, and I hate my mind for not saving me from it. Life is too hard, I cannot do it anymore. I roll away from her and curl up in a ball. She cannot help me now, no one can. I am helpless and useless. I can't be bothered to move myself, there is no point, I will only end up hurting someone. I know now that I am a worthless welp who needs putting down. I must tell Fern tomorrow to put me out of my misery and do the right thing. Take Sophia and use her to end my life. The pain shoots through my mind all night, and I fall into a dozing state. Not awake but not sleeping either, I am trapped here underneath the cloud. I am broken by the time sunrise comes, and this body will not be able to handle anything today. I will wait here for something to help me succumb to death. I hit my head, not out of violence, but to try to move the cloud on, as I can hardly think with it covering me. I should not have used nature's spells on that field, I know this now. I should have stayed seated and waited for the end at the point of a spear or bolt. My mind swirls, it moves away from the images that plague me, images of men's limbs being ripped off or the screams of men and horses crushed into the earth. Now, I think, hopefully, I can see the God of death coming towards me, a black creature, with a void of nothingness at its heart. I open my eyes; it is not death, but a shadow at the window.

'Are you okay?' A sweet sing-song voice calls to me.

I shrug and close my eyes once more, hoping death comes back willingly with an outstretched hand I can hold on to.

'Ariel, are you alright?' the voice calls again, and I hear a scuffling.

Diana hops through the open window and moves over to me. She grabs my hand and holds it tight, but it's not the hand I was hoping for.

'I am useless, please leave me here to die,' I say weakly.

The grip tightens further. 'No, you are a beautiful being. I am glad you made it back safely. Thank you for your sacrifice.' She says this in a hushed tone.

I have no energy left for talk, but can't stop staring into her eyes; they pierce into me and I feel as if I am floating. I hold her hand too, never wanting to let go now. Her hair falls on the bed and it breaks my dark thoughts for a moment. I can smell a sweet note of lavender and I inhale, bringing it deep into my lungs. She is truly a beautiful human to hold me so. Given how broken my face is, I am very surprised to see her so close. As she leans in, I am overcome by a hard beating of my heart. She leans her head on my chest and I breathe out in a long, slow exhale. I half thought she might have kissed me there. But that is silly of me – how could she find me attractive in that way? She is just thankful her head is not on a spike and her family no longer starves. It is true, she has much to thank me for, but she does not know the cost. I will die now, here in this bed as my final resting place. I do not understand why she stays, but she waits with me for quite a while, and the time ticks by slowly as I breathe into her hair. There are more footsteps, and then a noise.

'Oh, hello, you have come to see him then? Here give him some tea, he needs to regain his strength,' Fern says, and Di moves to collect the tea.

I am sorrowful that she has left my side. I would have stayed like that, with her head on me, for eternity. Diana comes back into view and puts the cup carefully to my lips. I sip as I cannot say no to her. The liquid is hot but I take a few more mouthfuls before rolling onto my back.

'How is he?' Fern's voice resonates inside me. I hate her suddenly – she should leave me, why does she not go away?

'I don't know, he won't speak much.' Di is hushed in tone as well.

I open my eyes again for a second and see the two women whispering in the corner, presumably trying to work out what to do with me. Di returns to my side.

'Whatever you need, just tell us. We're here to help you, dear.' Di strokes my hair and lets out a slow, pained sigh.

I nod to myself more than to her, and move my hand back to hers. I am too weak and feeble to use words so we wait. I shake as I think about how I was so close to happiness that I almost tasted its rich and complex flavour, but it was not to be. After all, I am hideous to behold, and those dreams I had of the three of us in the forest are well and truly over. I retreat into myself and let time pass by me. I no longer control time, it washes through me and passes quickly. I muster up some energy and look at Diana again into those beautiful eyes.

'Kill me,' I say forcefully, but also quietly, hoping she will do me this favour.

'Never,' she smiles at me, 'you will survive this, whatever it is. Fern says you did it before, why can't you do it again?'

I shake myself and roll my head away from her radiance which I can stomach no more. Knowing I will never be to her what she is to me. She is too much for me, too beautiful, too strong. I should never have laid eyes on her, it would have been a happier life, instead of this constant longing and wanting that I find so repulsive now. If she did feel the same way, she would kill me now, as it is my wish to die. But no, she sits and stares at me, hoping for what? That I will rise again so easily because I have done it before? She does not understand, she has never been in the malaise. I sigh, and feel the hand loosening. Diana has risen and disappears out of the room. It is for the best. Perhaps Fern will come with Sophia and end it all for me? Please, please do it, I shout in my mind.

'I thought this may happen.' Agatha's old, stern voice appears from somewhere. I hear the door slam shut and little legs hobble towards my bedside.

I open my eyes for a moment to check it is her. She smiles at me and comes ever closer.

'Kill me, please, you have to. I cannot endure this again,' I say weakly to Agatha, as the other women stand behind her.

'Drink this, we have much work to do.' She hands me a cup and it tastes disgusting – must be the poultice again.

I gulp it down, regardless. Fern brings a stool through for the old woman and we begin.

'Tell me, how did it feel to kill those men? You are very powerful but not strong, eh?' she asks me and pats my shoulder.

I cough and splutter on the poultice. 'I am very strong. They could not defeat me with ten thousand men. Never mind the five I stood against.'

'Yes, it is indeed true you are powerful. But strong enough in the mind to kill those and feel nothing? I do not think so. Ariel, you must know that you are still recovering from the last malaise. It will take a lot of time and strength to get through it.'

I nod. She is right, I am not strong in the mind. To kill like that takes unimaginable strength, perhaps no one has it. I definitely do not possess such a trait.

'It's a good thing though, not a failure. If you were that brutal I don't think the girls would hang around and look after you, would they?' Agatha continues.

I shake my head slightly. Is she right? Is it good that I cannot take life without a toll being paid? I wonder for a moment, stuck with the cloud and my mind. I struggle to speak so must push inwards, to find a path back to the light.

'I know you have been going around doing good deeds to help you recover. It is a good idea if you keep it up, remember that. The smile on a child's face or the pleasure of helping someone out of trouble.' Agatha speaks so softly that it wisps around my head.

I have done some deeds one might describe as good. I remember Sash and his nightmares, I remember his face after we were done, how it shone so brightly and innocently.

'How can I keep it up? I am stuck in bed again. I do not wish to move, nor have the motivation to help those who murdered innocent traders who made bad decisions. Not all deserved their fate . . .' I trail off as the tears start to come.

'You will be out of this bed when your body is ready. It is okay that it is not yet. The girls will continue to look after you and I will stay until you are well enough to stand on your own again.' Agatha looks at my tears. 'Mourn the men yes, but do not punish a whole town because of the acts of a few.'

When my body is ready. When will it be ready? I think never. It will waste away for the second time. I should have ended it before I found these humans, whom I care too much for. Agatha takes her leave and the women come to my side.

'What do you need, Ariel?' Fern asks me and I shrug.

'We will be here when you are ready, do not lose hope, Ariel.' Di's voice appears from my opposite side.

We all hold hands now and I look to the ceiling. I feel like crying, like bellowing to the gods to take me, but have none of the energy to ask for it. They do not listen anyway; they never helped me last time, only those who came to the keep helped. Real and alive humans.

'What have I done? You should all leave now, I am a murderer. Best forgotten to history,' I say to no one in particular.

A hand strokes my head and I fall into a daydreaming doze. There is nothing else for it, no one will help me to die, so I must persevere. I must endure and outlast the cloud; it may dissipate with time, it is true. It did last time. I was helped to my feet by these women here, and Diana remains too, so I have even more help than before. Maybe I can do it, even with a vulnerable, fragile mind that needs stitching up every now and again. If I can hold it together, if I can pull my mind back on track and change the outcome for the better, maybe I can live.

'Here, have some food, Ariel.' I sit up a little in the bed and eat.

The food is as ash in my mouth, so dry is the bread, but I force it down. I also find there is fruit in my hand, which tastes fresher and nice to the palate. The juice flows and I open my eyes to it, and a weak smile appears on my face.

'Better? You have been resting a few days,' Fern says and lays a hand upon mine.

'Yes, a little, thank you.'

I nod to myself, munching the fruit and hear the women humming a tune I find most pleasing. I am not strong enough yet to move, so snuggle down in the bed and let sleep take me. I find myself on a plain field, sword in hand, awaiting something. A horse appears from a misty background, I cannot focus on the form that sits atop the beast. I can tell it is hooded and a blackness emerges from it. The dark mist comes closer and closer to me, inching its way forward. It reaches me, but I do not run, I feel stuck to the ground. The darkness reaches for my legs and spirals upward towards my chest. I awake later, sweating and panting. I feel I am alone in this room now, and I stir my eyes to open and look around. It is dark, and I feel afraid. I cannot quite put my finger on where the feeling comes from, yet it sticks to me anyway.

'Fern? Di? Agatha?' I call out into the darkness.

A rush of feet comes towards the door and I hide under the covers to protect myself. The door creaks and I hear it swing open. A fresh breeze follows and then hands are on the covers.

'Are you okay, Ariel?' It is Fern and I breathe a sigh of relief.

'No, I am afraid and I don't know why,' I say as loud as I can.

'It's okay to be scared, you have been through the wars, literally,' she replies and lifts the covers from my face.

I see her face in the darkness, bright eyes still shine here. She looks directly into my eyes and smiles. Then a hand comes to my face. I jump but let it feel me, warmth. The warmth is back, and I start to cry.

'Don't worry, you have a long rest ahead, try to get some more sleep and tomorrow I will bring you food.' Fern budges me over and gets into the bed.

Chapter Sixteen

A broken spirit,

A destructive mind attacks,

I need a reprieve.

I lay a hand on her side and try to dream of something less frightening. But, I do not find rest. Instead, I am haunted by faces I do not know. Screaming in fury and agony, they writhe and try to squirm out of the tentacles ripping them apart. I did that, with nature's help. I did not know them, yet I feel a sadness for them; they did not deserve that. Nor did their families. I am a killer whether I used my sword for slicing, or for magic. I need to die, that I know I deserve, to be with their souls and send out my apologies and explain why I did what I had to, in order to save Fern, Diana and the rest of the innocents that reside in this town. Fern breathes deeply, at least she managed to find sleep. I roll onto my back, half off the bed and wipe my tears away. Tomorrow, I will find a way out, one way or another.

When the sun begins to climb and peeps into the window, I am resolute in the knowledge that this is the last time I will see the rising. I try to enjoy the sight of the light; it begins slowly, then seems to break free and stream into the room. Fern shuffles and awakens as the light hits her face.

'Ariel?' she says. I lean over to see her face, and she closes her eyes again.

'Still here, for now,' I whisper.

Fern turns and cuddles me. I stroke her hair and back. I am sorry to leave her all alone, but I know she will be okay in the long run and safe from me and the darkness I bring along.

Diana breezes into the room, looking fresh and happy.

'Morning everyone, how are we feeling?' she asks us both.

Fern moans, 'Is it morning already? I need some more sleep.' She promptly falls silent.

Di comes to my side of the bed. 'Come with me if you can.'

I nod and lift my legs out of the bed. I cannot refuse her on my last day, especially when she is shining so brightly. We hobble over to the doorway and she lays a hand on my back as we go through. It tingles and electrifies me, and my spine feels amazing as we step out of the house. I stretch out my limbs; it feels like an age since I tasted fresh air, and I breathe it in deeply.

'Come, come with me,' she says with a glow.

'Of course, I will follow you,' I say as she takes my hand and leads me out of the town.

'Where are we going?' I ask and she shushes me.

'You'll see soon, just be patient.' I shrug and carry on.

We reach a hillock and beyond I can see the town's people working away in the field.

'What are they doing?' I ask, curious as to what my surprise is.

'We have decided, as a community, to replant the forest!' Diana does a little jump and points her hand out. 'Isn't it amazing?'

I nod and look over them all. 'How?'

'We took seeds from the old forest and are planting them instead of crops.' She looks at me and smiles.

'For me?' I drop to my knees as I ask.

'Yes Ariel, as thanks for keeping us safe.'

'Thank you so much, Diana. I have no words.' I reach out a hand to hers, and grasp it tightly to stop the tears from flowing.

She helps me up to standing again and we take a stroll through the fields. As the humans begin to notice me, they stand and salute my hulking figure. I smile at them and wave so that they go back to work. This will be a fine forest one day, I am sure. But not for many years; the people planting will never see the conclusion of their results. It is a shame, but nature does not care, she will grow as the seasons pass, until all around us is a forest. I breathe in intensely, smelling as much as I can of the new trees and the dirt which has been dug at. I feel a sense of pleasure in my bones, a sensation I thought was long gone. But humans, again, have brought it back to me.

'The elders are so angry at the people, but they carry on regardless because they like and respect you, after what you did for them.' Diana continues to talk, while I look at all the glory.

I go to a man who is working, leaving Di's hand. He is old and feeble, but digs with all the might left in his body.

He looks up to me, then bows. 'My lord, are you proud of us? We are very proud of you. Sorry, my old back struggles with the digging but I will do my best, as you did.'

'Allow me to help you,' I say, taking the spade from his small hands.

I begin to dig and the man says, 'Your strength is tenfold mine! I think that will be enough, Lord, maybe we can put the seed in together?'

I nod and back away from the hole. He hands me a large acorn and we hold it with a hand each and deliver it to its resting place. He begins to cover it with dirt. I help and find this a good experience, creating something. I can't believe this man works with so few years left to live.

'Should you not be resting or out fishing? Or doing what you love? You must have only a few years left,' I say and the man looks up, slightly angry.

'I have many years to go, my boy. This is what I love, helping my fellow man, or demon of course. There is nowhere I'd rather be,' he says wistfully, 'after all, you saved my family and I must repay you somehow. My daughters, who work hard and have done nothing wrong would burn if not for your actions.'

I nod, knowing this to be a truth. I am happy to help the man and he is happy to help my vision.

'What is your name?' I ask.

'Jack, though most call me "old man" now,' he says with a chuckle.

'How can I thank you for your work?'

'If you can mend fishing nets, it would be most helpful. My daughter is pregnant with her first! But she cannot work any longer and bring in gold for us to live on.' He says this with a bit of sorrow but mostly jubilation.

'Of course, when I return to town, I will see what I can do. What is her name?' I ask, knowing that this may be mutually beneficial.

'Sara, my lord. You can't miss her, big as a house now!' He chuckles again and gets back to work as I rise.

I have never seen humans reproducing. It will be very interesting to meet this Sara. I return to Diana, and she holds my hand again.

'Good chat?' she asks with a beam.

'More humans to help, I guess,' I reply.

'Excellent, it helped before so keep it up. Come now, there is more to show you.' She leads me further through the fields.

'More? I do not require anything more, Di. You have given me all I need for now,' I say to this great woman responsible for setting this up.

'You'll definitely want to see this, Ariel,' she says with a smirk, 'I think you'll be even more pleased.'

Diana guides me through the throng of workers, and further past them she turns.

'Close your eyes, don't worry, just follow me and my voice,' she says with a giggle.

I do as I am told and follow her for many steps, unable to even lift a lid for a peek after being given her instructions. Her hand clenches mine and we come to a stop.

'Okay, open up!' she shouts.

I open a single eye first, then both wide. We are at the edge of the old forest. In front of me is a house – not just any house, though. It has been beautifully built and made with care and attention. The thatched roof is thick, and a chimney pot sticks out of it. The wooden timbers holding the house up have intricate designs on them, and I grow closer, entranced by it. I see there are names that have been carved, beside the wood.

'We did not cut a single timber from the old forest, I promise you. Instead, these are all parts or spares from the town's people. Their way of saying thanks, and each name is where it comes from.' She finishes speaking and jumps, clapping her hands.

I see now that some timbers are short and some are just pieces of old wood. It's perfect, though. I can see all their names and I break into tears. I lay a hand on the wood to steady myself.

'This is my house?' I ask.

'Of course! Didn't bring you here to show you someone else's.' Di winks at me and I go back to examining the work that went into building the structure.

My own house. It looks old, as if built by my hand an age ago, with pristine carpentry. The wood feels strong under my hand, and I cannot believe it is real, yet here it stands, glorious.

'Do you want to see the inside?' Di asks, grinning.

'Of course, I'm sorry, this is just so . . . overwhelming.'

We take a step towards the door and I see Fern's name scrawled across the face of the door. It is unmistakable, and I trace my fingers over the carving.

'She wanted to gift it to you. I think it was most appropriate, as you'll see her name every day. Come on! Let's open it!'

I push the door and it all comes into focus. The room is lavishly furnished. The window on the back wall illuminates the whole room. Paintings which much be Fern's line the walls. I take a step in and find I can finally stand tall in a house. There is a large table and chairs, and the floor is soft, made of wood which feels nice on my feet. This is my home, and it is perfect. A chair sits in the corner that I recognise from the keep; it is slightly burned but still looks in great condition. I go to it and sit, not believing my eyes.

'We managed to find that in the rubble! Isn't it gorgeous? I love this room, Fern did such a good job. But there's more! Come through!' Di takes my hand and I follow.

The next room has a huge bed and window in it. Beside the window, my own easel, canvas and paints. The bed is definitely big enough for my frame and is covered in blankets of wool. Better than skins, I think to myself. I make my way to the bed and lie down. It is extremely comfortable, and I roll over as Diana joins me.

'Perfection, isn't it?' Di says, stroking my hair.

'It is the only word to describe this. I love that the windows look over the wood, I think I'm in the forest again. It feels safe and warm,' I say.

Di lays a hand on my chest, almost tickling me. She plants a kiss on my cheek, then backs away.

'You deserve this place. Make it your real home, Ariel. Last night, Fern said she would come up later, to paint with you, and see how you are doing. I couldn't wait to show you all we have done, in thanks for your sacrifice. I know you are struggling now, but hopefully, this is a good thing we have done.' Diana looks me deep in the eyes, tilting her face down.

'What is that look for? I love it, Diana. I am so touched you all put in the effort. I am tired though, and I may sleep now,' I say and roll towards her.

Diana embraces me and asks, 'Do you mind if I stay with you? I'm on orders to look after you.'

She holds me close and I feel my breath quicken and my heart beats like a drum. I am afraid she will notice but can't stop myself and do not want to move ever again. Di lets the embrace go, and turns over, pressing herself into me. I feel electric and confused at the same time. My face is in her hair, and the smell is divine. I breathe in and out more cautiously, hoping it will not put her off this position. I put an arm around her, gently stroking her stomach, fearing letting my hand drift higher or lower. She sighs deeply, and I am pleased. I snuggle in deeper and find my perfect resting place.

'Fern told me how you feel about me,' Di says in a whispering voice.

I lift my head to see if I can discern her facial expression but can only see her cheek and nose.

'Oh. I'm sorry,' I say, regretting our position.

'No need to apologise. I've never met anyone who can destroy armies, and loves nature as much as I do before. It's really scary. But I know you are kind, in your heart.'

'You are afraid of me?' I ask with a trembling lip.

'Yes, no, oh, I don't know. We're different beings. Could it ever work?' she sighs once more.

'I want to try,' I say softly.

'Once you're ready come see me, and we'll see how it goes. You should rest now and I don't think I am helping. I will sleep in the main room, I think.' Diana rises and my arm drops to the bed.

I roll onto my back, the excitement dissipating like dust on the wind. Diana nods at me and waves a shy goodbye. The bedroom door closes and I breathe normally once more. So, it isn't out of the question, somehow, that she could like me like that too. I feel like springing from the bed, but find I cannot, my limbs ache and feel too heavy. I huff with my body and get under the covers instead. I bring my knees up to nearly my chest and try to sleep.

My mind circles around what just happened. I touched her, I felt her warmth and she did not reel away in anger or fear. It is my first love I think, at least, whatever love is. I find it such a foreign subject. Fern is so mischievous for telling her! But I am glad, I would never have plucked up the courage anyway. My hands still tremble, remembering the feeling, so I grip them tight and close my eyes. I must think of what is next, apart from Diana. The king will surely not let this defeat go; humans are a proud race.

I should get strong again. I should be able to meet the king and show my strength, but I am so tired of warring with these humans all the time. It never ends. The cycle of violence will continue until either I fall, or I kill every human outside of this region. It seems unlikely I will be killed, and as for killing the humans, I just don't have the energy for that. Plus it might be morally wrong . . . I laugh to myself – I am not that evil. Stuck between these two ideas, I don't have a clear vision of what to do. It is like the old days, when they just kept coming at me, without fear of death and the bodies piling up on the banks of the river. I still can't even believe what happened on the battlefield not so long ago. So many dead in the earth, and many more strangled on the field. Maybe I should properly bury the bodies, as a sign of peace. I shift and pull a leg out of the bed, then the other. I stand in my home and wobble but stay strong.

Diana is sleeping on the plush armchair I use the walls to make my way to the front door, when suddenly there is a banging.

Chapter Seventeen

Is there someone here?

One who could pray for my soul,

I wish it to rise.

'I was going to let myself in, but this is your house now. Settling in okay?' Fern's bright face brings a warmth to me.

Diana opens an eyelid and smiles at me, I blush. She pushes herself out of the chair and comes to give Fern an encapsulating hug. They smile at each other, then Di rubs Fern's arms and looks back to me.

'I should go,' she says simply, 'I will see you again though, Ariel. Look after yourself, and come to my house soon,' she strolls into the meadow and Fern gives me a quizzical look.

'What happened last night? You both look, different.' She shrugs and embraces me. My mind has turned to other thoughts before Di has left my sight.

'I must go. The bodies of the dead need burying,' I say.

'You will do no such thing. The villagers will deal with it. Come and sit, you silly fool, you're in no condition to go galivanting about.' Fern pushes me easily back into the house and coerces me into my chair, it is still warm from Diana's body.

'I must do something. War will soon find me again and I am afraid I cannot fight anymore.' I hold my head in my hands and start to bash it, forcing out the bad thoughts.

Fern leaps over and grasps my hands. 'Stop! You must rest. No one is coming yet, so gather your strength.' She holds tighter.

I bolt upright and storm to the bedroom if I must rest. I lie down and tears begin to form as I stare into the ceiling.

'I am so tired of this, Fern. What can I do? I am nothing but a killer, a thief of souls.' I cannot shake the feeling now, and the cloud is back to stay it would seem.

Fern holds my hand, and we sit in silence as she too begins to weep. I don't look at her, though I know that face is pitying me. I cover my face with my other hand and let the thoughts flood through my mind. I will be known as the death dealer, the murderer. What must humans say about me in other towns now? They must think me a monster, a hulking great demon who sucks life and souls out of men. Who enslaves humans to do his bidding. A tortured face, horrid to look at, and a magic inside that leaves all in ruin. I know in my mind this all must be true. Fern knows this of me, yet does Diana? She has not seen that dark side of me; she even called me 'kind'. How wrong she is. Does she not remember how I enslaved humans for my own gain? I am not kind or benevolent. I can't believe my body prevented me from being hanged and now is not willing to remove itself from this bed. What did my body do that for? I was ready for death moments before. Now they romanticise me and call me a hero. They built me this place, far from the town though, perhaps to keep me away from them. Even though I am their 'hero' they still fear me. They are even building a forest between me and the town. What does that say of their true intentions? I should never have protected so few and killed so many, it just doesn't make sense anymore.

'What are you thinking?' Fern sniffs and dries her eyes.

It must have been a while since we said anything and I do not know how long she has been sitting by my side. Can I really trust her? She keeps me close, or always has someone watching me like her friend or Agatha. Could it be that Diana is her friend, not mine? She could easily be trying to manipulate me into falling for Diana for her own scheme. What is the scheme though, what is the end game? Do they just prop me up so that I can fight when they require it because they are weak?

'Much to think about. Why are you here, Fern? Do you use me to fight when you need help? Is that why you all keep me around? To kill?' I ask, my voice becoming louder and more powerful.

'No! Of course not! How dare you even think such things. I am here because you saved me once and I love you for it.' She slaps my hand from my face. 'Look at me, can you really think that of me?'

I turn my head, but looking into her eyes I still cannot tell what goes on behind them.

'I did save you, it is true, I saved all of you humans because you had nowhere else to go.'

'Then believe us when we say what we mean in our hearts! I am here to help you. You must trust me, Ariel, I would never wish you harm or put you in harm's way. You will get through this and I will be here along the way, whether you like it or not.'

I nod at her small face. Maybe I can trust her. Doubt still creeps in but it does not matter at this moment, I think. My goal is to rise again, to feel the tree's bark on my face and roots beneath my feet. Nature is my only thought now, it keeps the darkness at bay, and allows me to believe in a future where none appears in my mind, and all seems uncertain. But I know the forest and all its glory. It will shade me from this malaise I know it, if only I could reach out and touch it. Instead, I am trapped in dead wood, with humans by my side who always want something from me. This 'home' as they called it, seems like a coffin, just a little larger than I have seen before. It makes me shiver and shake, rather than be the supposed thanks that they say it is. It should be somewhere I can feel at peace, I know this to be true. It's not. It is the opposite of what I need, no more roofs over my head, but the sky above. So, I will try to escape tonight. Once they are sleeping, I'll make my way to the only home I have ever felt comfortable in. I turn away from Fern again, to stare out of the window. I can see the edge of the forest and it makes me smile – not far to go.

'Ariel, could you talk to me, please? I'm so scared for you, you don't seem right,' Fern pleads.

'I am fine, Fern, see I can easily talk. I like to think is all,' I reply harshly.

'Ok, if you are sure. Won't you come paint with me again? I would really like to see you happy once more.' Tears start rolling down her face, and I feel I cannot deny her.

'Bring the easel to me, and I will paint with you, my dear,' I say, hoping this will appease her till nightfall.

Fern drags the art instruments over and I pull each leg till I am seated. She smiles to see me try, and I know it means a lot to her. I take the brush from her hand and she points over to the other window.

'Look deep into the forest, Ariel, can you see something you love?'

I peer through the hole in the wall and can indeed see a tree, gnarled and old. It is ready to fall any day, I can tell. It would be an honour to paint you before you go, I think, and bow my head. I nod to Fern.

'Yes, that tree there, the one that is falling slowly. It leans, do you see? It will not be long before it is a home for the insects,' I say and she nods quickly.

'Then we will paint it before it goes.' Fern watches me dip my brush in a pale green to start the background.

We sit for a few hours, making little strokes with the brush till the tree begins to form on the canvas. When I lack aptitude, Fern corrects and assists.

'I do find this peaceful, you know. I wish we could stay here forever. You are improving, you know that right? I am sorry I wasn't very helpful earlier. I hope now you feel more at ease?' Fern stops my brush moving with a tight grip.

I look down at her fingers wrapped around my massive hand. I smile – she is so small and fragile. Yet, when the time comes, she can stop me with no problem whatsoever. I am dazed by her, and cannot focus on the painting any longer. I turn my head to hers, and stare into eyes full of hope and a wish for my safety. But she will never understand why I have to go, why I can't stay here forever as she asks. The sun is lowering in the sky, so my time has nearly come.

'I enjoy your company, thank you for everything Fern. I would never have noticed this tree were it not for you, again I must thank you for this.' I am telling the truth.

'Great. I am so glad to hear you say that. I very much enjoy your company too. I want you to know that I am here for you, whenever you need me, okay?' she says with a lean in towards me.

'I understand, thank you,' I say then we continue back to the activity at hand. The scene is taking shape, and I want to get the outline finished before dark.

I had nearly forgotten my task when nightfall loomed. We kept painting until the sun was completely gone. Then I remembered in a sudden rush; it was time. Once Fern has fallen asleep, I will take my leave. I know she will be fine without my presence.

'Okay, I think we have run out of light, unfortunately – time for rest. I have set up a makeshift bed in the living room so you may have peace in here. Goodnight, Ariel, try to rest, please. We can start again in the morning, and hopefully before the tree falls we will finish.' Fern lights a small candle, and creeps out of the room.

'Goodnight, Fern, sleep well,' I say.

I am still sitting so that is a good start, and I must make my way to the window and slink out of it, with no noise. But before that, I will have to wait till she sleeps. So, I begin to meditate and call out to the forest in my mind that I am coming home. I hope it will welcome me, as there is no other place I can go. After a while, I believe it is the right time and I bend forward. Missing the canvas, I put my hands on the floor. I hear the wood creak, and it feels a bit jagged, but I continue slowly. The window is on the other side of the room and looks straight to the forest. I focus my attention on that instead of my shaking limbs. There are no obstacles to my goal, I am thankful for that, and sneak further. A large creak in the boards results in a call.

'Are you up, Ariel? Go to sleep, you need your rest,' Fern says, but does not come through.

'No, I am just fine, thank you. I'll be sleeping soon,' I reply in a put-on happy voice.

It is so difficult to move these limbs, one at a time. I try to stretch them but the pain of holding my weight is intense. Finally, I feel the breeze and know the outside world awaits. I lift one hand up, trying to keep silent, grab the windowsill and pull. I make it to my knees by the window, then push myself up to stand. I force myself inelegantly out of the window and fall into some shrubbery. Now on my back, I must be quick to disappear lest Fern becomes suspicious and tries to find me.

I can walk now, from tree to tree, wobbling from one to the other, and a sense of anger starts to grow. Why am I like this? I can run for miles faster than a horse, and yet here I am, trudging along metre by metre to an unknown goal. I stop leaning on trees and try to put my steps in order. My legs fail me, and they collapse my body down to hands and knees again. So I will crawl instead, if I must.

After a few hours of crawling, bit by bit, I have made it into the heart of the forest. I haven't seen my animal friends yet as it is dead of night so I lean my back on a tree to meditate once more, and wait. I am safe here, I think to myself, feeling the forest floor beneath my toes and hands. I am safe here, away from humans and their constructions and their plots. I am safe here, I repeat the mantra, hoping it will bring me solace. I now clear my mind of all thought and feeling, experiencing and observing my mind from afar. Any thoughts that come I look at in curiosity and then let it go. I am amazed at what I see, from the town burning to Fern and Di being murdered. Also, thoughts of my own death, bleeding profusely, till the last drop falls. I can see that drop and watch it in slow motion, following its path down to the floor to merge with the pool beneath it. Then the body collapses and the mind is finally gone. I feel emotions, rage mixed with love, an ambivalence towards humans perpendicular to the elation of seeing Diana. I watch these without judgement; they are only thoughts and feelings, I am not them. I am so much more. I creak my body from out of its position and open my eyes.

It is the dawn, so I continue my travels, strong in each limb now, though I don't quite trust my legs yet, so I steady myself back on the vines hanging down. They brush my face in a very fulfilling way, thousands of them hanging from every tree. The feeling is infinite and brushes my whole body in a most pleasing fashion. My first friend has awoken; the birds. I hear their song – it sounds different, but perhaps that is my fault for being away so long. I cannot find them in my vision, being obscured by the endless vines, but am not disheartened as I will see them later. I look to the ground for more signs of living beasts and animals. Under some bark, I see the insects scurrying; it makes me chuckle and I put down a single finger to be with them. But instead of crawling towards me, a circle begins to appear around my finger. This I find curious and displeasing. The insects should be happy. I put the bark back down to keep them safe and move on. I step back through the vines, brushing them away from my face now as they become heavier, obscuring the light. I come to the fallen tree from which I once made my makeshift shield in case the villagers were not welcoming. I touch the tree – it is cold and wet now, grainy, and I remove my hand as it feels unpleasant. I hear a noise and turn; it was the crack of a branch. In a bush not far from my person a very welcome face appears, my first friend. This time she neither runs nor comes hither, but stares intently. I find it unnerving, those eyes so bright and wide; I cannot grasp the feeling behind them. I know, though, that it is not a friendly look. The deer turns towards me and I take a step back towards the vines. She charges with a spring out of the bush and runs straight for me. I jump on the vines, using my arm strength to pull upward before we hurt each other. What is happening? This was so different before, what has changed to put me so out of favour? I grip tightly to the large vines as she circles beneath. I hear more footsteps, and a wolf slinks into the clearing.

'Run, my friend!' I bellow to the deer.

But it seems the wolf's prey is not the deer, but myself. They take up position below me; the deer's squealing bleats and the wolf's snarls are formidable. More emerge from the surrounding forest. I gasp – there are hundreds.

'Why?' I cry to them, but there is no reply.

I wrap myself tighter in the vines. I can hear the birds closer now, the crows and hawks and even the little ones swoop down from above trying to knock me down to the angry crowd. The scratches hurt, but I am safe up here. I must find a way home. I look around for a way out of this. I am too deep in the forest, I never should have come. I used nature's favour for death, but she knew that, surely? I came with an open heart, but maybe I haven't changed enough.

'I did what had to be done! Can't you see?' Tears are now dripping from my swollen face, red with fear.

I grip tighter to the vines and they begin to feel as if they cling to me. They curl around my legs and arms, then start to pull. Below, a howling begins, and the animals seem excited. I am spreading outward I realise and try to pull back, but more vines wrap themselves around my limbs and force me wide. The strain is great and I feel as if my arms and legs will be ripped off my body.

'Don't do this! I am your friend, not your enemy! I saved you all, I looked after you. Please don't,' I say weeping and coughing.

Now I am petrified, stretched out to my fullest form. A single vine comes out in front of my face, it looks truly alive, as if thinking what to do next. Then it stabs at my throat and I let out a garbled gasp for air. It bends and twists around my neck. I feel like I did when I was nearly hung by the villagers.

'You won't do this . . .' I choke out.

The vine tightens so much I think my head will pop off. I clench my jaw, and try to squirm my way out of this hold. Did I come here to die? Was that my wish? Did I know she would be angry and take my life? I know there is a large part of my mind that is ready to give up and let the last of my held breath out. Something comes into mind –Fern and Diana. Their faces stay strong and, for a moment, I feel no cloud over my mind. It is as clear as the sky above. It is no use fighting physically, and I know what I must do now. It pains me unimaginably, but she has given me no choice. It will break our bond forever. Never will an animal trust me again after this, but I cannot see another way. I must live, I have so much left to do. I grasp onto the vines at my sides and scream louder than I ever have before. Flames start to lick from my fingertips and toes. The fire spreads quickly up the vine, and soon it is a blackened plant, burning away to its strong core. I am running out of time; I can feel myself starting to get dizzy. I must not fail.

Chapter Eighteen

Punished by the gods,

Beaten down and made to crawl,

For reasons unknown.

With a snap, the vines break around me as the fire spreads ever upwards. All that is left is the one around my neck. My hands free, I touch that last vine and it shirks backwards in fear. I fall, straight towards the awaiting mouths and teeth that definitely want to take chunks out of my body. But it is too late for them, too. I land on one knee and fire spreads out from my body through the ground. Some are caught and screech and run, the rest back away and scarper. The grasses burn as I stand to full height.

'Is this what you wanted? Is this better? Now we both have no one!' I cry out to the air.

I turn back through the vines, leaving fiery footsteps on the ground, burning the moss which once gave me shelter and cooled me. My hands outstretched, I burn the vines away and it is like a curtain as they spread away from me. But they cannot be allowed to escape my rage; I burn faster, spewing out flame in all directions and they blaze. Once through the vines, I turn my attention to the old trees and set them alight. I am so angry with her that I do not care any longer, I do not wish her to live near my home anymore. The leaves burn, the trees cannot move and I am a flaming torch spreading light where there was none before. Soon the inner forest is a raging fire and I make my way to the outskirts, destroying wood that I know is ages old. I am still swooped by birds so I turn my attention to them, wings so frail to fire, they stand no chance.

As I near my home, the tree I painted groans at me and begins its descent, intent on disabling me. But I am too quick and too strong. It is hollow I know and I punch my way through it as it comes down. At the edge now, I turn and throw one final ball of fire deep into the forest, and the explosion is catastrophic. I feel the blast and the hot air that follows. I lift my hand, and the fire on my body is extinguished. I wave her goodbye and smile. It is a heartbroken one, but my grin is for pity on the living. I walk steadily now, my magic solid and robust, carrying me forward to the house. I walk in through the door and am confronted by Diana and Fern, standing and talking to one another. They are alarmed about the smoke they have seen in the forest and where I might have disappeared to.

'Ariel! Thank goodness! What has happened? Are you okay?' The words flow from Fern in quick succession.

She runs to me and holds me tight, nearly knocking me off balance. I am still smouldering, I notice, so do not hug her back in case I am still hot. Fern pulls back and begins to check me for wounds.

'I am okay, Fern. Do not be alarmed. We had a disagreement of sorts in the forest,' I say calmly.

'With whom? Why is there a fire?'

'Nature, she has not taken to me as I thought. I had to escape.'

'Oh gods, this is horrible,' Fern says and turns towards Diana.

Diana steps in my direction. 'That must have been awful for you. What is going on with the forest? Does she not accept you anymore?' she asks.

'No, I am not accepted anymore. I think she is angry I killed so many in her name, but it is hard to be sure.' I let out a sigh, putting my hands to my face to hide my shame and tears. 'I did this and now she burns because of me. She is not at fault, I am.'

'No, you are not at fault, Ariel. You did what you had to, and if nature is angry we will go find somewhere else where the forest is your friend once more.' Fern punches me lightly. 'You disappeared on me! You should have talked, I could have stopped you and avoided all this mess.'

'I am not sure I could have avoided this. I had to go there and see her, she was my protector, you see? This is a war for my soul, Fern. I am attacked on all sides! The king, the elders, my mind and now nature herself!' I start to pace the room in angst.

I close off to their voices and feel stuck in my head. Walking up and down the room calms me a little. I am at war now, for real. What can I do? There is nowhere to go, and I am stuck with my mind rattling with these ideas. I shake and my lips tremble, tears flow freely. I must get out, I must find relief. There is nothing else to do but fight my way to safety and not let them all win against me. I am powerful, I can defeat one after another, but not all at the same time. Not without nature by my side, helping me; she has forsaken me and will destroy me. I still do not fully believe it – maybe someone put a spell on the forest! That is an explanation, but who? Who is that powerful? None on this island . . . I think. Or I have another adversary, unknown and in the shade. No, it is nature herself who damns me. It must be so. I drop to my knees, legs giving up after the torture they have been through. I collapse, fully and definitely into the ground, hoping it will swallow me up in a gaping maw.

It is Diana's voice that penetrates through to me. 'Ariel! Speak to us! What is going on?'

'She has forsaken me, hasn't she? My ally, my friend has gone! Can't you both see? I am damned, you should leave this place and let me rot,' I shout at her through drool and tears.

Diana comes to my level and kneels, holding my head. I feel her warmth and let out an audible breath.

'Please, don't leave, I didn't mean it. I need you Di, help me.' I tug on her blouse and draw her close.

Diana also draws in a deep breath and looks up to Fern who is standing above. I look over to her and reach out a hand, and she grabs it quickly and kisses it.

'We are here, we are not going anywhere, are we, Di?' Fern says forcefully. It fills me with hope.

Maybe I am not truly without allies. The women both hold me tight and I feel a calmness wash over my body; the fear is gone now. But a darkness still remains. My mind is not fixed, or well. It can't be, after all it has been through. The strife of life is taking its toll on me now. I relax my body fully and flop into the ground. Like I am dead and letting my soul drift fully upwards. They shake me quickly and I can feel myself coming back into the room, aware of all around me. The fire can still be heard crackling away outside, and if we don't leave here soon, we will be engulfed also.

'We must go now, far from the forest, it will burn quickly and fully,' I say and the women help me to my feet.

'You are right, Ariel, let's go before something happens to us,' Diana replies quietly and holds me on her shoulder, Fern taking my other side.

We struggle to move towards the door, and the closer we get, the more my heart aches to leave this place that could have been sanctuary. I will never feel calm, never get myself together, I know this. But through the door we manage our way, and start the journey to the town. The town's people, who were planting, have disappeared. Probably after seeing the smoke they have run to the town for safety. Good, I think to myself, she will never grow here, never spread back across the land chasing for my soul. We hobble onwards, and come over the rise before nightfall, and I can now see the town. I think we breathe a collective sigh of relief and hurry down the hill with more vigour in our muscles. By the time we reach the square, the moon has risen and shines a hazy white light along our path to Diana's house. She lets me go and opens the door, and I am ushered in only to be faced with her father and brother.

'What is going on, Diana? Do you know the time? There's a fire in the forest up north, and now you bring him in here. Why?' the father blurts out.

'Oh please, he's fine, don't worry. The fire will burn out I'm sure.' Diana briskly walks past them.

I follow with Fern still under my arm, straining with the weight. I am dropped onto a bed and breathe a sigh. It is better here, with the women safe and me allowed to rest. I curl up in the bed, needing to sleep, feeling burned out, literally. I hear the door close and am alone. I fall into a daze, and begin my road to sleep. Even in the place between awake and asleep, I can still hear their voices.

'What are we going to do with him? He started the fire, didn't he? Nothing but trouble if you ask me.'

'He had no choice! Calm down. We will look after him, you don't have to do anything, anyway. Remember, we all owe him.'

'Fine, Di! Keep your pet. Just keep him out of our way.'

'He's no pet! He's a real being, a good one at that! So just watch your tone.' Fern's voice wades in.

'Go home, Fern, this is not your business anymore.' A gruff and manly voice curses out.

I hear the front door slam, and then there is silence for a while, allowing me to crash down mentally. I awake what feels like a few moments later, to the sound of the door creaking open.

'Ariel? Are you awake yet? It's been two days.' Di's voice is soft and warm, and I feel like cuddling up in it.

'I am, sorry I thought it wasn't long. Let me get up,' I say and begin to stretch and move my limbs.

'It's okay, rest. I will bring you some water and food.' Di disappears behind the door again.

I decide to move, regardless. My body feels so stiff and broken, so I crack my neck and shake it off. I stoop and step to the door, opening it. I am in front of Diana, she looks at me expectantly and I blush, feelings coming to the surface all too quickly. Trying to hide the emotions coursing through me, I lower my gaze and take the water she holds.

'Thank you, Diana. I don't know if I should stay long, your family don't need me hanging around,' I say, rubbing my neck, then taking a large gulp of water.

'Don't be silly. Did you hear us argue? It's all sorted now, you will stay and I will look after you. Here, have an apple.'

I crunch down some of the fruit and then ask, 'Where are your family?' I look past her, and see no one else in the room.

'They're both out working, a lot of the town's people have gone to bury the dead for you . . . ' She trails off, and I nod my head slowly.

'Good, that is very good. They should find rest in the ground,' I say and move towards the table to take a seat. The wooden chair creaks and bends, but holds me.

I lay my head on the table. Many I killed, many to dig a grave for. I feel terrible, for all those lives I took so quickly and lightly. Now, nature has taken a turn against me for it. I am at war, yet I do not know what to do next. What is the step I must take to rectify all the chaos and death? I am stumped, lost in the void. It feels extremely dark in this room now, all around me, with no way out. I feel one hand on my head, stroking what is left of my hair. It calms me, and lets me think more clearly. I must do my best to save her from whatever comes next, that is all I know for the moment.

'Please, speak to me, Ariel, I know you hurt. Maybe I can help, if you let me in?' Another hand holds mine shakily.

'I don't know what to do, Diana. I am lost and scared of myself. I am a murderer, a force of death's hand,' I say, not moving my head from the table.

'That is simply not true, I know it in my heart. Come now, pick up that head and look at me.' Diana pulls my head upwards and I let her, looking straight into those dazzling eyes.

'I can't believe you, I am sorry. You didn't see the battle. It was a massacre, so many bodies, Diana. Just so many, I couldn't count,' I say.

There is nothing in her eyes and nothing comes from her mouth. She bites her lip and brings her forehead to mine. We breathe together, in this darkened room, like we are the only people on the island. I feel her breath and notice her smell, a delightful one and it drifts into me.

'We can get through this together. Just trust me, Ariel, we can do it. No one else matters, just us two now.' She leans further in.

I let her come close to my mouth and she nearly kisses me. I feel a stirring in my mind towards her and trust her fully now; no matter what happens, I will have her at my side. She retreats back. I am not sure why, and I stay looking up at her. I have eyes for no other, I should really tell her that, but the words cannot come out of my mouth. I am tongue-tied for some reason and cough instead.

'Are you okay? Here, have some more water.' She pushes the cup towards me and I take it and finish the drink.

'Yes, just finding it hard to think. What should we do now?' I ask, with hope.

Diana rocks back into her chair and has a puzzled look on her face.

'I don't have the answer for you, Ariel, I am sorry. We will figure it out though.' Diana sighs and lifts herself from the chair. 'Let's get out and walk for a time, maybe that will clear your head and show you the path.' She takes my hand and leads me up to stand.

'Okay, let's see some sunlight,' I agree and drift along in her flow, to the outside world.

Chapter Nineteen

Judgment breeds judgment,
Be at peace with those around,
It would serve you well.

Walking the street, I feel a sense of calm. It is early so the humans are starting to wake up for the day, and look sleepy. Diana waves at a few and does some small talk, but then we start to walk further out of town. She takes my hand, it starts my breathing and heart-pounding effects again, but she is too far away to notice, this time, I think. Having lost the town and put it behind us, she takes me up a small hill and sits, motioning for me to do the same. I dutifully follow and look out over the town.

'It's a beautiful place, isn't it?' Diana says wistfully.

'I suppose, I wish I could have enjoyed that place of my own though, the fire will have ripped through it by now, it looked like it could have been a magical, idyllic home' I reply and she cuddles into me.

'It's alright, we'll build you another. How are you feeling?' Diana peeks up into my eyes.

'I feel . . . I don't know to be honest. Still under fire and attacked, but I am glad I have you by my side, Di. I don't think I can do this alone.' I look down at her and smile a little.

She turns away, and lifts an arm to hold mine. We sit together for a while in silence. I am hoping that something will come to change my feeling of dread and loss. I can't tell her I feel this way, when she is so hopeful that I am better. I must hide it and pretend everything is headed in the right direction. Then she may grow a feeling for me, a feeling that is not fleeting but a true one, something tangible and amazing. I cannot stop myself now – I think about her with a focus I never have had before. She is everything to me at this moment. I hold her arm a little tighter and she smiles, letting out a noise I do not comprehend, it is a sigh mixed with another emotion. Maybe happiness, but I am not sure. I have never made such a sound. I do not feel happiness, I think, only another emotion that is all-consuming for Diana, so I will stick with her until she leaves me. She will inevitably escape and find another better suited to her, why would she stay? Who would with a monster such as I?

'What are you thinking?' I ask, hoping I can enjoy this time with her while it lasts.

'Just watching the people. I like it. People-watching. It pleases me to see them all milling around,' Diana replies and a quizzical look must cover my face, as she laughs at me and then points towards town. 'Look, they are all so happy with their jobs or chatting with one another, it's nice.'

'Little do they know they march towards death all too quickly,' I reply, 'I have watched many fade away just like you will one day.' I am mournful at this thought.

'We are here now and that is all that matters. Just watch them and revel in their beauty,' she says, hugging me tighter still.

I look down with her now, and start to see what she does. They do look happy, saying 'mornings' to each other and going to face whatever they must achieve today.

'I live at a much slower pace, Diana. I will watch them and envy their speed,' I say out loud.

'Good job, Ariel, you watch with me for a while. I like it here.'

She is right, it is a nice day and pleasant to watch the humans. It takes my mind away from horror, to a place of rest. We wait till the sun is at its peak. Diana stretches and yawns, then rises.

'Come on, let's see if we can do anything to help someone today. I think it would be good for you.' She reaches out a hand and I take it with ease.

'Okay, I am sure someone will need something, humans always do,' I say with a smirk. Diana laughs and pushes me with her shoulder, rocking me away and back to her side.

'I suppose we do require a lot of help. But that is what you are for, helping.' Her voice raises in pitch at the end and she looks happily at me.

We start a slow, easy walk towards town and I wonder what is going to happen next. With Diana, everything seems right. I hope this does not change. As we reach the town, I lead her to the few traders who have returned, hoping for gold and not the noose. Their eyes sparkle when they catch my eye, thinking I am the lord still, and wealthy. I wave them away, I have no use for their wares. But a necklace does catch my eye, and the trader sees me looking at it.

'Sir, would you like this? I will give it to you freely,' he says.

I am curious as to why he would do such a thing, probably he is hoping to be in my good graces after what happened before. I pick up the necklace and it shimmers gold in the light. The stone in the middle is a sort of red ruby; I don't believe it to be real, but in any case, it does look pleasing.

'Thank you, my good sir, I will remember your generosity. Here, for you, Diana.' I unclasp the necklace and drape it round her neck. She lifts her hair so that I may fix it for her.

'Thank you, Ariel, it's very pretty. Is this a ruby?' she asks me. I shake my head a little with a smile, and lead her away from the market.

A crowd has gathered around a house I know. It is huge by comparison to the others around it. Three stories high into the sky and ornate woodwork is carved into every inch of it. It has been painted red and gold, too opulent for my taste, but we are drawn into the gathering. There is a lot of clamouring and shouting, so I part the group with my arms. They move uneasily, all trying to get a peek at what is happening at the front. I force my way through, hearing gasps at who is pushing them away. I come to the front to find a man. He is tall and fair, but lying on the ground, shaking. Another man, the head elder, holds the man's head and is crying out. I move closer, and feel Diana's hand on mine.

'Please! You must help my boy!' the elder shouts as loud as he can over the mob's voice.

'Get back, let him work!' Diana calls taking charge of the crowd, and she pushes me forward, 'you can save him, can't you? He is innocent of his father's crimes, remember that Ariel.'

I look round to Diana and nod. I will forgive this man's father. The son is not at fault.

'What happened? You must tell me everything,' I say, kneeling beside them both.

'He has had a fever for days, and I found him here like this. He is dying, please help.' The elder's eyes pour with tears.

I do my duty, imagining the man to be a deer, ill in the woods. I would help that animal, so I will help him. I lay one hand on the burning hot head, and another on the chest. I can feel the disease within him; it creeps through his lungs and into his mind. I look down at him and can see the blackness inside. Blood is rushing into his lungs now, and it must be evacuated before he dies. I allow my magic to take hold of us both, letting my hands make us as one. A light spews from my fingers.

'Roll him onto his side,' I say calmly.

Diana drops down to our level and drags the body over. The father simply sits and cries. I engage with the man's body and force the blood up and out of his gullet. He throws up a lot of deep, red mucus, and the mob screams all at once.

'He's killing him! Stop him!'

I do not turn from my task. Now free to breathe, the man takes in a long gasp of air and opens his eyes.

'Do not fear, boy. Stay still as you can, I will help you.' I look him in the eye and he accepts by closing his eyes and then screaming out in agony.

I keep my hands connected with his body, now to draw out the fever. I hold his forehead, and concentrate on the heat, feeling it move from him to me. He shivers and shakes but slowly his temperature drops to a more comfortable level. The man opens his eyes once more.

'The pain, it is gone.' He holds his chest as I release him, coughing a little more but only from lack of air.

'The disease has gone.' I start to turn to the elder, but he jumps, quicker than I thought an old man could, into the embrace of his son.

'Oh, thank you, thank you. Truly you feel well again?' the old man asks his son.

'Yes, Father, I think I am well.' He turns his head towards me, wiping the last of the blood from his lips. 'Thank you for your kindness, my lord.' He coughs again but reaches out a hand to me.

I shake it and smile at him. 'You are welcome, it should not trouble you anymore. Rise and find rest, your body has been through a lot.'

He is helped to his feet by the crowd that comes rushing in. There are cheers and jubilation at the feat they have witnessed. They flood past me and I stand, being bumped around by them. I laugh and look round for Diana, still standing by me. I grab her hand and pull her from the throng. We both laugh as we become clear of the humans.

'Well done, Ariel, I knew you could do it!' Diana hugs my waist and presses into me, and I have no choice but to put my arms back round her.

It took a toll, I know. It might not come now, but it is present in my mind.

'I need a place to rest, Diana. Can we go now?' I ask.

'Let's get out of here before they turn to you,' she says, nodding towards the humans that have lifted the man up and are taking him into the house.

Diana leads me by the hand again. This time, passing her house, we go on down the street. I know we are going to Fern's. I am looking forward to seeing her, since she had to leave Diana's home in such a rush. We come upon the little house, with its thatch and the river running behind. Diana politely knocks on the door, and it creaks open slowly. A head peers out into the sun.

'Aw! You're better! Come in, come in, I am just working on pieces.' The door swings open and I crouch through it.

'Thank you, Fern, how are you?' I ask.

Fern turns back round with a smile, but her expression turns to horror as she looks at me fully. I look down, to see the blood-covered clothes sticking to me.

'Oh, it's not mine. We helped the elder's son, he had a disease you see,' I say, and pat myself to show it is not my blood.

'Oh my god! Get in the river now, the pair of you! You'll stain the floor at this rate. I will fetch new clothes.' Fern ushers us back outside.

We walk round the house to the stream, I feel like we are bonding, becoming one but am not sure how to proceed, it is an excitement beyond what I thought I could produce. Emotions stirring in me we dip into the water. It is good and cleansing, and I wash my face and torso. Diana is washing her hands, and up her arms, and I begin to feel myself staring.

'What is it?' she asks curiously.

'I just . . . nothing. I am getting clean,' I reply.

She giggles and continues to wash. I throw some water at her, trying to be playful, but I throw too hard and drench her head.

'Ariel! How rude!' Diana throws some water back, and then twists her hair to drip herself dry.

Her hair shimmers in the light as she does so. I am entranced and stare once more.

'Get yourself clean and stop staring, sir.' Diana laughs and shakes her head.

I get back to my task. 'Sorry, Di, you are just so beautiful in this light is all,' I say, hoping for a nice response.

'Aw, thank you, Ariel. You look handsome, but still very bloody. I would wash more.' She winks at me then stands, and walks back towards Fern's house.

I almost leave the stream to follow her, but she is right, I am still drenched in the blood of the elder's son. So I wash it away as quickly as I can. It is not a great job, but the best I can do. I rise from the water and make my way back to the house, shivering from the cold.

'Better?' Fern asks as I open the door.

'Yes, thank you.'

'I have left some clothes on the bed, go and change.' She does not look at me, as she is brushing Diana's hair back to its natural style.

I make my way through the other doorway and find some small trousers and a shirt to stretch on. I really must find some new clothes – what must Diana think of me? I will make some, I decide, once I am well enough to concentrate on such a task. I rub my head. It still lingers, that feeling inside my mind, watching her hair shining bright. I emerge back into the room with the women in it.

'Oh dear, I am sorry, they will not do at all! Go to the market and find something better, Ariel.' Fern shoos me out of the house with a wave of her hand.

'Goodbye Ariel, see you soon,' Diana calls after me, and I wave back to her.

Chapter Twenty

I once crossed rivers,

Flooded with death's cold embrace,

Waded deep and lived.

Now I walk, back towards the centre of town. I am lost in my mind, unsure of what I actually feel. Nothing makes me happy, so why should I try to put Diana through that? Would she be able to change me? Save me from myself? I do not know, and brush my hand up and down my hair. I lumber up the street, wandering as far as I can, away from the thoughts. The market is starting to bustle once more, and this pleases me. I look through the wares, finding a stall with cloth that I have not encountered before.

'What is this fabric?' I ask the trader.

'Sir, it is fine kett, very nice. Much softer and stronger than silk. You would suit it. Much better than what you wear now. It is expensive, though I am sure a lord will have the funds.' He smiles broadly.

A cough from behind makes me turn. It is the head elder, 'I will purchase this for my lord,' he says, and throws a few gold coins in the direction of the trader.

'Thank you, sir! Most generous. Enjoy, my good lord.' He bows slightly to me.

I take the kett from his hands and drape it over my shoulder.

'May I have a word in private, my lord?' The elder is still with me, I notice.

'It is only Ariel now, and thank you for your contribution, I seem to lack any funds now the keep is gone. I have never asked your name,' I say.

'Ah, yes I know. Come with me if you please. There is much to discuss.' He hesitates. 'I am known as Grace, the head of the elders.'

I follow Grace to the main hall, where a group has assembled on the chairs around the long table. We sit, me in an uneasy fashion, fearing I will be attacked once more.

'Do not shake, erm, Ariel, we only wish to talk.' Grace motions for the rest to start.

'The king is unwell, we hear from the traders. I think the next king to be crowned will not be long away,' one says.

'Yes, this boy is known for his cruelty and is young and bold. We should be wary of him,' another replies.

'What do you think we should do, Ariel?' Grace leans towards me.

'I would look to home first. There has been a lot of death around here, caused by you men predominantly . . .' I trail off, expecting an uproar.

'It is true, we have been led by the mob too long. How would you change us?' Grace peers at me through old eyes.

'I would vote on some council members, from the people, like a forum rather than elders. It was my mistake to create this situation, and I wish to rectify it,' I say to silence.

'We will discuss this, but what of the new king?' Grace asks.

'I think if we leave him well alone, he will do the same for us?' I say in a tone of a question rather than knowledge.

'You see, we do not believe that will be true. You defeated his father, and he will be forced to prove himself in battle. Who is a better foe than the demon that destroyed an army?' Grace leans back in his chair.

'That will be a problem, then. I don't seem to have nature on my side anymore, and without her, I may lose a major battle.' There are gasps from the elders, but not from Grace.

'I know, we saw the fire, Ariel. I knew something was wrong. So, we will have to avoid a battle for the time being. Leave it in our hands. We will discuss what you have said today,' Grace says, and turns back to his peers.

'Okay, I will leave it in your hands for now. Let me know of any developments. I kindly ask that you take me seriously, though, when I say that things need to change around here.' There are some grunts, and Grace nods in a slow manner.

I remove myself from the table, making my way back onto the street and into the marketplace. I have my fabric now, but how shall I tailor it? It is definitely a job to be completed, as I am practically naked in Fern's clothes. If I am to rise and not decay, I must be the part and look it. I wander down the street, away from the bustle. I know where to go, the blacksmith is closest and I am in need of a new outfit. Is making armour the same as making clothes? Probably. I lurch in that direction, to his home. I knock on the door and hear scuffling behind it.

'Yes?' a voice calls out, old and frail.

'It is Ariel, your previous lord. I am looking for the blacksmith,' I reply softly so as not to cause fear.

The door creaks open and a face I know appears – his grandmother. She ushers me with 'come in' hands. I do so and am greeted by the rest of the family. I bow to them and then look around for the man I need.

'He is not here, but at the smithy. Thank you by the way, we are forever in your debt for ridding my son of the waking nightmares.' The mother, Glen I think, smiles at me.

'Ah, yes, I hope he is well? I need some clothes made, unfortunately. These I am wearing simply will not do you see,' I say to her.

'My boy is well and playing with friends, thanks to you. I can make your clothes,' Glen laughs, 'those are not clothes for any lord. Come let us measure you. Grandma, can you help? I need a stool as well, you are so tall!'

I stand for her while she takes string around and up me.

'There, I have the measurements, now give me the fabric. You are back staying with Fern? I heard about the wretched fire,' she shakes her head, 'a terrible loss for you, I'm sure.'

'It was my fault.' I hang my head down in shame. 'I started that fire, nature has turned on me. Yes, I am back with Fern.'

'Oh my dear, she will forgive you I am sure. Trust an old woman, they will always forgive if you do your penance.' The grandmother whispers this up to me, so I must bow down to her level.

'Thank you, I will try to make amends,' I say and start to retreat from the house.

'I will bring your clothes as soon as I can, my lord,' Glen calls after me.

I wave them goodbye and make my way onto the street once more. Another task completed, and I feel a sense of relief. I sigh and stretch in the sunlight; it feels nice to be out in the air. I take some time to wander the streets before I return to Fern and Di. I must work out my next steps, metaphorically. I may have to fight now, if the elders are correct. It is a disconcerting feeling, to know I must face death again, if this new king is also bent on war. But is that a bad thing? Protecting is my job now, that is the main goal. I meander, like the stream and follow my feet, hoping they take me to where I need to be, without thinking of where I am going.

I am trapped here between life and death, hovering between the both of them. Where will I land? The men of this world continue to try and crush me. The elders will conspire again I know it, a new king will come to kill me and the forest seethes with hate for me now. Damn the powerful. I have no hand to play. I find a quiet corner on a side street and sit down. I cover my head with my arms and try to shut out the hate that fills my mind. I should be strong and able to stand up to the tides that try to wash me away! I am floundering here, a nothing-being, a useless, fearful youngling. I hit my head with my fists, then let my arms fall, feeling despondent. How can one take so much and still stand? I should be angry, I should be hate-filled. All I feel is loss, that I am far from a home and far from peace. I wish for my death, to depart the land and crumble into dust. I roll onto one side, scratching at the dirt beneath me hoping to claw my way back to Fern's house. The tears pour out and I bang my head on the floor till I feel dizzy, then stop. Everything calms and becomes silent. I cannot hear the words of the man standing above me. He holds out a hand, it is all I can focus on. He brings me to my feet. Holding my hand still, I hug the man with my other arm, and weep out all my sorrows. When no more tears are forthcoming, I stagger backwards and turn from him. I still cannot see properly and use the walls to propel myself forward. The blurriness subsides, I find the stream and wade upwards towards the little house that I built for her. I clamber up the bank and, finally, reach the door. I use my head to knock.

'Ariel? What is going on?' Fern looks at me with worried eyes when she sees my state of being.

'I don't know what to do, Fern. The elders can only plot, the new king will come for me and nature has damned me. I cannot defeat them all and they will bring about my slow, savage death.' I say through heaving breaths.

Diana rises from her seat and rushes towards me to hug me. 'We are your people, Ariel, just be calm and let us help,' Diana says in a muffled voice, pressing herself into me.

'Exactly. We are here for you, Ariel. Try not to give up on those who know no better. You are much stronger than them, I see it in your heart.'

Fern looks up at me and I turn my head, thinking about all I have been through to reach this point.

I stand up straight, these two special women have drawn the fear out and into the air, it fades for now. I put my arms around them both and sigh, breathing deeply.

'I don't know what to do now. They are all after me, I can't outrun them,' I say, overcome with the devastating words.

'Well, we could always escape, Ariel . . .' Diana trails off.

'How?' I ask curiously.

'Well, there are plenty of boats here, why don't we commandeer one and travel away?' Diana says, straight-faced and to the point.

'I hadn't thought of just running away,' I say.

'It wouldn't be running away, but moving somewhere better,' Fern pipes up.

'We talked about it while you were gone. We think it's the best decision,' Diana says.

I smile down at her. 'What about protecting the people? And nature, what of her?'

'We think you should go back to the forest and heal her, she will forgive you. At least that's what we hope. Then, when you return, we may disappear in the night,' Fern suggests.

I bow my head low and huff. Could it be that easy? These humans are the most precious to me. I have formed a link with them, it cannot be broken now. They think of me, even when I am not here, to try to help me and formulate plans. I could not ask for more, it is what I was always asking for, somewhere in my mind.

'What do think, Ariel? Shall we go?' Diana says.

'Yes, I think we have to,' I say, 'maybe on a distant shore I will find peace and you both will too. But what of the town's people? I am their protector . . .' I shuffle my feet, looking down upon them.

'You can't save everyone, and besides, with you gone, maybe the king will not come again as you have an agreement, don't you?' Fern asks me. I must tell her the whole truth.

'The king is dying, and a new one will rise soon. The elders think he will come for me,' I say, solemnly.

'Even more reason to go! We owe them nothing now, and you couldn't defeat the new king in this state anyway, could you? Let us go!' Fern dances around the room.

I hold tight to Diana, and she to me. We watch Fern's movements with a little glee. I am proud to know these two; they make life so much more spectacular. There is nothing more I need from the island, it has given me a beautiful bounty. But I have to make amends with nature, they are right. How may we sail without her favour? We would never make it across the water to somewhere new. She would swallow us up, and leave us to drown with no mercy. So, I will go, to bend the knee, and hopefully she will forgive. My magic is not enough to heal her, I must use my words and actions. I will go and do my best. That is all they ask of me now. Not to be a demon, only alive in my mind like them.

'What do you say, Ariel?' Diana asks me.

'I say that I must face the forest and gain her favour again. It is the only course. Then we will sail, I promise you both. Thank you.' I wrap my arms around Diana.

Fern is breathless but still has enough energy to say, 'Okay! We have a plan then. Are you ready to go? We can come with you, if you like?'

'No, I will do this alone one last time. It is my fault she is burned, after all. But after that, we will never part, you both promise?' I ask, knowing the answer.

'Of course!' they chime together.

I breathe in and out. Once my clothes arrive, and we rest, then I will walk to the forest. It is a daunting prospect, but it needs to happen. I squeeze Diana once more, then let her go.

'I will rest now. Then tomorrow I will go – hopefully my new clothes will arrive in time,' I say, feeling a little dizzy from all the conversation.

'Yes, come on, let's get you to bed,' Diana says and helps me face the doorway to the bedroom, 'have a good sleep and we will talk some more about our plans.'

I walk to the bed and collapse into it. I can't keep my eyes open any longer. I start to drift in and out of the sleep world. I can hear the women from here, but only just.

'Well, that went well, better than I thought when he came through the door.' Diana's mellow voice drifts through the door to me.

'Let's let him rest, then we shall put it all into action. Freedom at last is in all our hands, almost. If we can just get him to settle his score with nature, I think it will be time to go,' Fern says back to Diana, and I can hear a hopeful note.

I can listen no more, I cannot focus now. So, I let it all go, the king, the elders, all will not matter. We will be free, Fern is right. Free to roam the world. I have seen enough of the island. Leave it to the humans as it should be. I am upsetting the balance and it simply cannot continue. I fall into a deep sleep to rest for the work ahead.

Chapter Twenty-One

Give to me my mind,

Do not tarry; little time,

I crack and crumble.

When I do properly wake, the room looks still in the light. I put out a hand to touch the sunlight, and feel her warmth. I shake the bed covers off and put my feet to the floor. I stretch and yawn, then make my way to the main room of the house. The women are sleeping together on a makeshift bed. I feel quite sorry, I really should have given them the bed, but no matter, it is done now.

'Fern?' I whisper, but there is no movement.

'Diana?' I call a little louder.

'Hmm? Yes, I am awake.' Diana sits up in bed. She should be looking sleepy but still, she shines for me. 'Your clothes arrived yesterday, over there. Are you going to the forest now?' She rubs her eyes.

'I think so, I must see what I can do to repair the damage, in any case, even if she does not completely forgive me,' I say in hushed tones.

She nods and falls back to the bed.

'I will find you both later,' I say.

'Okay, be careful though,' I hear from the covers.

I find my new clothes, they feel nice and I dress. They are a purple top and red trousers. Not what I would choose, I think black suits me better for this task, but I will have to wear something. Maybe some colour will brighten my mind.

'You look nice.' Diana is still awake then, did she see me dress? And watch?

This thought excites me a little, but I must keep my head on straight. No more thoughts of Diana, only the work I must do.

'Goodbye, Di, see you soon,' I say and head towards the door.

'Bye, darling, good luck,' she replies sweetly.

It sends an electric shock through me to hear the word 'darling'. I love it and I smile broadly as I walk out of the door. I shake it off and march to the main street. Many are already awake and going to their jobs too. A few nod, a few wave and I return their hellos. I can see the traders are already in full swing, so I avoid the throng and head up the little hill towards the forest.

I walk through the fields; the planting of trees has ceased since the fire. It saddens me but maybe some will still grow. I hope so, she deserves to grow further into this land. I make my way past them to my old house. I say house, but there is nothing except charred remains. The roof has collapsed onto the ground and still smoulders. The carvings cannot be seen anymore. It was a wonderful gift that they gave to me, but now gone, as I will be soon. I draw near to the trees and stop. I peer through into the darkness and lay a hand on the first tree I find at the edge.

'I am so sorry, please accept my apologies and learn to forgive. I know what I did with your power was wrong. I know that I am a monster in your eyes, but let me help you regardless,' I say to the tree.

The blackened wood groans, and I let my magic start to get to work. I feel a lightness within, and let it flow through me into the wood. The tree groans louder and I am afraid that I will break the tree in half, but continue to flow myself into the forest. I can see the light travelling through my arm into the bark, healing it. I feel a tightness around my leg and look down to see a new vine has grown around me. I let my light find it too. It saps my strength to let both take my magic but I continue to force the light outwards. The grip of the vine tightens, and I am not sure whether it is friend or foe. It starts to pull on me. I am weak physically from all this effort, so my leg starts to drag into the forest. I am wide-eyed as it then tugs me down to the floor, and begins to pull my weight.

I let this event happen. More vines reach out as I go further into the forest, wrapping around my torso and arms. I begin to speed up. If this is a march towards death, so be it. I will heal you, I think to myself. I let the light come from all of my body – it is painful and tiring, but I let it occur. I am a conduit of healing now, and as I am dragged, flowers and grass spring up in my wake. The pain starts to become an agony. I am not sure where this is going, but I find myself deeper and further, closer to the heart of the forest, where she awaits me. I am uncourteously dropped in a clearing that I recognise.

'So, we meet again. Have you seen what I can do with my power? It is not simply for destruction, you know this. Come to me now, let me help you,' I say out to the forest. Nothing happens.

I sit up and begin to meditate, still with light pouring out of me, still in great pain. I let my mind shift and wander into the ground and force the light down to the tree roots. This is good magic, and I feel pleased using it. I have never stretched myself over such a big area before. I shut my eyes and pray that it is working. There is nothing for it now, I must try my hardest. I do not watch what is coming towards me. It could be a vine, but then I begin to hear paws on the ground. I hear growling and open a lid to peek at what is going on. There is a wolf in front and centre of me. Drooling, a little limp, and larger than I have seen in this world for a while.

'Where have you been hiding? Come feel the light and be healed, too. There is nothing to fear from me.' I breathe out to it, letting my magic work on the animal.

The wolf snarls deeply, as the limp leg snaps back into place, and she backs away. The agony increases, as my power is melted with the forest. I look around to see moss growing back and the bark of the trees slowly becoming strong and firm again. I can't lift my limbs now, I feel so drained, but the work is not completely finished. My flesh feels pulled to the ground and I scream. I must heal all I can before I fall into unconsciousness. I struggle to lift my head now, my legs are popping out of their sockets and I feel a warm rush of liquid from my nose and mouth.

'Please, is that enough? Or will you draw out my life?' I cry, burbling into the empty hollow ground.

There is a sense of relief, and my light begins to dampen. Like a fire, I beat and flash, then the light within me dies and I crumple into the ground.

I awake to the night, and with eyes still closed I sit up. I can hear the chirruping of insects but nothing else. Leaves rustle, and I open my eyes wide, remembering what has occurred. I look down at my legs, twisted and broken, but repairing slowly. My arms still work, and I rub the blood from my face, spitting a large clot of it from my lungs. I can see a vine now, through blurry eyes. It strokes my face, not in malice but in thanks, I hope. It is hard to determine, but I think I have done all I can.

'Can you forgive me? After all the hurt and pain I caused?' I ask the vine.

It shrinks backwards, almost thinking to itself, then wraps itself around my torso. I do not even try to stop it. The dragging begins again, and I am pulled along the forest floor. More vines reach down to speed me to my destination. They wrap around all my limbs now, even my legs which is enough to make me cry in agony. I do not scream though, too exhausted to vocalise what I am feeling throughout my body. We come to a sudden halt, and I am laid up against a tree on the edge of the forest. My vision has cleared and I can see the fields reaching out towards the town.

'I'll never make it,' I say with some force, 'allow me to pass here and trouble none anymore.'

There is a snarling to my left and I turn my head slowly.

'So, am I dinner or will you help me?' I ask the wolf. I can see now by the size of the beast, that it could easily carry me to town.

I reach out a hand and the wolf comes closer, nuzzling under my arm into my chest. The snarling dissipates, and is replaced by a relaxing snuffle. I smile and sniff.

'Thank you. So I am forgiven, after all. Good. Stay with me, or help me to town, I leave the choice to you,' I say quietly to the night.

The wolf lies at my feet, crouched, awaiting my body. I heave myself forward, letting my legs go where they may, and I reach out and grab the neck fur of the wolf. I clamber on and hear the groaning under my weight. She rises and begins to pad towards town. The pace picks up, as she becomes used to me. We gallop through the fields and arrive at the crest of the hill. I can see down and it is so unbearably close now. The wolf halts as she peers at the few town's folk still awake, cleaning the marketplace.

'It's okay, I can manage from here, I am sure the people will help now. Go back to the forest and be free. We have made our peace, I will now be leaving the island forever, let her know,' I say.

The wolf lets out a short howl and crouches again. I roll off in an ungainly style and heap myself into the grass. She licks my face, snorts on me, then runs back in the direction we came. I look back to the town. The people definitely heard the howl and are coming to investigate, swords at the ready.

'It is just I, Ariel! I need your help! Please follow my voice!' I shout down to the collecting humans.

They race up the hill, having seen my hand reaching up out of the grass.

'What the hell happened to you? Were you attacked by a wolf? We heard the howl!' the first rescuer screams at me and my mangled legs.

'She is gone. I need dragging to Fern's, if you please,' I say calmly.

He nods and calls for a stretcher. I am hastily put on a thick piece of wood and carried towards the square. I nearly fall off several times as the humans trip, or are crushed under the load. Luckily, we all arrive at the square unharmed. An elder appears.

'What in the blazes is going on at this time of night?' He sounds angry but I am still calm.

'I went to heal the forest, it cost me a bit of energy is all. I must be returned to Fern's house immediately,' I say to the man.

His face becomes pale as he looks over my body, he backs away and ushers the men forward. They up their speed and trample down the cobbles and round corners before I am dumped down on the ground. They are breathless and heaving, but have done their job, as I have done mine. One knocks on the door and a sleepy-faced Fern appears.

'Yes?' she asks before noticing my body on the stretcher and rushing to my side.

'I am okay, Fern, just a little broken. I need rest I think, I definitely deserve it after that.'

'What? What happened to you? Did the forest do this? Are we safe?' The quick-fire questions come at me.

'I did this to myself, as I said, I am okay. Now let us go inside,' I say and point to the door.

Fern backs inside and I am rolled into the house. My legs are healed enough for me to crawl now, so I make my way to bed.

'Are you okay, Ariel? Did you manage?' Diana asks and steps over to me, helping my legs to move.

'Yes, I think I managed. We will be able to get out of here,' I reply, and am finally in the bed, and free.

I clamber in, feeling the soft bedding I snuggle up in the cosy blankets.

'Thank you, Di, we'll leave soon I promise,' I say to her and stroke her face.

'That might not be possible now,' she says, 'the king is on his deathbed; news arrived in the town not long after you left. The elders want to speak with you.'

I nod in contemplation. What do they want from me now? I am broken and ready to leave, it is time. There is nothing that can stop me from leaving. I must go with Fern and Diana to somewhere safe, where we are able to build a home and future. There isn't a future for us here, they must all know that by now.

'Did you tell them we must leave?' I ask Diana.

'Yes, I told them, but they still need to speak to you apparently.' She rolls her eyes and sighs. She drops her head onto my chest and I breathe deeply for her.

I stroke Diana's hair until I fall into rest. A dream world takes me and I fight off the darkness that still resides in me. I must find a boat and a way out of here. In the dream world, I am searching for a vessel to carry us, but everything burns before I can touch it. Falling to ash. I am completely alone and start to cry. My tears flow down my cheeks onto the sand. I turn to see the town burning too, and I shout for Diana and Fern but no noise comes forth from my gaping mouth. I am so terrified, I wake up. It is daytime once more.

I sigh in relief; they are safe. Diana has climbed in the bed with me and my heart suddenly speeds up. Her legs are wrapped round me, her arms round my torso. It feels exhilarating. I tingle and feel every ounce of her being. I breathe faster and know why now. I think I am in love after all, there is no other explanation as to how this feels. I have slept beside Fern before and only feel a sense that I need to protect her, but this is much different.

'Are you awake?' I whisper to her.

Diana groans and starts to move. She looks up at me through her red locks and grins.

'Hello you, how are we feeling?' she asks.

'Good, very good now, thank you for staying with me,' I reply as straight-faced as I can, holding in the nerves.

'It was nice to lie together again, wasn't it?' Again a wide grin comes across her face. 'Why do you look at me like that?' I guess she knows the answer as well as I do.

'It was. I'm sorry, I can't control my face,' I say to laughter, it sets me off too and we giggle together.

I shake my head and wipe the tears from my eyes. I have never been so happy to wake up. But can I tell her, or is it the wrong time? I do not know what to do with myself. She reaches up and squishes my face.

'Oh, Ariel, we are a pair.' Diana then rolls out of the bed, leaving me soaking with sweat. 'Come, let's see what the elders have to say. I will go with you of course.' Diana starts to change into outdoor clothes.

'Okay, I suppose we should hear them out, thank you,' I say.

'Stop thanking me!' Diana bows to me laughing and skips out of the room.

I smile to see her go, and reach out of the bed for my own full dress. I put on the now-ripped clothes, they will have to do for now. I make my way through the doorway into the studio room. Fern awaits us, and the women are whispering to each other. Diana shushes Fern as I come through fully.

'So, we need to go?' I ask them both.

'Yes, we will go. Fern will stay to pack for us,' Diana replies and reaches out a hand for me to clasp.

Chapter Twenty-Two

Love drives us forward,

It encapsulates our life,

Grasp it with both hands.

I am thrilled by this holding of hands, it is not like before, I think. Before, it was out of pity and to help me. Now she does it freely and wishes to go outside with me by her side. How glorious life can be. I am trapped in my head now. So, the king is dead and the new king will come for me, if the elders are right. Why shouldn't we leave before that happens? I know I should feel daylight, but don't register it. Diana guides me through the back alleys to the main street.

'What will your family do?' I ask her.

'I have chosen my path now, it lies with you and with Fern, my new family. My old family will survive without me,' she says with a slightly wistful tone.

I nod and ponder all the humans that will be left behind. I will leave it to the witches to protect the humans. They are my last chance to remove myself from the island. It brightens me to know that Diana has thrown in her lot with us. We seem to be a good team. I walk the street with her to the main hall. I feel a sense of trepidation now, and hang my head low. We walk in and all chatter comes to a stop. They look round at us and stare almost in disbelief.

'Ah, you have arrived, welcome my friend. Who is your guest? Diana, I believe?' Grace asks as head elder.

'Yes, Diana, here to support Ariel.' Diana steps forward and looks like a queen to me. Strong and powerful she walks into the hall and takes a seat. She draws another chair out and motions me to sit as well.

'Okay, welcome. We have much to discuss with you, my lord.' Grace nods a bow to us both.

'May I remind you, I am no longer your lord, or sire, or any such thing. Just Ariel, if you please,' I say.

The chatter starts up again and Grace raises a hand to silence them.

'The new king formally requests your presence. A runner came with the message while you were gone. The old king died and the runner was sent immediately, not a good sign. I believe you should go, as a sign of good faith,' Grace says, gravely.

'Why? He will try to kill me, you must know that. I no longer have the power of death, I am now the healing light alone,' I say flatly.

The room bursts into talk – worried talk.

'He has three more armies to send! Are you saying you will not fight them off?' another elder shouts.

'I will fight no longer, as I said, I only heal now. The world has changed, and I have decided to as well. I will leave this island, there is nothing that could stop me. So, why would I go and meet the king?' I ask again.

'Maybe, if you cannot fight, you must convince him that we pose no threat to his reign. It is our only hope of survival now. You will meet him south of our border, at a town called Thrung.' Grace leans onto the table and looks me dead in the eye.

I avoid his glare. Must I go? It seems unlikely I will survive, but if I can save the people? Should I risk my life, in the hopes that they are spared? My last chance at protecting them. I must go then, and meet this human. He will not stop until we speak, and that is better than a battle I cannot win.

'Okay,' I pause, 'I will go. But only if the elders are disbanded and a vote taken so new humans will take their place.'

A clamouring erupts from all mouths. Diana simply looks round at me and smiles; she holds my hand and squeezes gently. I hope she is proud of me in this moment.

'Settle down. I said, settle down!' Grace tries to calm his elders. 'We accept. Your command is rightful, after all. Should you not return, then we will see what happens.' This settles the men.

'Time to go, come with me,' Diana says, standing and looking so majestic, I think she would make an excellent elder, I think to myself, but an even better wife.

I nod and rise. They will not listen unless I make them, and complete this task. I must steel myself, and show I still have much mettle. The king does not know I will not fight. He must be fearful of me, somewhere in his mind. I can use that fear to secure the town's folk their freedom, as I take my leave.

'Well done, Ariel, so we will go?' Diana asks and I hesitate.

'We? Are you sure? We may be walking to our deaths,' I say, hopeful she will change her mind and let me go alone.

'Definitely. Fern and I will escort you, and keep you safe. Is it true you only heal now?' She peers into my eyes.

I nod. 'Yes, it is true. I can only use my magic for the good of the land now.'

'That is good, Ariel, there is no need for further death. You will be a diplomat for the people, and when we return, the elders will let go of power and we will leave!' Her voice raises at the end.

I am less convinced. I do not believe we will return, but we must try. If the king will not listen, we will run for the boat.

We walk through the sunlight, and return to where we began the day. Knocking on the door, a sleepy Fern answers.

'Well, how did it go?' she asks.

'We are going on an adventure. Fern, do you think you could ready a boat for all three of us while we see the king?' Diana speaks first, and I am glad to hear her words.

'Of course, I will prepare for our departure. Will you two be okay?' Fern looks to me now.

'Yes, we will be fine, Fern. I have Diana here with me, I do not fear for our safety,' I lie.

Fern nods in thought but opens the door wider so we may enter. Diana drags me in by the hand, I sigh and sit on a stool.

'We will leave immediately. But I haven't been South in so long I don't know the road.' I say to the room.

'Yes, let's get it over with. I know where the town is, I will guide you.' Diana grabs both my hands now, and kneels in front of me.

I smile down at her. 'Okay, let's get it done.'

'I have something for you, before you go. Into the bedroom with you.' Fern smiles and gestures a hand towards the door.

I stand up and stride strong legs towards the door. What could she possibly have for me? Opening the door, I see it immediately. My new sword, Sophia, lies on the bed. It may come in useful, if only for putting fear into him. I walk to the bed and lift it, and she feels good in my hand once more. Useless, but comforting. I return to the studio room, sword in hand.

'Thank you, Fern. It is much appreciated. I will only use her for good,' I say.

'Glad to hear it. Now go and get ready, I will do the same.' Fern brushes past me with a pat on the ribs, and leaves the room.

I look to Diana, and she looks back to me and stands.

'What do we need? I think we have everything, maybe some horses? I'm afraid it's quite a way,' she says with a smile.

'Okay, I don't suppose we can just run there.' We both laugh.

'Oh, no we can't run. Horses are a much more civilised way to travel.' She shakes her head and makes for the door.

With Fern preparing for our adventure across the waters after we return, I take Diana's hand this time but still she leads me through the town, towards the stables, I am guessing. We turn a corner, where I can see six large horses and a human scrubbing them with a brush.

'Hello, Amin, we are in need of horses, but you guessed that right?' Diana beams at him and Amin smiles back, bowing to her.

'Of course, Diana. I'm afraid they are rather expensive, but my lord can surely pay?' Amin looks round at me with a golden glint in his eye.

'Go see the elders, they will pay of course,' Diana suggests to him.

'Hmm, I suppose, will he fit on one?' he asks.

'No, I can move as quickly as any horse, one will be required for Diana alone.' I say. We look at the horses, some too weak for the journey but a few are in great condition.

'Pick your horse, these three all look in good condition.' I say

Diana lets go of my hand and begins to inspect the horses. She touches them with grace, and I smile at her. She chooses one and makes it ready for travel.

I help Diana onto the horse and we march up the street. The three of us march up the streets, Amin leading the way. We trot along the cobbles, to the main hall. Amin disappears inside and returns in a flash with a huge smile on his face.

'They pay Diana, I will feed my family well tonight!' Amin counts his gold and runs back down the street in glee.

Diana whips the reigns and gallops off towards the outskirts of town. I start to chase her. I catch her and run alongside, both of us full of joy, laughing at our speedy exit. We escape for the road out of town. When we reach it, she slows to a walk.

'This is a fine horse indeed,' Di strokes its black mane, 'I couldn't walk all the way.' she says to me.

We can clearly see the remnants of my keep now, I had not thought to look to it before now.

'That place has brought a lot of pain for everyone, I curse the day I built it now. But all my possessions stolen I feel slightly aggrieved.' I say.

'True, many went and destroyed the place. But you don't need material things, Ariel, especially not a dark place such as that was,' she smiles and winks at me, 'now, let's get this show on the road, there's a lot of ground to cover before dark.' Diana is above my head height. 'It's nice to look down on you, for once.' She chuckles and so do I, and we continue our travels.

The way is long, she is right. I do not know where we are headed; it has been a long time since I travelled far south of my fiefdom. I have not been to the bridge again, and this sends me into a panic. I cannot believe I am going back through that place, where so many were left in the sun to rot, and it was my fault. I did that, and it hurts me to know I've done it twice. All those souls lost, and only I could have taken them. Luckily, it is no more, I say to myself, no more killing only bright, light healing. Diana cannot know of how many souls I took, willingly.

'We will pass the battlefield, you know that? Are you okay with that? I know it must pain you, Ariel,' Diana says like she is reading my thoughts.

'I know, I have just been thinking about it,' I reply.

'I can see it on your face. I am sorry you had to do that. Come, hold my hand and we will get through it together. Just talk to me if you are feeling scared.'

I am glad she said that. I could not conceive of being alone with this right now. The pain is intense as we draw nearer. I dread it, but power on with my steps. At least I can lift my head now. I feel shame, but know that at least Diana believes in me.

'We are here? I am only guessing by your look.' Diana pulls me close to the horse.

'Yes, I stood up on that ridge and reigned down death. It was not me, I promise Di. I am that demon no more.' I tighten my grip of her and she reciprocates.

'You did what you had to. I am still hopeful we can implore the king not to do the same again.' Diana smiles down upon me and I shrug.

'Who knows, but we must try to make him see that we are of no threat, and will disappear shortly,' I say, looking up to the ridge.

I breathe a relieving burst of air as we pass it. There are still a few bodies in the field, and it crushes my heart. There are still vines clinging to the swordsmen at the bottom of the hill, and a few town's folk are in the field trying to pry them free for burial. They struggle to move the rotting corpses, and I nearly vomit. But, I think to myself, what could I have done differently? Did they not come to kill me and those I profess to love? The sword I carry becomes heavy and I wish to let her loose. Yes, they came for me and found their deaths, but who am I to place blame? Is it not the gods' place alone? Or do the gods watch, but not take part, until the end of our lives? Maybe there are some questions to be asked and souls to be accounted for in my afterlife. I feel it grows closer, as we meander through the fields and roads. We continue in silence a while, me lost in thought of my ever-closer death.

Chapter Twenty-Three

For it is said that,

'Many die for what you have,

You must live for them.'

The sky is darkening by the time we reach a village; it is a small hamlet, not one I have ever visited. The humans inhabiting the village do not notice our approach, but as I help Diana from her horse, they start to look round. There is some shouting and people leave the street.

'Do they fear me?' I ask Diana.

'I don't know, they all disappeared rather quickly,' she replies.

'Should we keep going and camp somewhere?' I say nervously.

'No, we need proper beds, Ariel. Come, we will see what is up.' Diana guides me forward.

We find the inn at the edge of the village. It is a broad house, with lanterns on either side of the door and a sign that simply says 'Inn'. Diana opens the door to a room full of humans. Stunned into silence, they stare at me, and it feels like daggers piercing into me. I wish we could go but Diana walks towards the barman.

'Barkeep, we need a room,' Diana simply says.

'Of course my lady,' he bows, 'are you with him?' He nods his head towards me.

'Yes, have you a concern?'

'No, of course not. My lady should not be travelling with the demon, though. He brings death and destruction with him. Did you see the battlefield? You must have passed the stinking corpses. Not that he saved us of course – many died hiding from the king's army. He is a walking bad omen.' He looks right at me now, eyes frozen in hate.

'He no longer is a threat, I promise you.' Diana turns to the crowd. 'Should anyone be in need of healing, come and find us,' she shouts proudly.

The barman nods, and shows us to our accommodation. I try to hide behind Diana, fearful of what I let happen to these humans and the repercussions. They can't hurt me, but maybe Diana is vulnerable here.

As I enter the room, the barman tsks at me, then returns to his job. I make my way to bed and flop facedown upon it.

'I let these people die. I failed.' I mumble through the pillow.

'It's okay, you didn't know. Just be calm and rest, Ariel.' Diana takes a seat beside me on the bed and strokes my back.

There is a sharp knock on the door, and Diana rises and answers.

'May we help you?' she asks, but I cannot see who she talks to.

'Please, the soldiers took my leg. I was running from them and an archer hit me. The leg was poisoned and had to be removed. Is it true he can heal me?' The voice is fearful and shaky.

'He will help you, come in and sit.' Diana creaks the door open further.

I hear the thud of the human walking, and turn to see what I will have to do. She is on crutches, much like the ones I had to use when I was walked to my near death. I don't know if I can restore a whole limb. I look her up and down as I come to a seated position in front of her. I have only ever healed, not regrown. I look to Diana for support and she mouths 'you can do it' and moves behind the woman.

'What is your name?' Diana asks for me.

'Helga. My lord, can you heal me please?' A tear runs down her face.

'I will try, but you must keep still, Helga,' I say.

I put one hand on the remnants of the knee, and she winces, but does not move. The other I take to her forehead. I close my eyes and as she follows me, I find the light within me. I feel it grow inside and slowly let it come to my hands. I can't regrow all that, can I? I must try. I feel the light passing from me to her, and a pain starts to grow inside me. So, I am healing something at least, I think to myself as the spiky feeling grows in my chest. It turns to agony as the light brightens so much that I can see it through my closed lids.

'Keep going, Ariel, it is working!' Diana gleefully says.

I do not reply, and concentrate harder. I shake and feel a great heat in my hands. I hold onto the pain and do not move. I hope it is enough to bring back the limb but I cannot see now. The light shines brighter still, and Helga begins to scream. She tries to move away from the pain, but I grip her head and leg and hold tight. She wrestles with me, shaking and sweating, as I am. Helga reaches out and claws me, dragging her nails into my face. Then she passes out, and I feel her go limp in my hands and hold her upright. I have heard nothing from Diana – I don't know if I have finished or not. The light begins to recede, and I open my eyes as the pain dies down and the heat comes to a halt. Helga is unconscious and Diana has stepped back, with hands over her eyes. I look downwards – the limb is now perfectly formed, even with a foot. It is done, then. I feel a sense of elation and my eyes grow wide.

'I did it, Diana, I did it,' I say in astonishment.

Diana lets her hands fall slowly from her face, and comes to inspect. We both examine my handiwork, and a proud look comes across her. She spreads her arms out wide, and hugs me.

'You did, Ariel. Good job.' Diana grabs my head and plants a big kiss on my forehead.

'Thank you. I never could have done it without you here supporting me,' I say and receive another kiss on the head for my words.

'You are very welcome. I'm not sure what I did, but if I help, that is enough for me.' Diana steps back as Helga starts to wake.

She looks at me, then downwards and touches her leg. She stares in disbelief for quite some time before looking back to me.

'Oh my god! You healed it, and there's no more pain! Oh thank you, truly thank you.' Helga grabs my hands and then my body, hugging me tight.

'Of course, spread the word, any will be helped,' I say.

Helga removes herself from me and starts to cry in floods. It gives me pleasure, I think, to have helped and shown myself my true power. She runs, skipping out of the door and shouting to all the folk in the tavern. Soon, a steady stream of injured and unwell come through the door. None as bad as Helga, which is lucky, as I don't know that I could stand much more pain. They come with all ailments, late into the night. I do not turn any away, even though it is late and I need to rest. Diana sits on the bed next to me, rubbing my back and holding my hand when she could. Finally, the stream becomes a trickle, and the last to come through is the barman, along with a small child that he carries.

'Please sir, my child has a fever. I'm not sure he will survive the night.' He turns to Diana. 'I know what I said, I am sorry. You have helped so many, will you help my son? Don't hold me against him, please.' He looks down to the floor in an agony I have not yet witnessed.

'I will help the child, it is what I am here for.' I raise my hand and the barman advances, letting me hold the small head.

I feel the darkness and pain, and the son wakes and starts to scream. The light flickers inside me and I remove the heat and illness, quite easily now I have had the practice. The child quietens down into sleep. I open my eyes and look at the barman once more.

'It is done, your son will survive the night.' I smile.

The barman looks at his sleeping baby and laughs through his tears.

'Thank you, sir, many will hear of what you have done this evening. Any traveller who comes my way will know of your good deeds, I promise.' He bows to me then, stroking his child's face, leaves the room.

I breathe in deeply and feel completely drained. I can feel my blood pumping through my body with increasing pressure. Diana holds me close, and I know she is proud. That is all that matters to me, but how will I protect her? How can I save her against the king when all I can do is heal humans now?

'I can't protect you, Di,' I say quietly.

'I will protect us both, don't you worry anymore my Ariel,' she whispers in my ear.

I turn to look her in the face. 'How? We are going to our deaths, you must know that.'

'Of course I know, but I have a secret I have hidden until now. When I was a little girl, the witches taught me a meagre amount of magic. I have been practising over the years, and I will protect us even when you can't, my dearest.' She pulls me in tight to her.

'You know magic?' I am baffled. 'Why did you not tell me?'

Diana looks lost in thought for a few moments. 'I did not believe in myself until now, until I saw your healing powers. You must hold onto them. I will deal great damage and you will get us out of there, should it be necessary.' She strokes my hair.

'Thank you, Diana, you mean the world to me, you know?' I say into her eyes.

'I know I do, and you mean a lot to me too. We are meant to be together through this, we will look after each other through all the chaos and storms to come.' She tilts her head forward, now forehead to forehead. 'So, just keep on doing you, and I will keep us from harm.'

I smile and try to round my head with this new information. She could be powerful, and I could teach her so much more.

'I will teach you on our travels then, anything you need, I am here. Remember that, please,' I say, hoping she will be able to handle the magic knowledge I can pass on.

'Okay Ariel, I will be your student for a while.' She sticks her tongue out at me.

I chuckle and brush her cheek. I feel so close to her now, alone together in this place, a long way from home, wherever that may be. I lean in close to her. I don't know where I am going or what is about to happen. My blood rushes to my head and I face her now, all vulnerable and curious.

'Can we do this, Ariel? Will it work between us? I won't give my heart completely unless you are sure,' she whispers.

I signal my agreement. 'I am sure, Diana, I have never felt love before and I think that is what I feel now, in here.' I take her hand to my chest so she can finally feel my heart racing for her.

A tear rolls down her cheek. 'Okay, then let's do it properly and find a priest when we return, yes?' she asks me. I accede to this, with all it means.

She leans in, I turn my head and we finally kiss. I have been waiting for this all my life, I know that now. I let her take my face in her hands and we stay here for some time. I never want to let go, but she finishes the kiss and backs slightly away and blushes.

'Good kiss. Was it your first?' She looks hopefully at me.

'Yes. I have never felt for anyone the way that I do you,' I say with all my heart.

'Then come rest with me. Put your arms around me and hold me tight. I never want you to let go.'

'I never will Di, I never will.' I say noticing I am crying now.

We lay back on the bed and I curl round her. I worry I am too large, too ugly for her to stay forever. I shake these thoughts out of my being. I settle into sleep, breathing in her scent and my face deep in her hair. I feel in the perfect place, but I also feel myself drifting. I don't want to rest, I want to stay with her and be here and now, present and aware. It can't be controlled though, and I crash.

I awake suddenly, without Diana in my arms, I quickly look round the room, startled.

'Don't worry, I am still here. I am just taking advantage of the break and brushing my hair.' She smiles at me. 'My Ariel, did you sleep well? I hope so, we have to get moving south today.' She glances downwards.

'What's wrong?' I ask, afraid of the answer. Maybe she regrets last night?

'Nothing, we just have to go and I don't want to,' she whispers.

I let out a relieved breath I had been holding it without knowing. I am glad she is not running away. I really thought she might.

'Okay, I will get up then. Can I teach you some of my magic as we go down the road?' I ask.

'Of course, we need all the help we can get, I think,' she says wistfully and sighs, tugging at her hair. 'This hair, Ariel can you help?' Diana holds out the brush.

I rise from bed and go to her. She turns away and I start to brush. I feel very nervous all of a sudden, as I get close to her again. She giggles and we both starts laughing at my ineptitude.

'Have you ever done this before?' she asks brightly, and helps my hands through her hair. 'My Ariel, you are doing fine, just relax please.'

My body feels shattered and completely overwhelmed. 'Okay Di, I am trying to relax, it's just very hard with you.'

'I bet it is, but that is okay.' She turns her head towards me. 'Kiss me again and know I love you too.'

I breathe in sharply, then quickly move in for another kiss. It is much shorter than last night's, but still lovely. I take my hand and hold her face now, but she pulls away, same as last night and pats my cheek lightly.

'I think that will have to do, now, shall we travel?' Diana smiles at me with bright eyes.

'Yes, okay, let's go.' I am a little deflated at the thought of our mission.

Chapter Twenty-Four

Do not despair friend,

I am always your servant,

To guide and to love.

As we walk to the door, my legs feel heavy; they do not want to leave either. However, it is time, we have a lot of ground to cover before the sun sets again. We leave the inn to a cheer from the barman.

'Have fun last night, after we left?' He winks at me.

I nod happily and Diana pulls me away, laughing. We make our way out to the horse, which has been fed and watered since we last saw it. I help Diana on and we march towards the edge of the village. I have much to teach her if we are to survive this ordeal. I am pleased that she has the gift too. It feels like we are more connected. I skip along the road, happy that we are moving forward together. Fern will be so pleased as well! She will obviously take credit for bringing Di and I together. I chuckle to myself.

'What's so funny?' Diana looks down on me.

'I bet Fern will be elated,' I say.

'What is it with you two? How do you know each other?'

I tell her the story of us, and how she is like my daughter, how I feel protective of her and she over me. That we are kindred spirits and her paintings helped keep me from going mad.

'That's beautiful, Ariel, I hope she is okay.' Diana looks backwards for a second, nervously.

'I hope so too, I can't imagine a world without either of you,' I say. 'Okay, I have a few tricks for you to learn if you like?'

'Let's do it!' she says with glee, 'I am looking forward to practising.'

We walk out of the village first, then I show her some simple spells to hurt people.

'We can only use these in dire circumstances, Diana.' I look at her seriously.

'Yes, only if the king tries to kill us, of course.' She puts a finger to her mouth, then reaches down and strokes my cheek, it soothes me greatly.

'It is best to remember that fire is your best friend, but she may burn you in kind.' I show Diana how to start a flame.

She begins to cup her hands and blows into her palms. The kindling flame bursts into life, and she sends a fireball of impressive size down the road. It explodes harmlessly a few lengths in front of us. We laugh and I hold her hand, proud of my Diana. I also show her how to create ice balls, which she manages without effort; a true witch.

'Here, this is how you make bolts if a ball is too big for the room.' I pull back one arm and fling a bolt into the air which explodes in a smaller, more direct manner, up the road.

'Excellent, let me try.' Diana concentrates, then copies my movement exactly.

The bolt comes to life in her hands, and she flings it further than mine. I am extremely impressed, but stop the lessons as dark magic pains me now. Diana sees my weary look and holds my hand tighter; she does not ask for more from me.

'So, this magic hurts you now? I can see how tired you get. I hope you are okay, my Ariel,' she says sorrowfully.

'I am okay, thank you, Di. It does take a lot from me now. Pain comes along with any magic, healing for example – it is an agony deep in my bones. I don't know why. Does it hurt you?' I ask, knowing I am probably the only one.

'I suppose I feel the heat, but no pain. It must be hard for you; I saw you sweating with the woman, Helga. You were brave.' She smiles down at me and puts her hand to my shoulder. 'I think that is enough for now. I hope one day you can teach me light magic.' Diana looks at me, I smile to hear that.

Two healers would be great. Us travelling the world, healing, instead of destroying. Destructive magic holds no use to me now, but Diana has an aptitude for it. Between us, we could actually survive an assault. The next village is now in sight, and we take off from the road to find some well-deserved rest. Here the villagers do not run, but greet us with cheers. I stand tall and proud, and wave to the gathering. Never have I had such a reception to my presence, and at last I am happy that we have had a positive impact on humans.

A little boy approaches us. 'Please, will you help my papa?' he says, pointing to a little house at the edge of town.

So they have heard of our deeds. I accede to his request. Good, I think, I am pleased to help and guide Diana's horse to the house. I help her dismount, and we enter. The boy takes us through the small abode to a back room, and on the bed lies a man bandaged from head to foot. Bloodied and dying. I can tell this will be painful for us both. I move towards him, but Diana grabs my hand and shakes her head.

'He is dying – that looks too much for even you. I can't stand the thought of you hurting yourself,' she whispers to me.

'I have to try, I've never seen it this bad,' I say and turn away.

I walk to the man, with Diana in tow. He wheezes and coughs some blood up. Dying indeed, and I think I will fail, but I must try – it is all I have left to give. I squeeze the man's hand, letting go of Diana.

'I can't promise you will survive. Do you want me to try?' I say solemnly.

He nods through dark eyes; he is nearly at the other side, I must work quickly. The boy comes forward and I take out a hand to back him off, and he hides behind Diana. Once again, I put my hand on the man's head, the other to the abdomen, where he bleeds worst. The man groans as I press down on him, then let the light start to grow. It passes through my hands and onto the man. He is in great pain and begins to shake already. I hold tight; I must break through this in order to heal. I let the magic do its work, feeling the pain in my chest grow also. The man sighs deeply and then starts to shake uncontrollably. I try to hold onto him it is too much; I need to remove my hands, but they are glued by light to him. He throws up a lot of blood, and then passes into the next world. I have failed, and the light retreats from his body. I shake my head to Diana. I am weary now, having lost the man. The boy is behind Diana, and he begins to step backwards.

'I am sorry,' I say, 'there is no life in him now.'

The boy turns and runs as I stand. Diana grabs me and hugs me tight as I cry for the passing of the man's soul. Suddenly, we can hear a clamouring outside, and we depart the room to investigate. The boy is shouting and runs when we appear at the door.

'Murderer!' a shout comes out.

'He took his soul, I told you!' screams another.

I step forward and try to hush the crowd.

'I tried to save him, but could not. I am sorry,' I say in a quiet tone, too quiet.

The crowd jeers and moves forward in a wave. Diana steps in front of me, pulling a bolt out of fire.

'Get back! Or you will burn!' she screams to the humans.

The wave dissipates, and some of the humans run for cover. Diana jumps on her horse quickly and motions that it is time to leave. I walk forward to her and what is left of the human crowd starts to move forward. I growl deeply like I may attack, and they part.

'Let's go! Now!' Diana shouts at me and we gallop to make a quick exit out of the village.

Once we are free of the humans, we slow to a walk and trot. I am breathless and still hurting; how quickly humans can turn when they feel attacked. I shake my head – it is too much to be their saviour. Now whoever else was hurting in that village will go without and may die. All because I couldn't save the man, inches from death. At least he is now at peace, unlike the rest of us, it would seem. My eyes are streaming, and I only notice now. I wipe the tears and sniff. Diana swings out on the horse and hugs my head with both arms. We move like this for some time, in silence and me with a hand on the horse, letting all the despair and sadness out. It is a great mourning I feel for the man and his child. Surely the man must have known I was his last chance at life; he said yes, after all, to my attempted help. Once my eyes are dry, Diana swerves back onto the horse and sits tall, looking out into the distance.

'I am sorry, Diana, I couldn't save him. He was already in death's embrace,' I say quietly.

'I know. It's not your fault,' she says without looking at me.

'Are you angry with me?'

'No, I am angry with them.' She tilts her head backwards towards the village.

'Oh, I see. I am used to the malice and anger of humans, it is not abnormal to me. I can see their point. It looked to the boy as if I killed his father, and I kind of did,' I say.

'No, he was dying! You tried your best, they should understand that!' She becomes red-faced and clenches her fists. 'You are good and light now, I hate that you go through so much pain just to be hated in return.'

I look to the sky and hope the man has reached his resting place. We move in silence once more. I can see she is still seething, and let her be in her mind until a calmness has approached.

'It's just not fair,' she says, unclenching her fists, 'I wish it had gone differently is all.'

I hold her open palm, letting my peace wash over her too. I hope she feels it and knows we are not alone, but a team.

'Thank you for saving us back there,' I finally say, 'could have gone a lot worse.'

Diana looks at me and smiles. 'That is true, I suppose. Come let us walk together, I am afraid it is not far to our meeting place now. The border approaches.' She points off to the distance.

'Yes, I know this place, we will soon pass the bridge . . .' I trail off before I start to unwind and cry again.

'What happened there?' She looks down on me quizzically.

I tell her the story of the first humans to arrive on the island, how they eventually drove my kin away and that I stayed to protect my land. It was mine, but is no longer I suppose, and I am glad inside to let it go. The land has only caused me trouble after all. Now, without the forest, I don't see a reason to stay.

'I cannot wait to leave this island, Di, we must depart at once when we return to Fern – promise me we will all go,' I say.

'I promise we will go together, we are all three of us bound now. I love you, I don't know where it came from, but it is here to stay. You are my first real love you know?' She beams at me.

The light in her eyes gives me hope. Hope that we can conquer this mission and extricate ourselves, then we will be free. That is the only thing that will bring me peace, I know that. First though, as we approach the bridge, I must face my fear. The bridge is not as I remember it. They have improved it, I see. Barely recognisable from the one I built and killed so many on. You could fool yourself that was another place. Flowers and meadows cover this land; it is a peaceful place, and I make a decision.

'Can we stop here for the night? Darkness approaches,' I say.

'Oh, you're so dramatic. Let's rest here, yes. Then tomorrow we will find our way out of your land.' Diana rolls her eyes at me and chuckles.

I suppose I am. But this is a grave place for me. I don't want to relive it with her; that was a darker me. Light only shines from me now and I must embrace that. I help her off the horse and we lie under the stars together. In this season, she will not feel cold, and I am grateful for that. I look up at the night sky – so beautiful. I cannot count the stars, so many sparkle so brightly. Like me now, light pours from them, and I smile.

I awake first this time, just as the sun is peeping over the horizon. I lean over to watch Diana as she slumbers – no star can compare.

'Diana?' I whisper and she peeks an eye open, beaming.

'Not the most comfortable bed, Ariel.' She yawns and rubs her eyes. 'Time for a wash since we are meeting a king today.'

I follow her down to the water's edge. It is refreshing and it pleases me to wash in a blue water, rather than the red it was on that night. I look at my fingers, and I see flashes of crimson – this can't be right. I stand and back away, staring at both hands in disbelief. I shake the last of it off and brush my hands through my hair, before collapsing on the ground in a dizzy haze. I do not see Diana approach, but hear steps running towards me, and I lash my hands out in a frenzy, scared I am under attack again.

'No! You can't take me!' I scream to the heavens.

'Ariel! Stop! Let me help you!' Diana's voice pierces through the clouded mess of my mind.

I let my arms go limp and suck the air in quickly and with force, sitting bolt upright. I open bleary eyes and can see a figure standing over me. I hope it is either Diana or death; either will allow me to rest and relax. The figure disappears then returns, pouring liquid all over me. So, not death after all. The water steams off me. I awake from the nightmare into the normal world. It is a shock, and I scrape about for a hand to help me. I find one, and the figure speaks to me, but I can't quite hear anymore. They grab me by my waist. I feel it, it is warm and kind, so I wrap one arm around it and breathe out. I shake my head and objects begin to focus in the distance. Then, my eyes move downwards and it is Diana's locks I see first. Relief spills over me; no death today, nor any enemies.

'Diana?' I finally say, my hearing returned.

Diana lets me go; she is very red. 'My Ariel, what happened?'

I hit myself on the head. 'I have no idea. The water turned red, like it did that night. Then everything was a blur.'

'You are sweating! Oh my gods, are you sure you are okay? Maybe we should rest today and meet the king tomorrow,' she says, head hung low.

I gather my strength and stand, and I feel okay now, I hope, though so hot. I walk to the river and let the water envelop me. I swirl and move around in it, letting all the heat escape. I raise my head out and look back to where I came from. Diana is watching, sitting peacefully on the grass. I sweep the hair from my face and beam at her.

'I think I'm okay, let's go today and get it done with!' I call to her.

I pull myself out of the swirling water and crawl up to land. My hands still shake a little, but it is hardly noticeable. We will find the king today. A daunting prospect, but the challenge has to be met. I heave myself to where Diana sits and plonk myself down beside her.

'Better? I'm worried.' Diana looks at my face.

'Yes, and I am sure today is the right time. Sorry about that, it's this place is all,' I say and lower my head.

'Okay, if you're sure, and don't be sorry. You are a ridiculous man, sometimes, it's not your fault.' She rubs my back.

I stand and pull Diana to her feet. We must still have a lot of ground to cover before reaching the town, so I help her to the horse and we make our way across the stone bridge. It feels sturdy, much better than the one I created. Once we have parted ways with the bridge I feel much better, stronger and a bit embarrassed that I made a fool of myself back there. No matter, Diana cares for me is all. It is still early in the morning, plenty of time to reach the town before nightfall.

'How far are we to go?' I ask.

'To the border then east. It is not far after that.'

We ride into midday, reaching the border of my land, and she stops at a fork in the road. I am nervous now, out of my land and onto foreign soils. Each step is a breaking of the truce that we made so long ago. I shiver. Surely it will be okay, though. We have been invited after all, and we will make another pact, then I can disappear without war.

We take the left fork, and move east. Diana begins to trot in front of me as a black image appears on the horizon.

'There. That's the fortress town. Let's see what they're up to.' Diana keeps up the pace.

'Fortress? How will we escape it?' I become fidgety.

'There is only a small castle, I am sure we will find a way.' Diana sighs and looks back to me. 'We will be okay.'

Chapter Twenty-Five

Hate the feeling of,

Loss of power and control,

Help me stand up friend.

We meander to the gates. A wooden barricade stands all around the buildings, probably to keep me out. It wouldn't hold an older version of myself, but this could be where I have my last meal and breath. I hold my head up as the metal gates swing open, pulled by soldiers. We walk cautiously now, and Diana gets off her horse and ties it up by the now-opened gates. We are met by a man in robes of black, what I should really be wearing, I chuckle to myself in my red and purple garments.

'Welcome, you found your way here, then. Come with me, the king has also arrived,' he says and turns around to walk up the street.

It is not at all like my town. More dirty and it does not appear that the people of this town clean it. The houses are more like hovels, broken in places without repair. Fires burn bright on every corner, with a soldier standing next to each lit torch. They carry long poleaxes, and are heavily armoured. There are no normal people that I can see, and this worries me. Where are they? Where is the market?

As we pass out of the town, and into the castle grounds, the feeling changes. Through a second set of gates, opened by soldiers again, the houses become large and perfectly formed. Banners fill the streets – a welcome for me? I laugh – they are for the king, I am sure. The castle is now a few paces away. It is not as large as I imagined; a fortress should be huge, surely? Like my old keep. But this one has no turrets, and it is only a square building, I could have mistaken it for another home, were we not heading right for it.

'Please, enter.' The man has stopped and bows with a smirk on his face.

I draw in my breath, ready with clenched fist, but Diana grabs my hand.

'Ariel, let us meet the king,' she says to me, and walks past the man.

On entering the castle, it is clear that outside appearances deceive. The lush pool in the middle of the hall, the banners of red and gold, and the people who stare, all look bright and fresh. The carvings on the wall are spectacular, and beautiful sculptures of women and men line the way forward. The paintings would impress Fern I am sure. Many are large and show nature in all its glory. I shake my head; it is not what I expected from the humans here.

'Wow. Glorious,' I say out loud.

Diana nearly laughs, and takes my hand again. She pulls me forward to a group who stares intently at us.

'Where is the king?' she asks the first man she sees.

'Right this way. You must be the Demon Lord,' he says to me. 'I can see they were right when they called you a monster,' he says carefully and begins to walk us up some stone steps.

'I am Ariel, a lord no longer,' I say as we climb.

'Of course, you are just the king's subject now.' He does not look back.

'We kneel for no king,' Diana says, and looks round to me and smiles.

As we climb, I can see more paintings of men this time, dressed in strange clothes and carrying weapons of death. So, this is how the humans see each other; masters of the realm. I know better; I am the only master of nature, the original master. But I will keep this to myself – after all, this is a diplomatic mission. Words will carry us through the day, not war. I hope that the king feels the same, but he is a boy, I have been told. Will youth win over age today? I do not know; sometimes the young can be threatened easily and either run or fight. With something to prove, this king may turn towards fighting. Diana is slightly breathless as we reach the top of the stairs.

'Well, that was quite a climb,' she says to me. 'Will the king arrive to greet us soon?' she asks the man.

'I do not know. You will wait in here for his majesty.' The man points to a door.

I am afraid now; I feel trapped, like we are walking into an ambush. But onward we continue. Diana opens the door, and we are welcomed by a large group of men. They sit at a long, heavy table and are chatting with one another. All heads turn, and scowls begin, aswell as much chatter between them. I bow my head as I walk through the doorway fully. I scout the room with my eyes, working out a plan to escape as soon as possible. I gather my strength and cough to clear my throat, hopefully my voice conveys my power.

'Hello there! We have travelled many miles to meet your king. Could we perchance have some food and water?' I say, with a little force in my voice.

A heavy man rises from his seat, near the end of the table. 'Good morn to you both, of course, there is plenty here.' He motions for the water, bread and meats to be brought to us.

'Thank you,' Diana says and takes a big glug of water then passes it to me. 'Where is your king, may I ask?'

The standing man bows. 'He will be along shortly. I am Vince, and these fine men are the emissaries of the realm. Gathered here as a sign of good faith, to negotiate the terms.'

Diana bows in return. 'That is a most welcome idea, and the terms are quite simple. Leave us alone. Now, what else do you have?'

There is a silence that washes over the men, and I see more than one turn pale. The silence is broken and the men start to shout to one another.

'And who are you? The negotiation is with him alone.' Vince points to me.

'The negotiation, as you call it, is between Ariel and the town's people. I am here to represent them, my name is Diana.' She bows once more, then stands up straight and tall.

'We can't talk with a woman! Get her out of here, Vince, she will only cause trouble,' one shouts over the men.

I step forward – it is time. I raise my hand, and silence comes again. I can see the fear in their eyes.

'Diana is my escort and will talk with you, whether you like it or not. She is here to stay, and *our* terms are as she described.' I calmly enunciate each word.

The men look at each other in disbelief. 'These are your only terms, Lord?' Vince asks.

'Indeed. I only wish to be left alone, as set out in the deal made so long ago. Before any here were born, the deal was to leave me and I would leave you,' I say, carefully.

The men look to one another again. Diana holds my hand and rubs my palm. It is the truth, and they know it. I feel a little stronger now, and lean onto the table.

'You all know the deal. I have destroyed one of your armies. How much more death do you require?' I ask Vince, staring him back down into his seat.

'A new deal must be made!' one calls to Vince.

Vince holds up his hand, and the men hush. 'A new deal must be brokered, my lord. The one you made aeons ago does not hold any longer,' he says calmly.

I am quizzical; I don't know why the men are so against the old deal. It worked for a long time. They must know something I do not, or are just bearing down and trying to cause me to fear them. It won't work, as I fear them no longer.

'Then we must wait for your king. Where might he be?' I say.

'He will be along soon, firstly we wanted to talk of our terms.' Vince smiles slightly.

'Your terms? What could they possibly be?' I ask.

'We hear you are a demon of the forest. Return there and do not come back. The town's people will be dealt with in accordance with our laws. Too many have escaped justice by your hand. We are prepared for war, but let it not come to that. We believe you are weak, my lord, and can't possibly defy your king any longer,' Vince states with a straight face.

I feel a rage growing, but know he is correct in a sense. I cannot fight them off anymore. It would be suicide to battle all their armies in my current healer state. I must make them believe, once more, that I am a force to be reckoned with.

'How dare you question me! I have ruled my land, on my own, for generations. This king says I am weak, but not so long ago you all lost an army to me. I think we should focus on diplomacy rather than threat, or you all may regret not taking me seriously,' I say through gritted teeth.

'Is he right, Emissary Vince? He could kill us where we sit?' The man closest to me asks, and I can see perspiration dripping down his face.

'No, our spies tell us you are lying, sir. Nature has forsaken you, and your forest has burned. Lie in your destruction, and let the rule of law take its course. There will be no gaping holes in the ground, nor vines to strangle our soldiers, will there?' Vince smiles cruelly.

There are spies in my lands? Who could do such a thing for gold? I would, and have, gladly shared my wealth. Maybe it's those damned traders. Or someone who wishes a knife in my back. Nevertheless, I must try, for all our sakes.

'I am the law in my lands. It is true that nature took a turn from me, but that is resolved, let me tell you.' I flick the sword's hilt. 'She is with me even now, and the sword glows for blood.' I slightly unsheathe the weapon, and she shines a bright green.

They gasp and start to murmur at each other. 'You never told us he reconciled! He is as strong as ever!'

'Now, calm down! He is simply lying, to save his own skin,' Vince reassures his comrades.

Diana comes to my side, laughing. 'You old fools! Of course he still has his powers! I have seen them for myself, and you are all in grave danger should you not accept the terms.' She can still be heard over all the clamouring.

'Why would we ever believe you, witch, I am guessing? Witches are famous for their lies and trickery. We have nothing to fear, I promise you.' Vince hushes them.

'Well, you can't say I didn't try to save your lives.' Diana's response causes an uproar.

They point their fingers and shout 'witch!' and 'liar!' I turn to Diana.

'What is the plan?' I whisper to her.

'Fear,' she replies.

I bang my fists on the table, which shakes them in their shoes. I can stand this no longer.

'Bring us the king! This negotiation is over until the boy arrives,' I say to the room.

'As you wish, my lord. He is no boy, but a man chosen by the gods to save us from your darkness. But, yes I think it appropriate now for our king to join us.' Vince swings his head round to one of the servants, who hurriedly disappears.

I look down to the floor, unable to conceive of what I should do next. Suddenly, two soldiers appear from nowhere, making me look up at the chair at the end of the table. It's closer to a throne really, and I start to notice its detail. Lions are carved on either side of the dark mahogany wood. The back panel shows some sort of battle scene. It does stick out from the rest, and I can't help but stare.

A hush comes over the men, none brave enough to speak now. Following more soldiers, out of a doorway at the corner of the room, come two trumpeters. They raise their instruments high, and begin to play. Not the best I have ever heard, but regal in some way nonetheless. More soldiers pour from the opening and then some beautifully dressed people, all in shades of purple. Last to arrive is a boy; he is small and thin, almost gaunt. He strides with confidence though and takes his place in the throne without batting an eyelid towards me or Diana.

'Who is the woman?' he says harshly, and I can tell this meeting will be a difficult one.

'Diana.' I look him in the eye. 'Who are you?' I say loudly.

'I am your king! You will address me as such, demon,' he scoffs and puts a hand to his cheek. 'Take the woman away.'

A soldier beside him marches down the table, but is only met by my grasp around his throat. I lift him, even though he is fully armoured, into the air. I let him hang a little before throwing him back to where he came from.

'I am here to speak for the town's people. We are not going anywhere.' Diana spits the words out to the table.

'Stand down soldiers. I am King Richard the Eighth, and you may both address me as your honour, your majesty, et cetera. Understand, mutant?' Richard smiles deviously.

'I understand. I am Ariel, Richard.' I smile back.

I know he was trying to goad me into showing my cards, but instead he shows his by slamming his hands on the table in anger. He then regains his composure, coughs and raises an arm. I hear a clattering of metal and look up to the gallery above that had escaped my attention. Crossbowmen. More than I can count appear, with triggers at the ready. They take aim at both myself and Diana, and I tilt my head for her to move behind me. She stands strong and shakes her head slightly. I turn back to my enemy, who is cackling, arms wrapped around himself in laughter. Vince puts out a hand to calm him but is stopped by another soldier.

'Your majesty,' Vince begins, 'we must strike a new deal.'

Richard stops his belly laughing and sits up in his chair. 'Plenty of time for that, Vince. Firstly, tell me, how did you defeat my father's army, Ariel? I simply must know. I heard it was quite a show of power.'

'If you remove your archers, I will tell you all,' I reply.

'Now, why would I do that? They are only here for my protection, don't mind them. They will not harm you unless I give the order.' Richard looks up at the crossbowmen and smiles. 'Do they frighten you? I was hoping they would be great for dramatic effect.' He opens his hands.

'It is quite simple to defeat an army. With a wave of my arm, the men will be struck down,' I say gravely, hoping he will not see through my charade.

He stares at me curiously and in silence for quite some time. The boy has seen maybe fourteen or fifteen summers, too young for this game. But he is a dangerous opponent nonetheless, with a lot of power, so I must tread carefully. I do not know what magic I have to keep us from harm. I lean back and sigh, look at Diana, and then turn back to my enemy. He tries to sit tall and powerful. But there is a hint of his age, and he tries too hard. I may be able to overpower him, metaphorically, soon. First, I must see what kind of deal they have for me, and try a diplomatic solution. If not, there may be no hope if he becomes hot-tempered. Diana and I will have to prove that we, too, are strong. I lightly lean back on the table, my fists clenched. After all this silence I become weary and shake my head.

'Boring you, are we?' Richard finally speaks.

'Not at all, just waiting for your deal to be brought to the table,' I reply.

'Fine. I will lay my cards on the table, then you will do the same. You are weak. I know this because I have spies in your home. Yes, you should be shocked. Some need the gold that you have kept from them. You no longer have nature's favour. Whatever magic you produced to kill my men, you no longer have!' Richard pushes himself up to standing and points a finger at me. 'You are a liar! You will die let me assure you. First though, you should know my soldiers will have reached your pitiful town and burned all within by now.' Richard laughs and holds up a hand, and the crossbowmen aim.

'We are leaving the island! Let us go in peace and none have to be hurt today!' Diana calls out to the table.

They snigger in disbelief, thinking they have won over us. It may be true though, and if he does have spies, this is extremely bad for us. Who would turn from the town? What could they possibly get out of it? I have given my keep freely with all its gold enclosed. This is a sad day.

'It is true, we are leaving. So I beg of you, see sense and let us go in peace.' I hold out my hands, palms upwards.

'Peace? After all this, you come to ask for peace? I should have my archers kill you both now. But I think time in the dungeon and some torture is in order.' Richard smiles evilly.

'We leave now,' I say, 'you cannot stop us. I have made peace with nature and regained her power. Your spies and soldiers are useless.'

I turn to Diana, hiding the tears in my eyes from the king. This is my final card to play; we never should have come, but we had to try.

Chapter Twenty-Six

Nature burned inside,

But it will rise again to,

Help you on your way.

'I am sorry, Diana,' I say, and close my eyes.

'Don't be,' is the reply and she takes my hands.

I hear the whooshing sound of a bolt first. I block Diana and feel the bolt break my skin, and I cry out in pain. Diana holds me close now, as we prepare for our deaths. I whimper and fall to my knees; the bolt has pierced deep. I cannot breathe properly and wheeze out some air.

'Who did that? I am the one to kill them!' Richard makes a strange huffing sound. 'Well, it is too late now. Fire at will,' he says apathetically.

The whole gallery fills with the sound of fingers pulling triggers. I curl my back and pray for the power to save Diana. I feel the light burst forth, blinding the company. The bolts hit something, and fall harmlessly to the floor. I look up to see that the light has created a bubble of safety; time to leave. I rise and try to pull Diana from the table.

'You die first!' she screams and thumps her hands on the table. The fire spreads so fast from her hands that in that split second, no one can run, catching the diplomats first and possibly the king, I hope.

I pull Diana to my shoulder and run, surging through the door and past the guards. My shoulder takes the weight and I run faster than I thought possible. The gates to the fort are my next barrier, and we move so quickly that the soldiers do not have time to close it. I am a blur as I jump through the town, and round corners towards my goal – the large gates at the town's entrance. I hold my shoulder low and keep Diana on the other, then headfirst I slam into the gates and wood explodes around us. Diana is still firing arrows of fire and ice backwards. The bubble protects us from the worst of the splinters, and I charge towards home.

I must make it back before the soldiers have their day of death. I don't know who in the town is strong enough, perhaps the witches who were able to bind me at my 'trial' not so long ago? I can only hope this is the truth. My legs weaken, and we start to slow. I can see the land clearly, so I lift my head up again and regain the speed. I pump my legs harder as they burn. We reach the boundary to my lands by the second nightfall and I still believe we can make it home before the soldiers tear through the village. As my sight turns to black I continue onwards, but my knees begin to buckle and we slow again. The feet that carried us so far, begin to fail me. I tumble downwards, reaching out a hand to the ground and darkness envelops me.

'Ariel! Wake up! You must wake up, please!' I can barely hear the words but feel myself being rolled onto one side.

'I can't,' I manage to whisper.

'You can! Just open your eyes!' Diana screams at me in a high-pitched, fearful tone that I have not heard before.

I accede and open my eyes. The world before me is a green haze, then a face appears.

'Keep your eyes open, stay with me. The bolt has gone far in. I will get it out, okay? This will hurt,' she says, far too calmly.

I scream as the bolt shifts and I feel the tearing. It explodes out of my shoulder in a last pull. I hear the clattering of the bolt on the ground and Diana pulls me round to my back so that I face upwards.

'Can you hear me, Ariel? It is out. But it has black stuff on it – what does that mean?' she asks.

My head swirls; that is why I fell. A normal bolt should not cause me much trouble. I am a quick healer, especially now with the light inside me.

'Poison,' I say quietly.

'What do we do?' she shouts in my face and shakes my body. 'What do we do, Ariel?'

I have never been poisoned before, and it is a curious feeling. Like I am on this plane, but not. I hold a hand up and see it shimmer in the light, and I smile. Diana bats my hand down.

'Listen to me! What do we do?' she asks again.

'Wait. I will try,' I say in my delirium.

I force the light out, grow it in my belly and breathe it up to my chest and then shoulder. I can barely breathe but I try my hardest. I must survive. For Fern and Diana, if no one else, so I focus as much as I can. I feel the darkness within. Some kind of plant-based poison. I call on nature, pleading for something to come to save me.

Diana jumps backwards suddenly, and I feel movement beneath the ground. I look round with opened eyes, and a vine rises, turns towards my body, and then digs into the hole. I wheeze and cry out, feeling the thick, green, slimy vine push further into me. I trust her though, and push the light to the pain's centre. I try to wriggle away but the vine pushes deeper. I arch my back and Diana's hands come to my head, holding it tight. This comforts me as I feel hot blood pouring out around the slime. Soon I will pass out, I know it, then I will be at peace. I may die, but then that is my wish, I suppose, that I have never lost. I see black, it invades my sight. It is that time again, and I promptly follow the darkness to find that peace.

I cough myself awake, spluttering into life. I sit up and heave in breath deeply. Diana comes to my side and holds my back, steadying me. I am alive. There is no time to celebrate though, and we must return home. I can only hope that at least Fern has escaped. My body shakes with the knowledge that she may have fallen already. I stand up wearily, and take Diana's hand for her to stand with me.

'We must keep going, Fern needs us immediately,' I say.

'Okay, if you are well enough, let us go. I don't know what will have happened by now. Just keep strong and calm.' Diana looks into my eyes.

We hold each other tightly, and I give her a squeeze, then lift her back on my shoulders. They feel as strong as ever, so I begin to run, pumping my legs once more towards home. I cross the bridge without giving it a second thought; there are lives that may be saved. We come across the two hamlets, both burned out husks of their former selves. It frightens me into more action, more haste. Through the night I keep the strain in my legs, running full speed. Day turns to night once more, Diana sleeps restlessly on my back while I continue the charge. In the morning, I can see the smoke from a fair distance away, black plumes rising across the darkened skies. Red light covers the cloud; many have died, it seems. I force myself onwards towards the billowing columns.

As we near the town, Diana bangs on my shoulder and I slow to a standstill. She jumps from me and looks with eyes of agony, at the town. She walks in front, and I follow with my head bowed. I have not saved them from their fate.

'Let's go, Ariel! We can still help the wounded!' she screams, but we both know it is too late.

The battle is over, and all there is left to see is the damage. I have not seen returning soldiers on our run, and this gives me hope. Diana starts to run; I follow at her speed, and can see the tears streaming from her face.

'Father, Father, please be alive,' she whispers audibly to herself.

I am hoping the same for Fern, but as we come over a ridge, we can see the marketplace on fire. From this distance, I can see heads on spikes. I don't think Diana has seen them yet, so I reach out a hand and slow her down.

'Wait, we should slow down, it's safer,' I say and hold her hand as we walk towards our shattered town.

When Diana sees the heads she gasps, and then screams. Leaving me, she runs towards them. I run after her, looking around for some sort of life. Only ghosts remain, I think to myself, and there is an eerie quietness now. Diana holds her hands to her face as she stares up at the heads.

'Who is it? I can't see! Ariel, who is it? Tell me!' she begs.

I lift the spike from the ground with a heave, then bring the head into focus for us both. A man, clean-shaven and young. His black hair is trimmed short.

'Soldiers,' I say and look at her, 'maybe the town's people are somewhere here, and survived.'

Diana nods vigorously, and races away. I know she is headed for her house so I hurriedly rush after her. I can't tell what awaits at every corner we turn. She pelts down the street and bangs through her own door.

'Father? It's Di! Where are you?' There is no answer, only the ghostly whisper of the wind and smoke.

We reverse out of the house, I come to rest beside her as she slouches downward to the ground. I know we must leave, but can't stop myself from mourning with her. There is no one here. Just fire and death roam the streets. I stand beside her and pull Diana to her feet. I can see in her eyes there is no hope left in her. Bodies of both soldiers in armour and town's people litter the street some burning. Diana hunches beside her people and looks for her father but does not find his face.

'We were too late. Oh gods, Ariel, tell me what we do now?' Diana asks.

'The humans have put those heads on spikes to ward off further attacks, therefore, it would seem that they survived the first attack and fled. We should find a boat and continue with our plan,' I say slowly.

'I can't leave till I know they are safe! Can't you see that? You always call us humans, like we are different from you, but we are still real! We can help!' she shouts at me, banging her hands on my chest.

'I know, I really do. But it's not too late for us to survive as well. Di, we must go.' I look downwards at her, and she nods.

'They are okay, I know it,' she says, mainly to herself. 'Fern.' She looks up to me, crying.

'She will be ready with a boat, I feel it,' I say and we walk further into the smoke to the harbour.

Dodging flames, we walk carefully away from crumbling buildings filled with ash. The harbour is small, I remember that, and is made of stone. It should not have burned, and if Fern has hidden out to sea, she will be safe. As we leave the town for a cobbled path that leads down to the sea, I look for boats on the horizon, but nothing appears. A small boat awaits us, however, and I feel my heartbeat race. This could be the boat she was readying! I know it is, I can feel it. Fern is a clever woman – she will have hidden during the attack and come to the boat in the aftermath. There are no words to express the joy I feel . . . nor the dread that occurs shortly after. It is not Fern who appears from the cabin of the boat, it is Agatha. My old friend made it. I feel a short relief, but then she looks me dead in the eye, and shakes her head. It can't be. Agatha waves me forward, and I grab Diana's hand. Before we get to the boat, I fall to my knees in dread. I can't face the news. If I stay here, I will never have to hear the words. If I stay here, I can pretend Fern is painting in the cabin, awaiting our departure. Diana comes to kneel beside me. She looks at me softly and brushes my hair from my eyes.

'Come on, it's okay Ariel. Together, okay?' she says.

Chapter Twenty-Seven

Where are you my friend?
Away like dust on the wind,
In my time of need.

Diana pulls me up to standing and like a hobbled couple, we face Agatha on the boat. She simply hugs me when we reach her. Tightly, she wraps herself round my waist, and I can feel her shaking too.

Through muffled crying, she says, 'I'm so sorry, my boy, I couldn't, I just couldn't save her.'

I begin to tremble uncontrollably, and sob. I fold over Agatha, and hold her. For what seems an age, we stand like this. So it is true. My daughter, my Fern, is gone from this island and the world. She will never paint again, never see the sun and never hold me like this once more. I should have brought her, saved her from this fate. I could have protected her then. I should have found the soldiers and stopped them before any of this occurred! They must have sneaked past, or hidden and watched us pass, gleefully. Agatha pulls away and she looks up at me.

'I have some of her paintings. I got them before the fire took everything,' Agatha whispers, biting her lip.

I nod, helpless with the feeling of bereavement. Diana moves forward and puts a hand on my back. I wipe the tears away, only for more to come.

'Come inside, there is much you should know.' Agatha motions for us to enter the cabin.

I wobble through the door, Diana at my back and Agatha behind. I fall into a seat and start to breathe so fast I may blackout.

'Calm, my Ariel, we are here for you. What happened, Agatha?' Diana asks the old woman.

Agatha takes a seat opposite, and shakes her head.

'The soldiers appeared at night, and many were taken unawares. It was cruel and devious. They set the fires while the people slept. Most burned and died from the smoke, and the rest came to fight. There must have been hundreds of them, killing indiscriminately, children, the old and the infirm. Oh, Ariel, it was nearly a slaughter. The witches saved us, being further into the town. I did my best to stop the soldiers too, as did Fern . . .' Agatha trails off.

'Where is she?' I ask.

'In the heavens, my dear. Her body? I do not know. I saw her fighting. But the soldiers were well armed. As I said, it was only the witches who destroyed them; their magic was enough to rout them and they were chased down. I am sure you noticed the heads coming into town?'

'Where are the humans now? They could come with us,' I say.

'Most have scattered. It's too dangerous here. But I knew you would come. Fern told me of your plan, and I would like to accompany you. Fern had the boat ready to sail.'

I think hard, my mind scattered like the humans. It swirls again like it used to and I feel my head fall into darkness. The deep despair overcomes me; I am helpless against this weight of knowledge. That damned king, I hope he burned for his treachery, he deserved much worse. Had I been stronger, more fatal, powerful, they wouldn't have dared come to my lands and cause such destruction. This is my fault; my plan is a waste now. What have I left? What have I to gain from anything now? There is no point in living with this pain. Even Diana is not enough to save me. But I must keep up pretences for these two that remain, until I can find that peace I deserve. I will be with Fern soon, keeping her safe from the gods. I hope they are kind to one so precious; they must be, or I will let my rage and pain out on them.

'Let's go, Ariel, before more soldiers come. We can fly from here and all the death. I have lost my family too – we are alone together now, aren't we?' Diana tugs on my arm.

I sit up and sigh, then look to Diana and smile bravely. 'Yes my darling, of course we are,' I lie, I will leave her soon too.

Diana smiles back with hope in her eyes. 'Agatha, you can come. Of course we need you,' she says.

'You are a couple? Oh my, Fern told me this was happening but I didn't believe it was real until now. I am so happy you found each other.' Agatha reaches her hands out, still weeping and we hold them.

I shake my head vigorously, then stand, letting go of the humans. I stride out of the cabin and check the boat is indeed ready to sail. I must get them out of here, they have nothing else left. I have my death to ponder over, ready to die as soon as possible, soon as I know they are safe and well enough to handle the rest of their short lives, alone but together. The boat is prepared; Fern was an excellent woman, she had the plan ready. Good girl. I lift the sail to full height and unwrap the lines from the harbour. The boat slowly begins to move out towards the open sea. I breathe in the air, fresh and pure. The wind blows in my face as we make our way further from the island.

They are free at last, no more kings or conquerors. Death is merely a memory for them now. Diana joins me, holding my hand at the wheel as I aim the boat straight out, and as far away as possible.

'Where do we go now?' Diana asks me.

'I don't know, maybe go until we hit land.'

There is a distance in my eyes, I know. Diana kisses me lightly, lets me go, and returns to the cabin. Alone, I feel free and more at ease. I can sort through my thoughts and not be hindered by humans. I feel a pang of regret, because I still love her, I just can't feel for her now. It is too late – I am dead inside, like I was before. A mere husk, that can be set aflame until there is nothing left but ash. I wish that were not only metaphorically true. That I could really burn down to my base elements, and be whisked away on this wind. The boat rocks in the waves. I have never been on the open sea like this, and I find it unnerving yet quite refreshing. Going into the unknown, like my kin before me. Maybe we will find their bones all washed up on a shore, and revel in their deaths. We will all die soon, a blink and we will achieve the goal. No one is here to stop me now. I cannot swim – maybe I should let go and jump now. Perish in the icy waters below. I peek over the side of the boat, desperate to end all this pain. Would the humans be safe? Probably not. I will have to wait, I tell myself.

Agatha peers round from the cabin. She looks at me for some time, without making herself known. I pretend not to see her and gaze out to the horizon, before she disappears. Good. I am in no mood for talk. She will only try to convince me of the other side, that I should live and be happy with Diana. Together, for this time and always. I don't know if my mind can hang on to Di anymore. I wish to see Fern again. She would bend my mind to her will again, to keep herself and Diana safe until their little lives and lights diminish. I am tired, so tired. I wish for no power other than over my own demise. How will I do it though? So far, nothing has worked. I am hung, I burn. I am faced with a thousand bolts and a bubble is created. They try to kill me and I protect myself every time, death fails to take me. Why can't I be more like Fern was? A fighter to the end, even though against the soldiers she stood no hope. My Fern, why did you not hide? I need you now. She could have taken the boat to sea and been alive right now. But she has gone by the wayside, alone. Without her father, her comrade to be there for her.

I settle my mind and move into a meditative state. I will not close my eyes but simply clear my mind of storms. The cloud is back, my old nemesis, I cannot stop thinking. I really should have done more, been powerful. I tilt my head down and sniff, biting my lip hard so as to draw blood. I spit it over the side. The pain is a release from this torture.

Relief seems to be short-lived at the moment. It comes back in waves, this malaise, over me. I have no tears left to cry, no wound could be deeper.

I look up to the sun and the gods. Why? Why do you do this to me? Please speak and tell me the reason so I may go on. Otherwise, I will have to come to find the knowledge. I let the wheel go; it does not matter where we end up. I lift both arms up to the sky and let my rage pour forth. I shriek to the heavens, calling them to action either against or in pity towards me. But there are no voices, no rumbles from up high. I breathe out all the fury, lighting the sky up, I hope, with anger. Still, the water ebbs calmly at the side of the boat, the simple waves lapping against the wood. No rage is felt in return, only calm. Diana rushes out from nowhere, pulling my arms down and grappling with me. I am confused at her frightened expression; I have never seen such a face before.

'Stop, Ariel! Please listen to me! I am here, talk to me.' Her voice quietens as she talks.

I look down upon her, the fear, the anger, the sadness, all make my heart break in two.

'I have nothing left to give, my Diana. Can't you see that?' I growl at her.

'Don't use that tone with me. I am at your side! Not you, nor the gods can stop that now.' She points her finger directly at my face.

I hold the finger, and feel something inside stirring. But the darkness soon envelops me and in my mind I am alone. I let her finger go, and she drops her hands to her sides.

'Whatever you need, we are here.' Her voice and expression return to normal, and she bows her head low, so I cannot see her face. The feeling I had is completely expunged but I still want to grab hold of her now. I put my hands round her waist and pull her close. She in turn wraps herself round me.

'Come now, we'll steer together,' Diana says, nodding to herself and guiding me back to the wheel.

I let one arm drape over her shoulder and control the boat with the other. I feel her warmth on my skin, but it is only flesh, and it decays even now. I do not heed her words. They ring hollow in my ears – there is nothing they can do. They talk a lot, these humans, but there is nothing behind those words. They will crumble in death, into this ocean, and dissolve in the currents. I feel my weight now; heavy in my legs. It wobbles my mind, making me disheartened. I quickly leap from Diana over to the side of the boat, and vomit.

'No sea legs, then? It's okay, my Ariel, you'll feel better soon,' Diana says, coming beside me and stroking my back as I void myself.

'What are sea legs?' I ask, wiping my mouth.

'You'll get them too, when you get used to being at sea,' Diana replies.

Once I am done, Diana helps me back to the wheel. I lull myself back into a meditative state, focusing on the fact that soon I will take my last breath in the world.

'Do you think we are getting close to land?' Diana pipes up and breaks my silence.

'I have no idea,' I shrug, and hope that it is true.

'We have enough water for another week. But hopefully, we'll find somewhere before that.' Diana beams up at me.

I feel the smile and can't help smiling back. It annoys me that she has this effect on me. I should be as stone, impenetrable and unbroken in the light. But cracks are apparent already. The darkness will pour from me soon, if she will not shortly leave. The light of the sun fades, and Diana yawns.

'I think it is time for bed. Will you come with me?' she asks.

'No, I will keep watch, I do not need the rest. You go though, I'll be here in the morning for you,' I reply.

'Okay, if you are sure. Give me a proper kiss goodnight.' She leans towards me.

I feel repulsion, but also the magnetic attraction of her. So, I lean down and kiss her firmly on the lips. She smiles and waves, skipping into the cabin. I regain my composure; after such a kiss I feel my face hot and flushed. I shake it off, and concentrate on the horizon again. There must be land somewhere, I am sure of it. A land pure of other humans, where the animals may free us all from sorrow and become our friends. A full circle, to where I was in the beginning. A fresh start for them, and a burial place for me. I will call on nature for a favour, to put an end to my misery and malaise. Diana and Agatha will be safe there. I will go as willingly as I can muster; she is the only one powerful enough to really take me down. Even though she failed before, this time it will be different. I will not allow my body to hurt her again. She must find a way of piercing through to my soul, plucking it out and sending it onwards. I would like that very much, no pain or turmoil, only peace and lightness to guide me up.

Chapter Twenty-Eight

It bites and hurts you,

Scares flesh and bones alike,

Fear into silence.

I carry on my charade for days and nights. Diana does not suspect. She believes I am happy in my travels, and hopeful too, that we will find a place to escape to. We joke around again by day, and at night I am able to breathe and be solemn in my soul. On the third night, I see a shadow in the corner of my eye. Agatha. The frail old woman comes out of hiding and heads directly for me.

'My dear, you may have fooled her, but me? No. You are thinking of ending it again, aren't you? You must reconsider this path of destruction. Live in peace,' she says quietly to the night.

I stare out to the sea, trying to ignore her, but my eyes flicker downwards and she catches me.

'I can see it, you know. The fear and dread in your eyes. There is no use hiding from it. You must face this and find that life is worth something to you.' Agatha pauses. 'She loves you, she professed it to me down below in the cabin. You love her back, and you may not want to feel it right now, but it cannot be dismissed.'

I let the wheel go. 'Agatha, this has nothing to do with you. Go back to bed and rest, for we may reach land soon and you will need your strength to look after Di once I am gone.' A slow tear trickles down my face.

I wipe it away quickly, like it never happened. *She sees through you*, a voice comes from the back of my mind.

'You can't hide, Ariel. You must face this one day, make the choice. Break her heart so much that she may die too, or live up to her idea of you and tell her what is happening.' Agatha sighs and turns away from me. 'I care a great deal for you, don't let it win.'

As Agatha hobbles and sways back into the cabin, I am left with this thought: what if this is not me? Am I truly lost, or only off course? I spin the wheel, heading for a new more northern route. I don't know why, but it feels right. Like I have been here before, nature must be guiding my thoughts, I hope. The boat groans, but does as it is told and we pick up speed with the wind fully behind us. I feel the breeze on my neck and my hair prickling in the cold. I am ready to find land now.

I look upwards and repeat, 'I am ready to find land now.'

I really hope that worked and the gods of nature are sailing our boat to land now. The ocean looks immense, I can appreciate that fact now. Looking around, all sides are pure water. Hitting land will be a challenge in all this emptiness. Nature is here too though, I feel it. I will the boat onwards and wait.

Diana comes out of the cabin once the sun has risen, and raises a hand to her eyes to peruse the horizon.

'Not much out there yet. You think we're lost out here forever?' she asks quizzically, like I would know the answer.

'I changed course in the night. I believe land is becoming closer, Gods willing,' I reply calmly.

'Well, you trust the gods, you are closer to them than any of us. I believe in you.' She comes to hug me tightly.

I shrug, and then hold her too. We both turn to watch the horizon; in each other's arms, everything should be right with the world. But it is not. I am shaking and Diana notices, looking up at me.

'What's wrong?' she asks, with a concerned look.

'I'm not sure, Di, I'm just not sure,' I say to the ocean. 'I feel a darkness clouding my vision again.'

Diana bites her lip, hesitating, obviously unsure as to how to help. I knew it would be so – there is no helping the damned.

'Don't worry. I'll be here with you through the darkness, my Ariel. We are stronger than it. I will be with you all the way.' Diana smiles, and points into the distant place where sky meets sea, repeating, 'all the way.'

Following her finger, I look out as far as I can. Movement. There is something black moving in the sky! I don't care what it is, we are heading in that direction. I swirl the wheel round and the boat rocks. I hold tight to Diana as the course shifts.

'What are you doing? I didn't mean to go that way!' Diana playfully slaps my chest.

'I saw something,' I say, 'something large moving in the distance. We should follow it to find land.'

Diana's look turns to exuberance, her cheeks flush and she jumps giddily into the air.

'I knew you could take us to land! See, I was right all along. What was it that moved, though? I don't see anything.' She peers into the distance.

'It's big and black. I don't know what it is yet. We will find out,' I say and smile at her, unable to be secretly happy that I accomplished my task.

'I must go and tell Agatha! She will be pleased with you.' Diana kisses my hand as she leaves it.

Land is near; no large bird would cross open waters for too long. The bird is slowly moving to the right. I will follow the left and see where it came from. It is fascinating to watch; I have never seen anything so large. Even a giant eagle could not be spotted from this far away. A small black dot appears. Finally, land – at least, that's what it looks like. Could be a huge rock sticking out of the ocean, I suppose. I hope it is not, and will the boat towards the speck. The bird eventually disappears into low cloud and is gone. I hope it is not the last we will see of it, I would enjoy the magnificence. The two women appear from the cabin, Diana dragging Agatha by the hand.

'Tell her what you saw, she won't believe me,' Diana giggles and says, 'please tell her land is close and we will all survive.'

I cough; the word 'survive' sticks in my throat like glass, scratching and tearing my gullet. Agatha looks at me with a glare, and raises her eyebrows. I nod to her and sigh, then point to the speck. They both turn and, I imagine, squint with young and old eyes. Humans have never had the gift of solid sight, it blurs and grows weak at seeing distant objects.

'There is land. I followed a large bird and can see the tip of some island,' I say.

'When will we be there, Ariel?' Diana's voice heightens and becomes giddy again. 'Oh, this is excellent! I can't wait to be on land again, can you, Ariel?'

I shake my head and roll my eyes. 'Yes there is land, and in a day or so we will be there. I am looking forward to planting my feet onto the soil again, I suppose.'

With that last word, Agatha turns and stares at me. I know the look, and what she is saying with it. There shouldn't be a suppose, I should be happy and ready to start my life anew. But it is not life that I crave! I wish to be twisted and torn up, and then allowed to rot in the soil we are heading for. They will not let me have peace in this lifetime, I know it. Clinging to me for support, they really are like the human children, with all their innocence and naivety. Will I cradle them and provide the necessary tools for survival? Or let them die in the forests? I do not know this yet, I do not know how long I will last before I must go.

We have a fair wind still, and it whisks us onwards to the land. As night is beginning to form, I see the last of the island. It is growing in size and is definitely not a barren rock. Darkness engulfs it though and I must keep our course steady, long into the night. It is not an easy task, watching the stars as anchors to our heading. I make my adjustments when required and yawn lazily with the rocking of the boat. By the time the sun comes up, I can see how well I have done. It is definitely an island, much closer than I suspected. I can see a green colour, trees I would expect, and a mountain in the middle, which must have been the speck I saw. The gods have smiled fortunately upon us, and I am glad in a way. Closer to a peaceful journey to Fern.

Diana pops out of the cabin as I steer the boat directly towards the island. She sways over to me and looks out to see the island fully for the first time.

'Beautiful! Isn't it amazing, Ariel? We are nearly at our new home!' she shouts to me.

I smile with the veil of malaise still drawn. Diana laughs and it is nice to see such happiness in a being. But I will never laugh like that or be happy for long, not until my task finishes. I hope Fern waits with a canvas, and brush in hand.

'We will be there by the end of the day, tell Agatha,' I say.

'Don't be so grumpy! Don't you see? Heaven is within our grasp.' Diana storms over to me and jumps to grab me. 'Kiss me, my Ariel.'

So I do, and we kiss long and deep, for what I do not know but it seems to please her greatly. She whisks herself away to the cabin and soon returns with Agatha.

'Amazing, you are right my dear, just beautiful,' Agatha says in wonder.

'A day's travel away,' is all I say.

Agatha turns. 'Good lad, well done.'

The women whisper to each other in starts and giggles. I do not eavesdrop but merely continue to guide the boat towards land. They eat and keep chatting about something that I cannot be bothered to listen to. Their drones are muted compared with my thoughts. Black as they are, and hopeless as I feel, there is still something within me that begs to live. I cannot shake this feeling; it comes from her, I know. I will have to wait and see which wins out. I do heed Agatha's words, it might be something Diana and I could share the burden of. But what will I do when she inevitably perishes? Then I will be alive but truly alone.

The sun is high, then it starts to dip and come down as we reach the shoreline. A brilliant, white beach awaits us and Diana is the epitome of joy. We hit land as it becomes dark.

'We should explore in the morning,' I say, 'maybe we will find some fresh water for you both.'

'Of course! Oh Ariel, good job! Come and rest with us, please? You haven't slept in a while.' Diana drags me to the cabin.

Inside, she pulls me further and I realise the boat is bigger than I thought. Cramped as it is, I find us in bed together. I fall into a rest that takes me from this hellish world and into a place of peaceful dreaming.

I awake with a start, sitting up and banging my head on the wooden ceiling that sits so close to our bodies.

'Ouch,' I say.

'Are you okay? Come, let's lie here a little longer, just a little. I've missed you.' Diana puts an arm over my chest as I lean back.

Chapter Twenty-Nine

Do not fear the light,

The undying shall rise up,

Be one with nature.

My rest with her is short-lived. I can hear a noise outside and it awakens my senses quickly. Voices – there are other people already here! I squeeze out of bed and sneak around the other side of the cabin from the noise, to get a look at them. They stand tall and I can hear them now.

'If it's humans, we'll kill them quick and see what they brought. You ready? Bruda! I said are you ready?' one of them says, and I can just see the tops of their heads now.

'We are being watched though,' this Bruda says.

I peep further knowing I have been spotted, then stand tall and get a look at them fully. It seems I have found my kin. Very worrying. They are dressed in red robes, and hold falchions in their large hands. They look at me in surprise and take a step back. So, they remember me then.

'You! Traitor!' Bruda exclaims.

'I am, but let me show you the light I have become,' I say.

'What are you talking about, light? Everyone knows you hid in the woods while your people were slaughtered, then came down to help the humans. You are not welcome here, ugly creature!' Bruda and her friend raise their weapons.

I hold my hands up. 'I carry no weapon, would you strike your kin without giving him a chance to explain fully?' I ask, hoping they also remember I was a warrior back then.

They lower their weapons. 'Well then, explain,' the large demon kin says.

I tell them I was left behind, I made a mistake in bloodlust, but then about the bridge and how I killed many, but couldn't stop the killing of our people.

'You will go before the elders for crimes against kin and treason. There is no other option but to die on this island,' Bruda says.

'I do not want to kill you. If you remember, I am quite able to. Let us go in peace, we will find somewhere else,' I say.

'Us? Who have you got crawling in that vessel?' the tall demon asks.

'Ah, well . . .' I am unsure what to say next.

'Humans!' shouts Diana and she creates a fire arrow ready to stab into one.

They both belly laugh. 'You think that arrow will save you, human?' They begin to march forward, swords once again raised.

I come between them before they can board. They back down again, stamping their feet in the sand.

'You should not protect these killers. They ruined our land and we have had to scratch and scrape to build it up again. You brought them again, traitor.' Bruda's face turns a deep red in anger.

'I am Ariel, protector of these humans and of nature. Should you attack I will be forced to kill you,' I say determinedly, trapped in a bluff.

A screech from the air breaks our stalemate. Bruda and the other demon look at each other worriedly.

'Leave this place! The drake approaches! We must fight it off,' Bruda says and both turn and run into the forest.

I look up. The black shape has appeared again and I can hear the screaming of my kin. I still remember that noise of fear and a rallying cry to fight. I take the chance to dive off the boat and begin to push it off the shoreline. As I am pushing, I start to think about all those lives lost. My kin, who have been through so much death already, are dying to nature just like I was. I push the boat harder and let it go once properly in the water.

'What are you doing, Ariel?' Diana shouts from the boat.

I back away. 'I must help my people – stay near the coast and I will return. Only come back when you see me.'

'They are not your people! Come get on with us quickly, and we can be safe and free,' Diana calls and starts to cry.

Agatha appears from the cabin, and hushes Diana, holding her. I wave at them and then bound into the trees. The forest is thick and hard to run through, but I can still hear the call to arms, so I force myself onwards. I don't know if this is a good plan, but I left them, killed them, it is true. I need to make amends, face my fears and the consequences that may arise. After all, I am a traitor; I caused the chaos and left my kin to die. The humans would have simply perished had I not helped them, and then my people would still be living in peace back on our island. I brush vines from my face, they stroke my shoulders in an odd manner, then start to part. She remembers, she forgives here and will help me with my task. Freed, I am like lightning, and run through to a clearing in the forest. Much has been cut down in order to create what is in front of me. I can see the whole town, wooden houses built to perfection, temples to the gods and properly built streets! But above, the screeching is deafening, so there is no time to admire their work. Over to the right it swoops, definitely this drake they spoke of. It is a huge and heavy-set beast. Not like any bird I have seen; so wide are its wings that it could block out the sun. Its head is horned and red, a gaping maw opens and it lands on two gigantic legs.

'Now!' I hear the call.

Archer's arrows ping harmlessly off its skin and mages start to use fire and ice on the beast. It screams and bites downwards at the demon warriors. I run, as fast as I can out of the trees and into the fray. I jump through the town and come to the warriors – the beast is upon them snarling and biting heads, legs and torsos by the dozen. I feel the light within grow and flashes come from my hands. The beast turns to me, great yellow eyes pierce through my bones. It growls, and white fangs attempt to devour me. But the light has already grown to a bubble; the beast is knocked backwards and it shakes its head. Talons reach out and try to grab me, then a spiny tail whips around my back but bounces off harmlessly. The beast looks a bit shocked, and I use this time wisely as it hesitates. I grow the bubble outwards to encapsulate my kin. They drop their arms and look curiously at me. The drake tries to bite another but is flummoxed by my magic. It screams again then takes to the air. It flies away from the town fast.

I let the light die within me, and the bubble disintegrates into air. There is cheering from the warriors and screams from those on the ground with missing limbs. My kin rush out of their hiding and help the wounded. A large demon, taller and wider than me approaches. He is dressed in finery, and his black cloak wisps in the wind.

'Impressive. You aren't from the town – you must be the traitor, yes?' He stares me down.

I pause, thinking, then say, 'My name is Ariel, but I am a traitor no longer, sir. I was left with the humans for many years.'

'Left behind? Is that your defence for bringing about the end of our civilisation? You murdered in cold blood. Guards! Take the ugly thing away,' he says.

Four very large demons appear from the town and escort me away. I am taken to a big house and pushed inside. A demon comes too and shackles me to a wall, then whispers to the binding. The room is almost black – fitting, I suppose, for a jail. There are no windows, and the only light dies when the door is closed.

I tremble. What have I done? Given my life away to help those who despise me, and rightly so. I start to mumble, chastising myself for not jumping back on that boat. A light appears in the corner of the room, and as I turn my attention towards it, I notice I am not alone.

'Thrown into the pit as well, eh?' the voice says. 'Do not fear, we'll be dead soon!' The laugh that accompanies the voice is dark and full of rage.

'Who are you? I am Ariel,' I say starting to crack and cry.

'Why, I am Gelard, master of beasts! They know I brought the drake here, so that is why I will die soon. Yes, we kill our kin for treason, my boy. You are the one I have seen before, the misfortunate? Let's see your face.' The light moves across the room and stops near me.

He cackles and claps. 'Yes! You and I are the same! Both treasonous villains. I have heard much of your story.'

'And what did you hear?' I ask.

'You brought the humans of course! Then let them kill half our kin! You helped them, eh? Thought you could rule the world? Me too! I found the drake on an island north of here, thought it would be a good pet and make me powerful. Turns out I made it very angry and it turned on me, chased me back here,' Gelard says, still cackling in apparent madness.

'How long have you been here?' I ask the demon.

'Oh, I don't know. Could be long, could be short, but I am sure they will kill me soon,' Gelard replies wistfully.

Could this all be true? Would they try to kill me as punishment? Half of me fills with glee, the other, with dread. I have not completed my mission to keep Diana safe yet. There is so much left to do, but maybe it is my time. It feels easy to wait here and rot with Gelard, to never try to escape. But something draws me from darkness. I could make amends; I could stop the drake if only they would let me help. I know nature and her ways – this Gelard scorned her, and now she takes revenge through the drake. I could calm them both. Then I could take Diana and Agatha further from this place where we are hated, somewhere good and pure. Not a scarred landscape where beings have hurt nature.

'I hope they don't kill us, Gelard. Tell me, where is the drake's nesting place?' I ask him.

The light travels back across the room, and I am thankful to see Gelard's face, bloodied and tortured as it is. It is twisted, and I find him more repulsive than a mirror reflection. But I pity the demon; no one should be locked away from the light and left to die so slowly. Eventually, he may perish from malnourishment; his eyes are yellow and teeth blackened. He holds out a hand for the light and I can see that he has been scraping his fingers against the wood; long marks are etched on the wall and his nails are ripped to the nub.

'North. About half a day's travel by sea. I found it I did, I am a beastmaster, so I thought I was in control, but it nearly killed me so I fled. This is all my fault.' I hear a weeping sound from him.

'It is not your fault, I am sure you have learned your lesson, as I have,' I say.

'Ha! Don't compare yourself to me!' Gelard spits in my direction, 'you used humans to bring about ruin. I would have ruled as a peaceful and strong king! Not this magus who cares not for the people.'

So, it was not a utopia at all, even before the drake arrived. I must meet this magus again to talk. Who knows where it may lead – if he is any kind of leader, he will listen to my proposal. I could appease the beast, I know it, I know it deep in my bones. This is my path to redemption now. I will help my people and then sail far away with my Diana, that is, if I am not put to death first.

'I will help my kin, Gelard. They will listen. Tell me more of the magus,' I say, ignoring his comments.

'You are a thief of life, bringer of death, how could you help?' he replies, still seething.

'I can, I know this. Now tell me of the magus,' I repeat sternly.

'He is a dark demon, and his rule has been difficult to say the least. A few homes were converted to dungeons in the early days, after the elders all died by human hands. We were scared so we voted him into the position of magus, but it was a terrible idea. Anyone who disagrees with him are put in these jails. Many have disappeared. There are few resources on this island, except for the trees, so on his command we cut them down. This is no paradise just a hell in which we are all trapped. You won't get an audience with him, let alone change his mind about you, mark my words.' Gelard takes a long breath in.

I sigh as he does – maybe it is all lost because of me. We were so happy and peaceful back on the island. They cast me out yes, but it made me who I am today, moulded me. I am happy to be nature's friend, and I do not need them, my kin. I should escape now and run, lest this magus kills me. I do not know what to do. I am trapped in a fear I have not felt for a long time, and near death, as I prayed I would be. But alive, I could improve this place, couldn't I? Is that my purpose here? I look up to the ceiling quizzically, asking the gods for a sign. There is no recourse but to try I suppose, and if the gods will it, I will survive this challenge and make it back to Diana. I do miss her now, and I feel a hollowness inside to be without her. I will live, I must live. She is currently bobbing on the waters not far from me, and I cannot let that be her fate, to die at sea. This thought somehow provides me with strength, and I can feel the power growing inside of my body. I look towards the bindings, push my feet to the wall and with all my might, try to free myself. I struggle and strain but it is no use. Something strong is at work here, the words spoken must be constraining my body.

Gelard sniggers. 'You can't escape. Don't you think I would be well away if I could just free myself that easily? We are dead beings, accept it. You, little treacherous demon, will have your time too.' He yanks on his binds and in the dark, I see his yellow smile.

'I told you, I am no traitor. And I must speak with the magus, please, you must know a way?' I plead with Gelard, who just shakes his head.

'They don't care. Don't you see? It's a poison-infested place, and the people you once knew are long gone. When we were bright-eyed and wise, we created a place of peace but it is lost to us now. You tore it down, brick by brick and made something dark. Something past the god's pasture to a hellish place. Just sit and accept your fate.' Gelard slumps down the wall.

'You like nature, don't you? I do too, Gelard. You want to protect it, and help give it the strength to rise up from the ground. We could be allies you know. We both want the same thing here, to save our people and promote nature to her rightful place.' I look intently at him for a response.

Gelard shrugs and bites on his nails. He holds the small light in his grasp, and I see the cogs turning within his mind. Who else should I have as an ally but one who shares my passions? He must see the sense in it. Both of us being outcasts, I know his pain.

'We will see when the time comes what nature has in store for us. I have little magic to use against them, that is why I needed the drake,' Gelard finally says.

He looks at me and I see the blackening of his eyes, devoid of light and hope. I turn towards the door.

'Bring me the magus! I demand to speak with him!' I shout and kick the wall.

Chapter Thirty

My mind tries to break,

Resilience is a need,

To brave the mind's flood.

Gelard shushes me. 'I am begging you, stop! They will only beat us and leave our bodies to slowly heal!' He brings himself towards me and kneels. 'Please, I will help you I promise, just stop making a noise.' He raises and lowers his hand to quieten me down.

I stop just in time and heed his words. From the outside, I can hear the guard.

'Better quieten down! Or we'll give you a good kicking again, and we'd love to do that to you, traitor,' a voice bellows through the door.

'See?' Gelard whispers over to me, 'you must listen to me. I have tried everything and it only ends in pain.'

I nod in apology, and I am beginning to care for Gelard. I see much of my young self in him, especially the fear. He nods back several times in quick succession, pleased that we have avoided being beaten.

I sit back down and breathe a sigh. Gelard chuckles with relief and follows suit. I definitely need a better plan than attracting attention, that will only serve to quicken my death it would seem. We are lost in our separate thoughts once more. The room becomes silent except for the occasional flickering of Gelard's flame. I play with the hay at my feet, while I try to figure out a plan. I know what I have to do, but I fear the consequences though. I must ask for nature's help yet again. But why would she aid me now? I ran into this, literally, so I must fix it.

The blast outside stuns me awake. A crashing, thunderous wave of noise blows through the room. Screaming follows a screeching that could only signal the drake's return. The beast must be one of nature's greatest devastators, and I wish I could speak to it in peace. But tied to this wall, I am helpless to aid my fellow demons. My kin scream as they are torn limb by limb, till the creature is satisfied.

I know they will come to me now, being the only one who has stopped the drake. Surely, they will see the sense in talking after the carnage has passed. I hear the guards clamouring, and worry for a second the drake has found us and wishes to take its revenge on Gelard. But the thumps pass our jail and collide with other wooden structures outside. I can hear the sound of archers and our wizards hopelessly attacking, then dying. I cry, the hardest I have in a long time. The pain flows through me and out in a deluge. I wish to scream for the dead, but know our best chance is to stay quiet. I clamp my hand over my mouth and curl up by the wall, terrified.

After some time, I am still bursting with sorrow, and the light comes towards me once more. Gelard seems to be studying me.

'You feel much pain for them. Why? They hate you,' Gelard says solemnly.

'Because this is my fault, and my kin are dying. It brings me much pain yes, but also fear. Fear that all is lost for my people. I know you all hate me, but I do not care, I will still love you regardless,' I reply.

The flame seems to flicker, and floats wearily back to its master. Gelard cups his hand round it. Tears begin to drip to the floor from his face.

'Then maybe we are the same, kin once again. Eh?' He shudders and looks towards the door. 'I will help you escape, but you must take me with you if you can. I also need to be free.'

'Yes, we are not a part of them any longer. We must leave this place forever. Of course, I will take you; we have a boat waiting for us at this very moment. You know where to sail?' I ask.

'Yes. I know the waters, and I will guide us. But how are we going to free ourselves? Neither of us has the magic.' He stares into the flame without looking at me.

The fighting outside has dissipated, but a few cries for help ring out still. The drake has departed at last, and I feel relieved for both my kin and the creature. I look around the dimly lit room for some hope of escape. The ceiling is too high to reach, and the walls too thick to break. I start to whisper to the wood, touching the wall and praying to it.

'Nature, guide me. I need your help again. I am sorry to ask so much of you with little in return. But you must understand the direness of my situation – see my friend, Gelard, he is also your friend. Help him overcome this despairing place,' I say quietly.

As I speak, Gelard looks to me. 'What are you doing?'

'I am praying to nature for guidance. We will not escape without her help.'

'I will do the same then, she has always listened to me too.' Gelard comes to kneeling and touches the wall.

The door shudders; she is listening. Perhaps our bonds will break, the door will smash open and we will be free. But the door only opens slowly, revealing a figure standing in the light.

'Magus,' Gelard says softly.

So, this is the magus. A tall powerful man, wrapped in robes with a staff in one hand and a flaming torch in the other. I cannot make out the colour of his long ringlets of hair. He looks bearded, but I cannot be sure.

'It is your time, traitors. You have desecrated our people for too long and escaped punishment. Do you have any words or shall we feed you to the drake in sacrifice?' The magus takes a step inside the room.

I can see his figure from the torchlight now. An old demon, but he stands straight and tall. I can smell the magic on him; he is not someone I can defeat now, I know this. His robes are of silver, his cloak of black. Maybe once he was a wizard of great power, but now faced with the drake and a depleted populace, he is just the ruler. He must have fought when the humans came for us. He knows my sins very well, so I must tread carefully.

'We are no traitors. I know you can't see this yet, but we are your allies. I can stop the drake, I know it, if only you would give us the chance to mend the wounds we have caused our people,' I say, staring right into his eyes, hopeful that he sees the change in me from all that time ago.

'I remember you, you know this? A creature we despised who brought our ruin. You, the broken-faced one. I couldn't believe it for many years, the havoc caused by such a tiny animal. You sat in the forest while we burned and fled. I was a wizard then, I fought hard against the humans.

What did you do but hide and then destroy us with pleasure?' the magus asks, staring downwards at me.

'I fought too, and you left me, not the other way around. I will admit I was naïve and let them in but we all should share the blame. We taught them magic and welcomed them into our homes, fed and watered them. I am not at fault for when they stabbed us in the back for asking them to leave, I admit to bloodlust but now I am pure,' I reply.

The magus looks startled and concerned. He thinks for some time, obviously pondering what to say next. A crowd has gathered behind him, and they stare in disbelief at me, mainly because they all know me, what I did.

'I am not that naïve creature anymore. I drove myself through a malaise and have grown through my sins. I kept my land and fought the humans whenever I needed to. I am not that demon now, only one of light magic. You must have seen it with the drake – only I can protect you and my kin,' I say.

'Pfft, you showed a little magic, and I do not consider you kin. Just look at your face, you are not one of us. You belonged with the animals, and you should have died with them.' The magus raises an eyebrow.

I look past him now, to the townsfolk, the ordinary kin. They look tired and weak, and I cry for them.

'I will never betray you the way I did before, you must all hear me. I can protect you; the drake is of nature's making and I have a relationship with her. You have all seen it.' I am cut off from saying more, as the magus blocks my view of them.

'It is only me you have to prove anything to. I led these people here. I looked after them and created this place, and there will be no dissidence, no one to break the order of things that I created.' He turns from me to Gelard. 'What do you say, Gelard?'

'He speaks the truth I believe. I am sorry I brought the drake here. Please release us and we will disappear forever. You will no longer have us as opponents.' Gelard's voice trembles and breaks.

'My people deserve their justice. You, Gelard, tried to bring about my ruin and you, tortured creature, you tried to bury us all in human filth. I have made my decision, and it pleases me to have you both here. Ready to die now?' he asks us both.

Gelard shakes and screams at the magus. 'This is not justice! You who holds my kin hostage to your whims. I do not fear you anymore!'

The magus laughs. 'You should not fear me! Fear the fire!'

With that, the magus throws his torch into the middle of the room and begins to retreat.

'Bar the doors. Let them burn and let it be a lesson to you all!' he shouts and the guards follow their orders.

The hay on the floor burns quickly. The fumes from the flames on the floor start to choke me, but I must be strong. I have burned before, I can do this. I look at Gelard – he will not survive.

'Pray to nature!' I shout across the room at him, 'she is our only hope now!'

He begins to pray quietly.

'No, shout with me, now!'

He bellows, following my lead as we scream for nature to listen. We beg, even as the flames start to lick our hands. I feel the heat coming then, searing pain, but I persist. She is the only one with the power to break these bonds. I feel a wind start to rise in the room, fresh and full of the smell of the meadows. I am taken back to those days when I used to be free with her. I breathe in deeply and choke on fumes no more. A mighty roar forces me to open my eyes as the door is smashed open. It is the drake's spiny face, almost smiling in the light. It barges through the wood, tearing down the walls as it moves towards us. The fire has all but been quashed, and the drake bends towards Gelard first.

'No! I am sorry, please don't kill me!' he screams.

But this is not its intention, I know. It breathes over the room and we are both unbound. Gelard's eyes brighten and widen, shocked at the power. He rubs his burned hands. The drake lays its head on the floor, and Gelard and I stare at one another for a second.

'Get on!' I cry at him.

He clambers up the neck to the back and grabs a spine. The drake looks at me, but I shake my head.

'No, I must see to my love first, and show the people I have changed. We will follow, I promise. Thank you.' I bow my head and the drake seems to shrug, then backs away out of the building.

I watch as it flies off to the North, and now I notice my kin in front of me, all dumbfounded at what has occurred. I march through them, parting the sea of demons. I turn towards them and ready myself for a speech, when a bolt zips past my head. I look over my kin's heads to see the magus holding a crossbow.

'Kill him, you fools! Now, before he escapes and brings more of the beasts with him!' the magus hollers.

I know already what magic they have, and let the light shine out of me, protecting my skin. Fire and ice flash around me, and I start to run. It would seem that they will never listen. I must lose them and make the boat, back to Diana. I swing around the trees, moving as fast as possible, and the vines clear a path for me to follow, collapsing back down behind me to slow the enemy. I feel elated and fleet-footed; I will make it. I must. The only hope is to find the drake's nesting place. It will know what to do next. I burst out into open ground, and I see the shore and the calming seas. I flood with relief, but the job is not over. The boat could be anywhere on this coast. Where did I land? I look around, filled with anxiety. There is a beach, and I bolt towards the shoreline. I skid to a halt on the sand, and cry out for Diana. Many times I shout, before I hear her! I follow the sound, and tears start to fall from my cheeks. I have run my legs into the ground now, and I start to slow but spot the boat round the corner of a rock. I gasp with relief; it is nearly over. I turn to look over my shoulder – the forest burns. Some demons have made it through and are chasing me. I leap towards the boat and dive into the waters; they are freezing to the bone and I lose all air as I hit the waves. I force myself to rise and try to swim for the first time in my life.

I can hear her screams for me to swim, yet I do not know how and start to dip under. I gurgle on salty water and flap my arms around. Suddenly a hand grabs me, her hand. It pulls me close and drags me forward to a boat.

'Kick your legs, Ariel! Come on! You can do this.' Diana's voice is sheer with fear yet still musical.

I kick hard and we power through the water, finally reaching the boat. I throw myself over the side and pull Diana from the sea. We embrace, as I yank her towards me. A fireball soars overhead, luckily missing the sail and we are startled into action. Diana lifts the sail further and hands me oars.

'Row with these for our lives!' Diana shouts.

I splash them into the water and start to pull then push. I get a rhythm, and we move at speed out into open water, too far to hear the screams of the demons on the shore. As we pass the point of their range, Diana puts a hand on my shoulder and I fall back, collapsing with the effort. Diana holds me tightly and kisses my cheeks repeatedly. I swing my arms around her, only just managing to move them, they feel so heavy and worn.

'We thought you weren't returning. That was very stupid of you, Ariel.' Diana smacks my chest, then closes her fist and thumps me.

'I will always return, my Diana. I had to try, but I failed them,' I say bluntly.

'You nearly failed us, my dear. Do not worry for them. They hated you, has anything changed?' she asks me.

I shake my head and start to wail with tears streaming. It swells with a rage, one for the magus who would not listen, one for my kin who never helped me. They are the damned after all, and I cannot help them, I cannot free them from their past. I slam my fists down on the boat and hear the wood crack.

'Calm now, my Ariel. You are safe, we are here.' Diana hugs me once more and I look up to see Agatha standing above us.

'Be free now, you have done all you can to mend the wound.' Agatha places a hand on my forehead, and I know she is right.

I sit up and look with joy at both women, my saviours, my protectors. Finally, I realise I have a family. They are bound to me as I am to them.

'We must make all speed to the north. Salvation for us all awaits us there,' I finally blurt out.

Chapter Thirty-One

Depression thinks that,

Being down, a disaster,

But hope still lingers.

The women nod, and Diana sniffs and wipes the tears from her eyes before readying the sail and wheel. The wind carries us forward quite unnaturally. I do not tell them why; I know nature guides us now. I sit, knees up and head resting on my hands, staring at the island as we leave. I can see the figures still watching us, but they fade in time and the island becomes smaller, then far from my mind. I become curious about what is in store for us. If I told them we were headed for the drake on this wind, they might settle into fear. I cannot put that burden on them, and we will be okay, I know it. We are under her protection now. I only hope the drake is accepting of humans too, and has not met the vicious side of them, as I have.

There is a day of sailing ahead of us, so I rise and stretch, looking towards Diana and smiling. I move to her, knowing I will always be greeted by a deep embrace. Diana lets the wheel look after itself, running and jumping into my arms.

'I thought we'd lost you again. You've been stuck in your mind a while now,' she whispers in my ear as I hold her up to my face.

'I will always come back to you, my Diana. I want you to trust me now. The wind guides us to a special place where we can be free. Do not question why.'

Diana leans back in my arms and looks me in the eyes, I am mesmerised, captured by her gaze. It is so true and right for me, my perfect partner. I could not ask for more. I regret that we will never marry as she wants, who is left to conduct a ceremony? But a life of bliss together will suffice, I hope.

The seas are calm, and we sail rapidly across them.

'Where are we going, Ariel?' Diana asks.

'I found a demon friend on the island, and we are now following him to a place where we will be safe,' I reply.

Though I have the lingering feeling of the dark malaise, I begin to hope that I will not die once the women are safe. I have asked nature for too much to keep me alive anyway, and I must use the time I have wisely, even if it is aeons. But maybe it is all for nothing. Maybe darkness follows me like the cloud, no matter how far I run from it. I cannot shake this worry, even with my future ahead and love in my grasp.

'Who is your demon friend? That's wonderful you finally found one of your own who accepts you.' Diana's gleeful voice sparkles for me.

'Well, he dislikes me, but we had a common goal of escape from that place. So I suppose ally is a better word.'

Diana shrugs. 'Better than nothing!' She claps a few times and returns with a skip to the wheel. 'Come guide us, Ariel, sounds like you know where to go.'

'The wind already guides us, don't you feel it?' I ask.

Diana bends her head to the side in confusion. 'Why do we need this wheel then?'

'We don't, at least I think we don't,' I say with a smile.

'Come on then! Let's settle in the cabin with Agatha for a while before it gets dark.' Diana leaves the wheel happily, takes my hand and pulls me inside.

It is not as gloomy in the cabin, as it was when we heard about Fern's fate. I have to hunch down to fit, but it is cosy and this brings me some comfort. It was spartanly built by the fishermen, who only needed it for sleeping. I sit down by Diana on a bare bench; Agatha has the only chair, which looks far more comfortable. I look at Agatha, knowing I can't hide my true feeling, but I smile anyway. She smiles back and reaches out a hand to mine, clasps it tight and gives it a squeeze.

'Well done for returning, my boy, I thought you might fall there with those demons. You are not them, you know this. They cast you out long ago and now you must do the same back. Let them leave your mind now, Ariel.' She looks a little pained, and I take it for concern.

'Yes, I do know, Agatha, thank you for waiting,' I say and put my other hand on top of hers.

Agatha nods thoughtfully, and Diana squeezes up to my side, cuddling into my body. I feel the warmth growing and a little light glows in my chest. We sit here, the three companions, and I feel almost whole. I look back to the doorway; clouds follow us still. The boat does not rock though, no rain comes, perhaps it never will, and I am safe. The cloud of my mind still returns and breaks my peace. I am unable to free myself. I clench my jaw as I continue to avoid Agatha's gaze, it is too much to bear at the moment, and I am tired after all the anger and death of my kin. So I lean my head to my arms, and start to nod off.

'Come, I'll look after you.' Diana looks at Agatha, both concerned. Diana takes me to the front of the cabin where a bed lies. I dive into it, collapsing fully in my being. I curl around Diana as she joins me. We do not talk, just hold each other, and be in the moment for a while.

I am entranced by the smell of her hair on my face; it is like coming home. I close my eyes and let rest come upon me. There is nothing to do now but wait, I say to my mind. Be quiet now and still, with her forever in this place. Diana leans into my chest and I feel that stirring once more. That feeling of elation and a pounding beating of the heart that only she can illicit. In a strange way, it brings me peace. I am nearly content, but something wrenches me back from slumber.

I quietly sneak out of the bed. Diana has found her rest, but I will not. Agatha has fallen asleep in the chair, and I put a blanket over her that I find at the foot of the bed. I move out of the cabin and into the open air. The night is dark and starry. I look up in awe, the spectacle appearing above is mesmerising. I am as a youngling again, so full of curiosity and wonder. I bask in the glory of the world, hopeful that this feeling stays a while. No one can stop us if I am this strong – we will reach the drake and nature will provide us with a home to settle into.

I say goodbye to the cloud of the mind, to the malaise. I am a brilliant light, free of struggle and despair. It is so liberating and I am conscious that this is my path and that I am alive! I feel my hands and rub them together in the cold night. They are rough to the touch, but it is a lovely feeling and I spread them out wide and look at them properly. I must be happy, I think. This is all so new to me. I feel overwhelmed for a moment and have to sit on the side of the boat. My feet reach the cool waters; it is pleasant, and I am not afraid of the next step we will take in the morning. So, I wait. I wait for the sun to peep from its hiding place. The moon's light eventually fades and bows to the greatness of the sun. Reds and blues shine through, and I feel the warmth start to grow on my face.

'Still up? Did you sleep? I was sad not to find you beside me, so I got up to see where you were.' I shake my head and Diana comes to sit beside me.

We admire the rising sun, flashing into us. No words are needed now, and I clasp onto her hand, looking towards her, smiling. Nodding to each other, we go back to watching.

'Look, there's an island coming up.' Diana rises and walks to the front of the boat.

I follow, eager to see what we have been brought to. A little wind still guides us towards it. The lapping of the water at the front of the boat is soothing and I sigh in relief that we made it. I see sandy beaches and tall trees, a forest so massive that it must be nature's homeland. A mountainous rock sticks up far on the other side of the island.

'Are we finally here, and free?' Diana asks me.

'Yes, Di. Nature has brought us here to live and be free. After all we put her through, she still looks after us.' I hug Diana, wrapping my arms around her neck.

Diana breathes out slowly, and reaches her hands up to hold my arms. We wait, unafraid and ready as the island grows close. A screech shocks us both out of the calm.

'Ariel, what was that?' Diana turns round to face me. 'What is this place?'

I smile and stroke her hair. 'Do not fear, this is nature's land, our new home.'

Diana nods, biting her lip. 'I trust you, my love. But what is that noise?'

'A drake will protect us here. It saved me and my friend back when my kin tried to kill us. It is a friend I assure you, my Diana,' I say.

Diana breathes in deeply, a little concern on her face. However, she looks me in the eye and I know what she is thinking. She would follow me anywhere.

'Okay. If you call it your friend, I will too. You are sure?' she asks me.

I nod. Yes, this is definitely the place we were meant to find. Gelard will be awaiting us and he will know what this place needs from us. The boat starts to grate on shallow waters and we jut to a halt on the rocks. Diana loses her balance but I catch her, and we both chuckle. I hear Agatha's steps behind and turn my head to look at her.

'Agatha, welcome to our new home,' I say, relishing the possibilities that are now in our future.

'My dear, I am so proud of you. Thank you for finding a place for us, but remember, we need you well,' she says with a stern voice, and a nod to me.

'Yes, I think I am well now. Come, let us explore.' I wave her towards me.

Agatha reaches me and places a hand on my side. I lift Diana first, then pick up Agatha too. I leap into the shallow sandy waters. They are so clear and I look down to see my feet moving up to the shore. I smile; this is definitely my path now. Reaching the beach, I let the women down.

'Thank you, sir.' Agatha hobbles up the beach and takes a seat on the sand. 'Paradise.' The word rings out over me like the water's waves.

It all looks so pure, so real, that tears stream from my eyes.

'Are you ok, my Ariel? Don't be sad, we did it, we are free at last.' I kneel down and Diana hugs me.

I hold her back and let it all out. There is nothing more than relief at the moment. I am uncontrollably happy. It is done, Diana is right. The golden sand wraps around my knees, and I sink into it.

I wish we could stay like this forever, however, I know there is land to cross. We must meet Gelard and ask the drake's permission to stay – it is a part of nature after all, so has a choice. A beast like that may not want to share, Gelard could already be dead, and what of my kin? Will the drake continue to hunt them? I don't know whether I hope it does not, or if it is better that they are wiped from the island for what they did to the land.

A rustling nearby breaks my thoughts, and I peer around Diana. It is my closest friend in nature, the deer, that finally emerges. I rise and walk towards the animal. She looks strong and well fed. She does not turn away from me, but comes closer.

'I am sorry for your losses. Will you, my first friend, forgive me and show us the way?' I ask her.

The deer bows its head and trots into the forest. I wave the women to follow. A forest so green and clean seems unnatural somehow. The vines are thick and grow everywhere, on every trunk of the trees. I look to the canopy; birds chatter to each other and whisk overhead. I touch the tree's bark as we follow the deer. It is rough and old but still fresh and healthy. The forest is noisy with life, and Diana gasps in wonder too.

'This is truly a beautiful place, Ariel. Where does this deer take us though? Can't we stay here?' Diana asks.

'No, we must ask the drake's favour first. Then we may start to build a life,' I say.

Diana shudders. 'Are you sure that is wise? What if it eats us?'

'Trust in Ariel my dear, see the animals? They trust him now.' Agatha's voice calls from the back.

We carry on slowly, the deer occasionally looking back to check we are following the path. The vines seem to move from its way, like curtains opening. I am full of joy and anticipation. We pass by some wild pigs, who start to follow behind. Diana laughs in surprise, stroking one that passes close to her. We walk for a long time, all in astonishment at what is occurring. Birds swoop and dive down to us, chirruping happily, and landing on my shoulders. Bright blues and reds; I have never encountered such birds before, they are magnificent. The forest becomes humid as we delve deeper, more animals joining the train. Even the rabbits have come to hop beside me. I feel as though in a dream, a magical one that I hope will never end.

'Hello there, do you want to walk with me?' I hear Diana's voice behind me and check backwards.

A great stag has appeared, and it stands as tall as me, with shimmering, white-coloured fur that almost blinds me. Its antlers are massive and old; this must be one of the caretakers of the forest. Diana strokes its side as it walks slightly in front of her. There are more noises now, ones I have never heard, and strange little animals swing from tree to tree above us. They howl and squeak in their language, talking to one another, probably about us. As we reach the edge of the forest, it is nearly dark.

'We will sleep here with them tonight. I think it best,' I say to the women behind.

Diana and Agatha nod and settle down on the soft, mossy bed of the forest. I sit, leaning on a tree and staring at the stag, who is now nuzzling with the deer.

'Thank you both, we are in your debt,' I say, 'I hope in time we can repay the kindness you have shown us.' I quietly listen to a small bleat.

'Ariel, my love, come and sleep with me. It is time for you to rest, there is nothing more to do now.' Diana curls up and I move to entwine myself with her.

I check that Agatha is okay, but she is already cuddled up with a bear she met on our travels. It is a warm night, and very still, and this lets me drift with ease into the land of dreams. I wander alone on the plane of sleep for the entire night.

Chapter Thirty-Two

You did not see it,

Nature guides you where it can,

Flowing green grass speaks.

When I awake, the sun is brushing our cheeks. My eyes are sleepy and I yawn. Sitting up on my elbow, I peer over to see Diana's closed eyes, before one pops open for a second and a broad smile appears across her face.

'Can we stay here a while?' Diana does not move as she asks.

'No, I am sorry my love, we must go to the drake. Come on, let's get up, sleepy,' I say to her, rocking her back and forth.

Diana giggles and falls onto her back, arms open and I have no choice but to move in for a kiss. I stroke her face as I do so. We embrace like this for what seems like an age. It is perfect, and I am unable to move. I feel a nuzzle on my back and break away from Diana. The deer looks me straight in the eye when I turn to face it, then looks round towards the mountain, and a grassy meadow that leads up to it. It is grey and dark still, not in keeping with what we have seen so far. I ponder leaving Diana here with Agatha where they are safe and braving it alone, but the choice does not seem to be mine. As soon as I stand and start to walk towards the mountain, Diana chases after me and takes my hand. I do not try to stop her. The deer waits on the edge of the forest, and I give it one last solemn look back.

'Will it be far? Are we heading for that mountain?' Diana asks me, and points towards the foreboding and dark rock.

'Do you see the smoke? That is where we are headed,' I say, after spotting the single plume reaching up into the sky.

I assume it is Gelard; I hope it is, anyway. We stroll through the grass and I stay in the moment, holding onto Diana and remembering each instant where she looks at me and smiles. We stay quiet; there is nothing more to say. A great roar reaches out from the mountain. I feel Diana recoil, but I grip her tightly and she comes back to my side. She shakes a little as we see the beast soaring around the mountain and coming down by the smoke rising from the bottom of the rock. Our meeting place is set.

'It's massive. I've never seen anything so big.' Diana stares in wonder.

'I know, but stay with me and we will survive, I promise you,' I reply.

'I am more afraid for you, my love. I don't know what I'd do without you now.'

I am apprehensive about the approach, but I keep strong for us both. Diana is stronger than me, we worry for each other, and I kind of like it. Actually, I love this feeling in a strange sense.

'I see the smoke, is that your friend?' Diana bites her lip.

'I am hoping so, yes. His name is Gelard, he is like me, a part of nature,' I say, trying not to let my voice waver.

'We are all a part of nature now, I hope?' Diana looks at me.

'You definitely are, my dear. She will protect you I promise it,' I say, knowing she is also a child like us, a lover of the trees and friend to the animals. Nature must see this as well. No longer of the new world, Diana will be a queen of the old and great treasures that nature provides.

I can see the fire now, and a figure sitting beside it. The drake has lowered itself downwards to the ground but the hump of its spiny back is easily visible. I hold one hand up straight and hope this signals our arrival. The figure rises, as tall as me, muscled and strong. Gelard. He starts to move towards us, at first walking, then running, waving his arms. I am gripping to the idea that this is a warm welcome, and not a sign to run back.

'Wow, he looks like you, Ariel. This is your friend?' Diana asks me.

'Indeed, let us hope he is coming to help us.'

As he approaches, we stop and wait to see what is going to happen next.

'My friend! You made it! And brought company, I see!' Gelard shouts and comes to a jog before jumping up and down and embracing me. I find it uncomfortable, but put a free hand around his back.

'Gelard,' I say as he moves back, 'this is the human, Diana.'

'Human, eh? Yes, I remember them well. So small, but so strong in number. Has she come with her hoard?' He raises an eyebrow in jest.

'I have no hoard, thank you very much. I am nature's human now. Ariel told me so,' she replies.

'I was only joking, of course you are! Or the animals and forest would not have let you get this far.' Gelard smiles at her. 'So Ariel, what now? Do you wish to approach the drake? She accepted me eventually, nearly lost a limb though! I hope you fare better and the human is not damaged.'

Diana gasps, shaking her head, but I know Gelard is still jesting. He waves us forward and jogs back towards the silhouetted drake, which has now lifted its head to spy us approaching.

Diana leads me forward, ready for whatever is coming. I admire her mettle, my love, my Diana. The drake will surely be convinced of her purity. Mine, on the other hand, is very much debatable. I have wronged nature in many ways. The drake will know this, being the old connection to her.

As we reach the stone, the drake rises to full height, standing on its back legs, an imposing figure to be sure. It huffs and stares at me, not Diana, thankfully. The drake stretches its claws and stamps forward, shaking the ground beneath us. We wobble to the fire, and Gelard sits beside it to await the decision. Still holding hands, Diana and I bow to the drake. I am unsure of what to do next. How can we communicate?

I try to talk to the great beast. 'You know me, I am Ariel, a friend of nature. This is my love, Diana. She is also nature's ally. We wish for sanctuary, friend.'

There is a long pause, and the drake seems to be thinking; it tilts its head and peers down at us. I audibly swallow, waiting for the next move. Diana steps forward, still clasping my hand.

'We would like sanctuary here on this island with you, if you will permit it. We ask for your favour.' Diana's voice is strong and confident.

The drake breathes in, then lets out a breath that nearly knocks both of us off our feet. She steps forward, almost like she is ready to attack, but instead opens her maw.

'Welcome, supposed children of nature. You come for sanctuary and protection from the outside world? I am not sure why I should grant this. I see you, Ariel, very well. You propose yourself as a friend, however, I have heard from nature about the fires you set with your magic. Now you bring a human in front of me. A mean race, the cruellest of all that we have seen in all our many ages.'

'What should we call you? Ariel here is a changed being. You must have seen much if you know all already. I have never been anything but an ally of nature, not like the other humans at all.' Diana forcefully argues her point.

'My name? Given by nature, I am Aranyani, protector of nature and her animals. I have taken many here to live out their lives in peace. It is true, human, you have been our ally for your life, but him? He destroys where he could create,' Aranyani booms at me.

I feel we are at a stalemate. How can I convince her that I am trustworthy? I fall to my knees, holding tight to Diana, and bow my head towards the floor.

'I am so sorry for my acts committed. I am no longer that demon. No longer one of my kin. I am a force for light and also protection, like yourself. We are one and the same. My Diana will tell you of the changes I have been through. Yes, I burned as nature took her revenge, but I also healed,' I say, starting to worry, believing she will kill us if we cannot come to an understanding.

'I have indeed witnessed your magic. I can see the great white light in your heart's centre now. I suppose you may stay and prove your worth, but I will need something from you first,' Aranyani huffs towards me.

'Anything,' I say, 'we are at your mercy, Aranyani.'

The drake reaches out a claw and lays it on my shoulder. The weight is massive and I shake under it, but hold and look into the eyes of Aranyani.

'You will sacrifice your magic to me and become mortal. It is within my power and it is what I ask. I will protect you, but you will age and die within a short time. It is also nature's request, of course. The light you hold will be used to keep the land safe as I raze the ground of your kin. There is no space for immortal demons now, your time is over. So, I can kill you or take this from you. Choose.' Aranyani's deep voice is serious.

'There is no choice there. I mean to live with Diana. I love at last, so let us live our short lives together. I give my power freely to you, and I hope it brings you protection too,' I say.

I am not afraid of losing my immortal status; it feels right that I should share my fate with Diana. We can live here, build something, and be alive. We will rise to the gods and I will finally see Fern once again. I cry and nod to myself.

'Come on, take it from me, I have no use for it anymore. I will live my life fully for the first time.' I finish speaking and feel a dragging in my soul.

'So be it, child. Keep still – this will be unpleasant.' Aranyani almost smiles.

She keeps her claw on my shoulder and begins to breathe in. My chest starts to burn. I feel everything slipping away, and the pain is intense, but I hold onto it. I need the pain. It shows I am alive. Diana grips my arm as the agony makes me cry out. I bend my head to the sky and begin to convulse. What I can see starts to blacken, then the world becomes dark and I am no longer in control of myself.

'Ariel? Are you awake?' Diana's sweet voice brings me back to life.

I open an eye – the world has returned. I stare into the sky, bright blue. Not a cloud in sight. I sit up and look at my hands; I am still large, nothing feels different.

'Did it work?' I ask Diana. 'Are we together now or have we died?'

'No, my love, we are definitely alive,' she strokes my head, 'it worked. Aranyani has gone to finish her work, she said.'

I know what that means – my kin will soon be gone from the land. Immortals are a thing of past times, not the future.

'How are you, friend? Don't worry, I had the same choice, but was told not to tell you.' Gelard is crouched beside me.

He smiles and I see a tear in his eye. He holds out a hand and lifts me to standing. I feel no light inside me now, no power.

'What do we do now?' I ask my comrades.

'I suppose we live, Ariel. We can do anything we like. Come, let us guide you back to the forest.' Diana is holding back tears.

'Why are you ready to cry, my dearest?' I ask her.

'I am just so happy, Ariel. I was afraid for you, all alone after I am gone. But now we can grow old together.' Diana embraces me and I hug her back.

It is better this way. I am ready for time to take me, away on its wings to the stars. It will be beautiful, and I no longer feel the need to ask nature to take me away from this land. I feel like I have no strength anymore as we meander back to the forest, slowly. I don't know if I will feel her anymore; will I still have a relationship with nature? Time will tell. We walk the meadow, and it is amazing to touch the grass with my hand knowing all is well. I still feel the creeping darkness but it is kept at bay by the feeling of love and brightness from Diana. We reach the edge of the forest, and Agatha awaits the three of us.

'What happened, my boy? You look drained. And who might you be?' Agatha smiles at Gelard.

'Gelard, my lady.' He bows low to her.

'I am Agatha. Don't worry, I will look after you all. So, tell me everything.' Agatha moves towards me and holds my hand.

I tell her that I am mortal, that the drake, Aranyani, will keep us safe as long as we look after the forest.

'I am weak now, I no longer hear her. What am I supposed to do?' I ask Agatha, nearly collapsing with my weight.

She grasps my hand tightly and Diana helps hold me up. 'Live and love Ariel, live and love. Nature is always here for us, it does not matter that you can't feel her. Just be with her.' Agatha looks proudly at my face.

I nod, hoping she is right. I move from them and grasp onto the nearest tree. It feels the same as before, the bark hardened and rough. A vine comes down, and I look at it with new eyes in wonder. It moves to my hand and touches me, and I clutch onto it and weep. Having her reach out to me is a blessing. I turn to check that my friends and love can see. They clap for us, and together we are strong. I need no special powers.

The walk back through the forest is long. We look for somewhere we might settle, and a deer rips across the forest, coming to a sliding halt in front of us. Breathless, it bows to us and starts to walk back the way it came. So we follow. There is nothing else to do but trust in her.

'Where do you think she takes us?' Gelard looks wide-eyed. 'I have never seen such a marvel. An animal leads us!' He chuckles and walks in front, looking at the deer and nothing else.

'Yes, my friend. The deer will lead us to our home. We are welcomed by them, and safe,' I say.

'You are truly blessed, Ariel. Now we all are,' Gelard says without turning to me.

At a clearing, the deer looks round at us and then sprints away through the trees and is gone in a flash. A great tree has fallen here, creating a break in the canopy and a perfect home. I know this is where we will live. I grab onto Diana's hand and pull her forward. We laugh and dance in the sunlight, both gleeful and happy. Agatha and Gelard look on, laughing too.

'My love, my Ariel, we must stop! We have much work to do!' Diana laughs at my movements, and guides me to the old tree. 'Can we use this, is that okay?'

'I think so, we can build with the wood, I believe,' I say nodding and rubbing my chin. 'We need tools though.'

'There was lots of broken rock at the mountainside. Perhaps we can fashion axes?' Gelard says. 'I will go. Where is that damned deer? I have no idea where we are.' He laughs as he speaks.

'They will lead you if you become lost, I am sure. Thank you, Gelard, follow the path back the way we came,' I tell him.

'On it!' he calls to me and salutes me with a large grin.

Once Gelard has left, Diana and I begin to dance close to one another again. We smile at each other's faces. She accepts my flawed features and I love her beauty. I stroke her hair.

'Do you love me truly, Diana?' I ask her.

'Yes, my Ariel. I will grow old with you, it is all I ever wanted. You are a part of nature like me, remember? And don't forget it!' Diana strokes my face in return and her big eyes beam.

Agatha comes into the clearing. 'I wish I could dance again, maybe once I find my peace.' I take her and hold her up to my shoulder, then twirl and jump around. Agatha claps as I do and wobbles a little but I have a good grip on her. After releasing her back to the ground, she bows to me and we all lie in the sunlight, many days we spend like this awaiting Gelard's return.

It is a joyous place, and the moss on the ground comforts me, like it used to. I feel like I am finally where I am meant to be. On the fourth day, I am dozing, holding Diana's hand. Before I feel like I am about to fall into a deep slumber, I am roused by a rustling and tramping into our clearing. It is Gelard I know, but accompanied by a menagerie of animals. He is laughing, a deep gleeful laugh, as the animals guide him. He is carrying rocks of all shapes and sizes.

'My friends, I have returned! With followers of course.' Gelard is nudged forward by a boar.

I open my eyes fully and smile at him; we have our materials. First I create all manner of axes, a memory of my time of killing in the forest hits me hard, but I continue. We start to work on building a shelter. Agatha watches on, supervising and cuddling with the animals that come by from time to time. The great tree provides much wood, enough for two houses I would think.

Gelard has not the gift of building, but becomes adept at collecting food to nourish us. The work is hard, cutting with the small axes, chipping away at the great tree, until nothing is left but enough wood for us to begin.

'I think we are ready to build, Di. What would you like our house to look like?' I ask her.

'Anything will be perfect, I know my Ariel.' She beams at me.

I look out at the scenery, a deep blue sky above and green leaves all around. The moss is lush, but below we find solid ground. I am pleased as I work away on the houses. They begin to form, without magic, with no special power, we just create heaven here on this island. Occasionally, Aranyani passes overhead but never stops to talk to us. She has no need of us now, and we don't need her in return. We sometimes wave at her but find no response, we laugh about it and continue our labours. Once the wooden structures are finished, we finish the roof with dry wood we find, and finally, it looks like a home.

Chapter Thirty-Three

Have you forgotten?

That you are strong and perfect,

Just as you are now.

Agatha is old now, and she barely leaves her house, Gelard takes the role of housekeeper. They laugh and joke at night beside the fire. We are allowed to take from the forest what has fallen to its death, which provides enough for us all easily. Diana and I explore the forest, eating berries and such wherever we find them. It is blissful. I love her deeply and I feel it in my bones. She loves me in return, full of life and the pleasures it provides.

Soon, Agatha passes to the sky. We mourn her, and bury her, but know she was happy at last and at peace like the rest of us.

I still have a darkness within me, it will always be so, I believe. The cloud comes and goes, and on the days when it fills my mind, Diana stays by my bedside and holds my hand till it passes. I will never be free, but I am at peace with it. The malaise no longer controls me, no longer lingers too long. I know it will end eventually and we can explore the forest calmly again. That is my true freedom, the fact that I have learned to live well, even through the storms. Diana is always there for me, no matter how deep the malaise is. I am afraid of dying yes, but know Fern still holds on for us, painting the stars for us to live in.

I find myself becoming frail as the years pass, the muscles no longer holding my weight the same. I use a wooden staff to walk, and find it more and more difficult to awaken in the mornings. I hide it from Diana, but I think she knows so I finally come out and say it.

'I think my soul is stretching to the stars, my love.' I am so nervous, I shake.

'It is as it should be. We have had a wonderful time together, I could not have wished for more. Will we meet again up there, do you think? My Ariel, my precious being, do not fear,' she says in a comforting manner.

'I am scared to die now. I fear the loss of everything we have built in this life,' I say, and look with old eyes into a wrinkled but still beautiful face, through everything, she has been a constant beauty inside and out.

'Thank you for giving me this life, my dearest. We truly have made something here, and the animals will not forget us. Come now, let us stay in the house a while.' She leads me home and I climb into the bed with her.

Gelard never got over Agatha's death, so he left the houses and went into the forest without a word of goodbye. But we understood; he has no partner to love but the animals, so I assume he left to attend to them. Someone must; I can barely lift a hand from Diana's side. I feel myself drifting, not like sleep but into something else.

'I love you always,' I say, 'follow me, my Diana.'

'I will follow you for eternity, my love.' Diana turns over and strokes my face as I let out my final breath.

I know I was loved. I know the darkness will pass with me. I think quickly, now, of all the wonderful things that have happened. My freedom from the keep, my Fern teaching me painting, and peace that I had never experienced before. I was a powerful lord of the animals and servant to nature. But I am weary of life, and it is time to leave. I hope Diana will follow quickly enough, after she too has finished her life. I will wait wherever the gods choose to send me.